PRAISE FOR

Elizabeth & Eli

'In Sue Williams' hands [Macarthur and Macquarie] become vividly real . . . I feel as if I have lived through these times with these two incredibly courageous women.' *Good Reading*

'Williams skillfully shows how both Elizabeths are moulded, pulled apart and pushed together by the times they live through . . . [*Elizabeth & Elizabeth*] provides a record of the too-often overlooked impact both women had on the early development of the colony.' Meg Keneally, *Weekend Australian*

'Williams draws a touching portrait of a friendship that manages to thrive despite difficulties small and large.' *Sydney Morning Herald/The Age*

'*Elizabeth & Elizabeth* is a fascinating look at how these two remarkable women navigated themselves through difficulties and heartbreaks to leave a legacy felt nearly two hundred years later.' *The Historical Novel Society*

'Gripping . . . pulls Elizabeth Macquarie and Elizabeth Macarthur out of their husbands' shadows to give them the attention they deserve.' *Weekly Times*

'Well-written, engaging and rich in historical detail, *Elizabeth & Elizabeth* is a lovely novel and recommended reading for those interested in Australia's past.' *Book'd Out*

Sue Williams is the best-selling author of the historical novel, *Elizabeth & Elizabeth*, set in early colonial Australia, and is an award-winning journalist, travel writer and non-fiction author. She has developed a writing style that tells a story as evocatively as possible, with a keen eye for detail. Sue's biographies include *Under Her Skin: The life and work of Professor Fiona Wood*; *Mean Streets, Kind Heart: The Father Chris Riley story*; *Father Bob: The larrikin priest*; *The Last Showman: Fred Brophy*; *No Time For Fear: Paul de Gelder*; *Peter Ryan: The inside story*; *Death of a Doctor*; and *The Girl Who Climbed Everest*. Other books are about travel, true crime and genetics, while she has also had a children's book published in the US. Sue's new historical novel, published in 2023, is called *That Bligh Girl*.

Elizabeth &
ELIZABETH

SUE WILLIAMS

This is a work of fiction. Names, characters, places and incidents are sometimes based on historical events, but are used fictitiously.

This edition published in 2023
First published in 2021

Allen & Unwin
83 Alexander Street
Crows Nest NSW 2065
Australia
Phone: (61 2) 8425 0100
Email: info@allenandunwin.com
Web: www.allenandunwin.com

A catalogue record for this book is available from the National Library of Australia

ISBN 978 1 76106 753 2

Typeset in 12.6/18.6 Garamond Premier Pro by Bookhouse, Sydney
Printed and bound in Australia by the Opus Group

10 9 8 7 6 5 4 3 2 1

The paper in this book is FSC® certified. FSC® promotes environmentally responsible, socially beneficial and economically viable management of the world's forests.

For Jimmy,
without whom none of this would be possible

AUTHOR'S NOTE

In 1809, Elizabeth 'Betsey' Macquarie, the wife of Major-General Lachlan Macquarie, accompanied him on the long voyage to Britain's most far-flung penal settlement, where he was to become Governor of the country that ultimately became Australia. The couple arrived in the colony after the Rum Rebellion of 1808 overthrew the sitting Governor, William Bligh, following a series of disagreements between Bligh and one of the coup d'état's ringleaders, powerful wool pioneer John Macarthur. Lachlan was appointed to bring stability back to New South Wales, and both he and Betsey were eager to leave their mark on the development of the nascent colony.

Elizabeth Macarthur arrived in Sydney in June 1790 with her husband John Macarthur. After a period in Sydney Town, they moved to Parramatta where they established Elizabeth Farm, which would become famous for its merino fleeces. When John journeyed back to London in 1809 with their two youngest sons to defend himself against possible charges of treason because of his role in the revolt, he left Elizabeth behind with their three daughters to look after the family's growing wool empire.

The two Elizabeths were women from strikingly different backgrounds. And they both had to contend with their husbands' sharply conflicting visions of the future of the new colony.

WARNING

This book is about colonial Australia and contains words and descriptions of Aboriginal people by non-Indigenous characters, as well as the recounting of events from a colonial standpoint, that today may be considered insulting or inappropriate.

Part ONE

I'm feeling so many mixed emotions. I'm relieved that our long, long voyage is over, but fearful of what awaits us in this new land with, by all reports, its strange creatures and hostile environment. The smudge on the horizon marks the beginning of our great adventure and, while I will be happy to be on dry land once more, my heart is racing at the thought of the unknown challenges ahead.

Betsey Macquarie's journal,
31ST DECEMBER 1809

Chapter 1

FIRST IMPRESSIONS

Betsey Macquarie

31ST DECEMBER 1809, SYDNEY

Oh my Lord, I'm going to be sick. That stink! It's like a punch to the gut. My eyes are beginning to water and I feel the bile rise in my throat. I tighten my grip on my husband's arm, lift my skirts and try to pin a smile on my face. First impressions are important. It would never do for the new First Lady of the colony of New South Wales to step ashore and immediately sink to the ground retching.

There are rows and rows of officials standing in the hot noon sun in Sydney Town waiting to greet us. Behind them, the crowd is ten deep either side, shouting greetings and waving and yelling. As we make our way slowly forward, shuffling through the stifling heat, I can see a slash of red uniforms and glitter of gold braid in amongst them. There are cries of 'God save the King!' and 'Huzzah!' I wasn't sure what kind of reception we would meet, but they sound keen to see their new Governor and his wife.

I nod to them, smile sweetly and wave back. But it's an effort. The light is so sharp and harsh, unlike anything I've ever experienced before, almost blinding. Already I have a pounding headache. I've waited for this moment so long, dreamed of it, prepared for it, I can barely believe it's finally here. But it is. And it is nothing like I expected.

I can feel a gentle touch from Lachlan on my hand and I smile up at him, gratefully. He knows I am nervous and he's trying to reassure me in his own quiet way. He probably thinks I'm anxious about the crowds and their scrutiny of us, particularly of him, an unknown quantity. In truth, I'm worried about a whole lot more, of which most he would have absolutely no clue.

But Lachlan is walking ram-rod straight, like the good soldier he's always been. He'll be smelling that same foul smell and feeling a little overwhelmed by the crowd, just like me, but he's showing few signs of any of it. The only outward hint of discomfort I can see is sweat glistening on his forehead; he must be suffering from the heat inside that stiff new uniform. I only just resist the temptation to blot his brow with my handkerchief. He carries on regardless, shaking all the hands reaching out to him, and saluting the army officers, making it clear he's in charge. I have to make a good impression, too. This feels like my first real test. I can't afford to let him down.

I look around furtively. It's wet and muddy underfoot and I can see a wash of fetid water a few feet away from where we're receiving our first greeting party. I nod my head politely at the men clustering around Lachlan, but am distracted by the sight of what looks suspiciously like human waste floating by. Open sewers, of course. I see a large pig snuffling around a mound of decaying rubbish, and a couple of mangy, probably feral, dogs beyond. One limps up then defecates on the path before us. What a charming welcome, I think to myself. But let's hope the people receive us with a little less disdain.

It's all very, very different to what I'd so fondly imagined back home. I'd heard many stories about Sydney being a distant paradise, and read letters from the First Fleet about how they'd finally landed in a utopia of balmy weather, fertile green plains, fresh water springs and towering gum trees. As we advance, however, that gorgeous mirage of Sydney is slowly transmuting into something quite hellish. The water lapping the port is brown and foamy, filthy with rubbish and excrement. The people coming to greet us look poor and hungry and dirty. And after disembarking with the initial pomp and pageantry, the part of the town I can see from here, after our first dozen steps on land, looks nothing at all like I'd hoped.

Of course, my world has been small. At thirty-one, I know little beyond Scotland, England and the ports we stopped at on the way here. Lachlan, sixteen years my senior, is so much wiser, having served in the British Army around the world, often facing terrible danger and privation to keep himself and his men alive. And I can't say he didn't warn me.

'Don't forget, Betsey,' he'd said at one point during the voyage, 'New South Wales is a penal settlement, and a relatively new colony. I don't believe it's going to be as pretty as you think, and nothing like as easy.'

I'd smiled sweetly. 'Yes, yes, I realise that,' I'd replied. 'But I've read many of the letters from the colony, so I think I have a fair idea of what to expect. Don't worry about me. I'm made of far sterner stuff than I look!'

He'd laughed at that, taking my hand and kissing it. 'I don't doubt it, my darling,' he'd said.

But now I am the one with the doubts. I realise that I really was not ready for what I'm now experiencing. The heat and the humidity are overpowering, and I can barely believe what I'm seeing . . . I quickly readjust my face again to make sure I'm smiling rather than showing any outward sign of my dismay.

This is worse, far worse, than even my darkest fears. Behind the ragged grey people and their own shabby infantry officers—now forming a line of honour from the wharf up to the grand building, which I assume must be Government House perched on the hillside looking down at us—the houses are little more than ramshackle huts hewn from mud and split wood. They're all sitting higgledy-piggledy in a jumble of narrow tracks around the place, with no sign of any order or even of the most rudimentary pride. The streets, if you can call them that, are simply rutted mud paths strewn with rubbish. And that smell.

We're guided to the front row of a set of seats positioned in front of a platform. Lachlan sits and I slump down beside him, just as my legs threaten to give way completely. Someone—I don't know who—hands me a parasol. I feel almost faint with gratitude as it finally blocks out that fearsome sun. I know there are sweat patches under the arms of my dress, so I keep them close to my sides. I cross my ankles and catch sight of my good cream silk shoes now caked in something that I fear is far worse than mud. I look away quickly and out into the crowd that is steadily amassing around us, everyone staring as if we're creatures from another planet. I imagine they're anxious about what Lachlan plans for this place. After so much upheaval in the governorship in the past few years, they'll be keen for a period of calm, order and, hopefully, prosperity.

One of our party from the ship, Mr Ellis Bent, takes to the platform, and unfurls his documents. As the man anointed to be our Judge Advocate, he's our master of ceremonies, but I can see he also looks nervous. At only twenty-six years old, this must be as daunting for him as it is for me. But at least he's had much longer to prepare for it. I've had time to get to know him on our long journey to this place, and found him hard-working, conscientious and very proper about what he sees will be his role in the upkeep of the rule of law in the colony. While he is always deferential to Lachlan, he's also extremely considerate towards me. He was very solicitous during my long bouts of seasickness on the voyage, even though he often didn't seem too well himself. I've decided I like him very much. I hope he'll be a good friend to us in whatever lies ahead.

I smile towards Mr Bent encouragingly in case he can see me. He draws a breath, and the crowd grows silent. Then he gravely reads out the official proclamation of Lachlan's commission as Governor. As the words tumble on, I steal a glance at Lachlan's face. He looks serious, solemn, giving nothing away of what he must be feeling. But what is he feeling? I realise with a jolt that I don't really have any idea. Sometimes I feel as if I don't know my husband at all. He's lived such a full life, travelled around the world, experienced things I could never dream about, and of which he'll never speak. Occasionally, he withdraws completely and goes to a very dark place, and I've learned to just let him go and wait patiently for him to return. At those times, he's almost a stranger to me.

Yet there have been moments when I've felt we've been as close as any two human beings could be. Our wedding day was one of the happiest of my life, and I believe of Lachlan's too. While we spent so much of our engagement apart, in the two years of our marriage we've known both great joy—and terrible heartache. I will never forget the day our baby daughter Jane died at just two and a half months old, and I saw this great courageous soldier let down his guard and actually weep with misery and despair. The sight cut me to the quick. I tried to console him but he pushed me away, embarrassed at what he saw as a terrible weakness. It made me only care for him more, want to protect him more fiercely and, most important of all, make him happy. A new start in a new land will be good for us both.

I look back out into the crowd. I am hoping to see one particular face there, that of Mrs Elizabeth Macarthur. I quickly scan everyone but I can't see her. Even though I last saw her twenty years ago, I feel sure I will recognise her. Elizabeth was always so beautiful and had a quiet elegance about her that would doubtless mark her out today in a crowd like this. She made such a strong impression on me as a young girl that I've been following her progress ever since. Indeed, I even have letters from home for her. I wonder why she isn't here? She surely would have known that this was the day of our arrival? I hope she's not sick or that she's not left and gone back to London with her husband. As the only woman of similar stature in this country, I hope she'll be a good and loyal friend. Otherwise this strange place is going to be extremely lonely.

It suddenly dawns on me that being the wife of the Governor of New South Wales is going to be nothing like I'd pictured, back home. Home. Today, Hogmanay back in Scotland, there'll be a frost on the grass crunching underfoot and it'll probably now be snowing. Our families and friends will be gathering, ready to see in another New Year with the kind of gusto only the Scots can summon. My family home, Airds House in Appin, in the West Highlands, will have a blazing fire in the hearth warming the house ready for all its visitors. I wonder if my brother John Campbell, the laird, will be missing me. I know my sister Jane, who lives close by on the Isle of Mull, certainly will be. I think, with a pang, of all my nieces and nephews growing up so far away. I wonder how long it will be before I see them again.

When we'd boarded our ship in Portsmouth, I hadn't thought too much about what I was leaving behind, so dazzled had I been by this extraordinary honour afforded my husband. It was to be the final distinction of his brilliant career, and his legacy. For me, it was my chance to broaden my horizons in a way I'd never dreamed possible and to put all my reading and education into action, and, most importantly, to help him make a difference in the new world. I'd spent the seven months of our voyage listening to Lachlan outlining his plans and his hopes, and writing my own journals of things I'd like to do to support him, studying my architectural pattern book of building designs I've brought with me, as well as drawing my own sketches of buildings I'd like to see take shape. Lachlan appreciated my suggestions—he had known when he met me that I can be quite independent-minded—but at various times he seemed determined to try to temper my aspirations.

'Hopefully we will be able to bring our ambitions to improve the colony to fruition,' he said one day while we were sitting on either side of his desk. 'However, I'm warning you that we'll have to be patient. Life in Sydney is going to be far harder than you imagine.'

I'd reassured him that I was quite clear about that, but he looked at me with uncertainty still in his eyes. 'The colony has been through terrible turmoil,' he continued. 'There'll still be deep scars from the rebellion. It's our role to establish stability first and then try to build on that. It'll take time. Plenty of time.'

I'd nodded but, in truth, felt he was being too cautious. These people were in dire need of strong leadership; they'd be eager for the colony to advance, and would want a fair deal. We were, at least, agreed on that. During the voyage, we'd found we both have very similar ideas about improving people's lots. The misery of the forced evictions of so many tenant farmers in the Scottish Highlands, cleared off the land by wealthy owners, mostly so they could consolidate bigger farms for their sheep, was still fresh for us both. Seeing those big, proud red-haired men reduced to begging on the streets of Edinburgh is a sight I will never forget. Before we were assigned to come here, Lachlan had been hoping to construct a model village at Salen on part of his estate on Mull, with comfortable homes, workshops and a post office. Perhaps there will be opportunities in New South Wales to make such towns a reality. Our excitement had grown with each passing day of the voyage.

On the way, we made welcome stops at Madeira, Rio de Janeiro and the Cape of Good Hope, all spectacularly beautiful towns with splendid wide tree-lined streets and graceful architecture. Our spirits were further buoyed. But looking around me now, at this forlorn town, I realise the challenges that lie ahead are indeed going to be huge; much, much bigger than I had anticipated. I feel sure Lachlan will cope most ably with everything in store for us, but I only hope to God I'll be equal to the task.

As the welcome speeches continue, I think about how much I'd been looking forward to this moment, especially as we grew closer. But as we'd finally sailed into Port Jackson, the wind had dropped and left us becalmed between the towering cliffs at the entrance to the harbour. As a result, instead of the much-anticipated arrival, we had to spend three more frustratingly tedious days within tantalising sight of the shore in the distance and all the bonfires lit to welcome us and the displays of fireworks that I couldn't help but notice became markedly more modest every evening that passed. Everyone was bad-tempered, our supplies were running low and even visitors rowed out from the shore weren't enough to relieve our tetchiness. They delivered all the latest news of the colony, the politics and the terrible floods of the previous year that had led to miserable food shortages, and Lachlan was soon engrossed in hushed discussions. But to me, to be honest, it felt a mere distraction from the hours we were all spending gazing longingly towards Sydney. There'd be plenty of time to get to grips with the nuances of the situation later, once we'd made land. That was all I could think of.

We'd received some supplies of fresh fruits and vegetables from the Convict Administrator in Sydney, Colonel Joseph Foveaux, who'd been amongst the first visitors to our ship, so at least we had a break from the usual rations. In truth, I would have been happy to be ferried over in a rowing boat, but Lachlan was insistent that kind of low-key arrival would be suited neither to his rank nor the expectation of the people awaiting us. It would send the wrong signal right from the start. So we had no choice but simply to wait, helplessly, and just long for the end of this journey.

Lachlan was frequently busy with our visitors, and he made one trip ashore to see a few of the more important bureaucrats prior to our official arrival. He was often bowed over piles of documents and correspondence, and while he sometimes shared bits and pieces of news, I knew he was intent on trying to get to grips with the situation in Sydney before he was appointed Governor. I tried to be there for him when he needed me, but I knew I was spending far too much time alone, thinking and worrying.

From our position by The Heads, Sydney appeared the very picture of a pretty town, with a few fine houses trickling down the hillside, almost all the way to the seashore. At night, they seemed to be lit by candlelight—a warm, welcoming glow. Mr Bent remarked that it looked 'a charming object from the water'. I smiled at him, knowing he was trying to keep my spirits up. He clearly had the romance of youth on his side.

'I do hope it will be charming from the land, too,' I replied.

When the wind finally returned and the captain received word we could proceed, we all craned our necks for the first real glimpse of what was to become our new home. Lachlan had his own regiment of soldiers dress smartly in their new uniforms and line up on the decks to make sure the local populace would be suitably impressed. Then we set off the customary fifteen-gun salute to announce our approach, and heard one back from the shore to heed our arrival and to welcome us in.

Now, actually sitting here in Sydney Town, I can see that the deposed Governor William Bligh's letters back to London painted a much more glowing picture of the colony and his work here than was strictly accurate. This place at the far end of the Earth appears, in fact, shockingly derelict and Godforsaken. But it's set to be our home for the next eight years and hopefully we'll be able, together, to help create a place of which Britain can be proud. I do wonder, however, if that's going to be possible.

I can feel Lachlan stir beside me, and I move to touch his shoulder. But he's already standing and doesn't notice. Instead, he steps forward to give his first speech in this new world. The hordes quieten, eager to hear what the man who is to decide their future has to say. I straighten and look out over these people who are to become our neighbours, our subjects, our friends, or even quite possibly our enemies.

Then I turn back to my husband and try to look enthralled by what he's saying and happy to be contemplating our future in this place. I want so dearly for this to be the fresh start together we both so desperately need after the death of our daughter but, for the first time, I have real fears.

In the days since our arrival, Lachlan's been busy meeting people each morning, reinstating officials sacked after the mutiny against Governor Bligh and re-examining land grants made by former leaders. He's also had to pore over a seemingly endless number of documents and inspect various parts of Sydney and its environs. Meanwhile, I've been left to organise dinner parties and entertain the wives of dignitaries, which is not at all what I came here for, nor see as my chief role. Naturally, I want to support Lachlan, but there's so much I have to give, and want to achieve, too. I'm growing impatient to put forward the plans Lachlan and I discussed for the advancement of the colony, for new buildings, new institutions and new ways of doing things.

When Lachlan had first courted me, I'd been clear that, as an older wife—twenty-nine when we'd married—I was never going to be some pretty young adornment to his life. For a start, I'd never been regarded as pretty, and my youth was well behind me. Instead, I'd had a good education and wanted to put it to use. Then, when this appointment came, we'd discussed it thoroughly and Lachlan had said he'd need my help, particularly as he wouldn't know who, at first, to trust. But now I feel like I'm being pushed aside, and Lachlan isn't taking me half as seriously as I'd hoped, and been led to believe, he would.

Whenever he has a spare moment, Lachlan tries to pacify me, saying things like, 'I know you have so many ideas about improving this place, and God knows it could do with them all, but as I've said, we have to spend our initial time here getting up to date with what's going on and working out who we can rely on and where the dangers lie. We simply can't afford to upset the wrong people.'

But this morning, Lachlan seemed to have been making a real effort to be more solicitous towards me and I had summoned my courage to bring up some of my ideas about improving Sydney again. He had listened and looked at me with such tenderness, that my heart had leaped. 'I love it that you're so—' he had said, as I smiled encouragingly at him '—headstrong.'

My smile froze and my heart plummeted, but Lachlan didn't even seem to notice, telling me yet again that we can't rush things.

I had looked down at the sewing in my lap to hide my annoyance. Even though we haven't known each other for long, I'd have thought he'd have realised by now that patience isn't my strong suit. I'm a woman of action. In fact, the tablecloth in my lap is proof positive of my impatience. I've been trying to embroider it ever since we left England but the white cotton has become almost grey from constant fingering. I've sewn and then unpicked my embroidery so much that it's now filthy.

I want to be involved in the discussions Lachlan is having with people about making positive changes to the colony during our time here, and I want to take an active role in the tasks that lie ahead. I have journals full of things I'd like to do to improve people's housing and ideas about the kind of formal public buildings and gardens every civilised society needs. After all, I am the niece of the fifth Duke of Argyll, who rebuilt the model village of Inveraray and helped build the township of Tobermory on the Isle of Mull, across the water from my home at Appin, for the victims of the Highland evictions. Instead, I'm left to conduct small talk with other women and do this damned embroidery!

My thoughts are interrupted by Lachlan striding into the room.

'I've been thinking about our discussion this morning,' he says. 'Maybe a change of air would do us both good. I have to go out to Parramatta for a few days to take a look at the countryside around there. Would you like to come too?'

'I'd love to!' I reply, standing so quickly my embroidery falls to the floor. 'When can we leave?'

'Well, I'd been thinking of heading up there later this week, but I haven't had a chance to make arrangements. So, perhaps we could go together tomorrow morning and I can send some messages from Parramatta to the people we'll be seeing. I'll talk to my aide-de-camp Captain Antill about getting the smaller Government House in Parramatta ready for us so we can use it as a base for a couple of nights.'

My heart leaps with a sudden thought. 'Can we visit Elizabeth Macarthur while we're there?' I ask. 'You know how much I've been looking forward to seeing her again.'

'Yes, of course,' Lachlan says with a smile, pleased to see me in better spirits.

I'm delighted. With Lachlan so busy, I've been feeling terribly lonely and homesick. I've met so many officers' wives, but I haven't warmed to many, quickly becoming impatient with their trivial chitter-chatter about the social life of the colony. Elizabeth Macarthur, I feel sure, will be very different, a woman of real substance with good standing in the colony and, hopefully, a friend and ally for me. I've always been close to my sisters and am yearning for some good female company. It's been so long.

The last time I saw Elizabeth was during a holiday in Devon with my mother. I must have been about ten years old and she would have been in her early twenties. I still vividly remember peering into the dining room in the house of one of my mother's friends, where a group of impossibly glamorous people were sitting around a grand table in fine clothes, chatting and laughing. When I was introduced to them, I thought Elizabeth seemed the ultimate in sophistication, in a fashionably low-cut silvery empire-line gown showing off her creamy décolletage, with a dark mass of curls framing her pale oval face. I was dazzled. She looked, to me, like an angel and smiled at me with such warmth that I've never forgotten it.

Over the ensuing years, I'd kept up with news of her. I'd worked for a while as governess to the grandchildren of the Reverend Owen Meyrick, a good friend and near-neighbour of the Reverend John Kingdon, who'd taken in Elizabeth as a small child when her father had died and her mother had married a man unwilling to take on another man's child. Reverend Kingdon had brought up the then Elizabeth Veale alongside his daughter Bridget and his younger son John as if she were his own.

I remember Reverend Meyrick telling me once how Elizabeth had met her husband-to-be John Macarthur while he was taking a break from the army and tutoring at the local school to earn more money. John was completely struck by Elizabeth and immediately began to woo her. And though her mother and several of her friends warned her against him, saying he had too grand an opinion of himself, and lacked both money and prospects, Elizabeth had disregarded their advice. Apparently Bridget Kingdon had told her father that Elizabeth was overjoyed to have someone absolutely devoted to her, after losing her father and feeling abandoned by her mother, and, in turn, became completely besotted with John, even falling pregnant to him—despite her strict upbringing—before their wedding.

The Kingdons and other close friends of Elizabeth's had been beside themselves with worry when she and John had joined the Second Fleet to New South Wales in 1789 with their son Edward, just eighteen months old. But by then Elizabeth was already pregnant with their second child.

I wonder what on earth Elizabeth felt about this place when she arrived twenty years ago. Back then, Sydney would have been even more primitive than it is today, and after her genteel life in England, she must have been horrified by the state of society here. What would she be like these days? I wonder. Although we have to be careful because of her husband and what he has done, we have agreed we can make her acquaintance. I smile at Lachlan.

'I am so looking forward to seeing her,' I tell him. 'She seems an extraordinary woman, not to mention utterly fearless to have come here back then and survived. I'd love to get to know her better.'

'And so you shall, my dear,' Lachlan says. 'I'll let Antill know to get the carriage ready this evening so we can set off as early as possible in the morning. But careful, what's that under your foot? It's not your embroidery, is it?'

Chapter 2

A REUNION OF SORTS

Betsey Macquarie

8TH JANUARY 1810, SYDNEY

The next day dawns bright and sunny—like most days here. Unlike the gentle sun in Scotland that bathes the fields in gold, the sun in Sydney glares so harshly that it pains my eyes. As soon as Lachlan and I step outside, I feel almost overwhelmed by the hot clammy air and experience a pang of longing for the cool green hills of Scotland, the iron-grey North Sea, and even the biting winds at this time of year.

Determined to put a good face on things, I climb into our carriage, relieved to be leaving town. After the staff finish loading our portmanteau, we set off towards the mountains. Ten minutes later we briefly stop on the outskirts of town so Lachlan can visit the camp of his 73rd Regiment. Then we're off again on the wide, tree-lined carriageway and soon I'm fascinated to see the undulating Cumberland Plain unfold before us, with its long, trembling grasses and spindly shrubs, studded by clumps of trees—which I later find out are forest red gums and ironbarks—wherever creeks flow. Every so often, we cross a bridge over a stream and catch glimpses of the Parramatta River beyond, and clusters of small farms and huts that settlers have built within easy access to the water. At one point, we pass a group of exhausted-looking convicts being marched by soldiers towards Parramatta. 'They'll be used for road gangs or building in Parramatta,' Lachlan tells me, as he salutes the captain in charge. After an hour and a half, my heart lifts to see a haze of mountains in the far distance, and we finally arrive in Parramatta.

I'm cheered too by my first glimpse of Government House there, which is a two-storey, white-washed mansion, and even more delighted as we pass through its beautifully kept gardens. Sadly, however, the interior of the house turns out to be in a terrible state of disrepair.

'What a shame!' I declare as we gaze around the derelict lobby. 'How could Commodore Bligh have let it deteriorate so?'

As we continue our inspection, I grow steadily gloomier. Though the house is well constructed, it's been neglected for so long there's evidence of termite damage everywhere. The ground-floor rooms are all in such a sorry mess that I can't quite summon the courage to look at the bedrooms upstairs, so instead Lachlan and I take a short rest and have tea in the drawing room.

'It's a disaster,' I say bluntly. 'Commodore Bligh must hardly have set foot in the place. And the building has such fine bones, too. I'm sure we could make something more of it.'

Lachlan nods in agreement. 'Yes, but all in good time.'

I prickle at the words, which seem to me to be his new favourite saying, but hold myself back from replying. Patience. I really should try to have more.

After finishing our tea, we complete our inspection, and despite the rooms upstairs being freshly cleaned for our arrival, their state is as bad as I feared. This will be our second home after Sydney Town, and doubtless we will spend a great deal of time here in the fresher, healthier air, especially if we are blessed with more children. So, I take copious notes of what needs to be done to make the house habitable for a family, smiling to myself as I picture us here with little ones. Practical projects like that interest me, particularly since I seem to have so little to do so far, and if Lachlan is prepared to leave such tasks to me, I can do them in good time. Then we set off along the river to Elizabeth Farm. I'm excited to be finally on my way to see Elizabeth Macarthur, impatient to find out what she's like after all these years.

As the carriage jolts along the rutted road, I gaze over the green bushland and catch glimpses of the blue of the river beyond. But as we draw closer I grow nervous. I wonder if she'll remember me or even recall that we once met. I hope we get on. I would so like to have a close friend in New South Wales. The women I've met in the colony so far are all content to stay at home drinking tea and gossiping, venturing out only to visit each other's homes. But Elizabeth sounds a much more interesting woman, from what the Reverend Meyrick told me of her letters. When her husband returned to England nine years ago under arrest after a duel with his commanding officer, she spent the four years of his absence looking after all their sheep, running their estate and proving, by all accounts, an excellent businesswoman in her own right. Now John Macarthur has again left the colony for England, back to face the courts this time for his role in the mutiny that unseated our predecessor, Governor Bligh, she is again alone and back in charge. I'm sure she could teach me a great deal about the colony and how to live here successfully.

I glance at Lachlan beside me, sitting with a faraway look in his eyes. He doesn't seem to mind visiting Elizabeth today, but I wonder if he'd approve of us striking up a friendship given that John is considered such an enemy of the establishment. Thank goodness our paths didn't cross on our respective voyages between England and New South Wales, because Lachlan had been under orders to arrest him on sight. That wouldn't have been the best of starts for any friendship with Elizabeth.

'I am so excited to see Elizabeth,' I say to Lachlan. 'Maybe it's a good thing that her husband isn't here now.'

Lachlan takes a moment to reply. 'Yes, I agree,' he says. 'I wasn't looking forward to dealing with him, but now he'll be England's problem.'

'Do you think she'll be lonely without him?' I ask.

'She does seem an extraordinarily capable woman,' Lachlan says. 'But it must be difficult for her without him, even though he seems like such a difficult, argumentative man. Maybe it would be better if you don't mention him in your conversation.'

'No, no, I won't,' I reply. In truth, I've been wondering what I *could* talk about with Elizabeth. I've been anticipating our meeting with such pleasure, and have such high hopes of a friendship, that

I suddenly start to grow nervous in case she proves not as keen to know me as I am to make her acquaintance.

We reach the Macarthurs' house after about fifteen minutes, and it's a stark contrast to the dire state of our accommodation. Despite being a far more modest single-level cottage, it appears wonderfully kept, with fresh paint on the facade, a good roof, some new building work, tidy fruit orchards all around, vegetable beds and what looks like a herb garden to the side of the home.

We climb down from the carriage and are just walking up the path to the front door when a young harried-looking woman wearing a dirty apron, her hair escaping her cap, comes out of the house and stops dead in her tracks, looking truly horror-struck. I imagine we must be an unusual sight out here in this rural setting, with Lachlan in his scarlet uniform and me in my favourite green taffeta dress.

'Hello there!' Lachlan calls. 'I'm Governor Macquarie and this is my wife, Mrs Macquarie. We're looking for Mrs Macarthur! Is she home?'

'Yes, s-s-s-s-sir,' she stutters. 'I'll call the . . . the . . . the . . . mistress. Please come in.'

'Thank you,' Lachlan replies genially, doffing his hat as the woman opens the wide cedar front door for us. We follow her inside to the lobby, where she opens another door which leads into a beautiful drawing room with a small pianoforte in the corner. That's excellent to see; I myself brought a grand piano over with us on the ship, as well as my violincello, so that will be something we have in common at least. The room also shows Elizabeth to be a woman of impeccable taste. It is decorated charmingly in pale green and yellow, fresh flowers are spilling out of large vases everywhere and intricately embroidered cushions are scattered on the chairs. I pick one up and study the embroidery more closely as we wait for her to appear, and my heart sinks at the love and dedication that has obviously gone into it. Then again, I tell myself, with any luck it mightn't have been Elizabeth who did the work.

When Elizabeth Macarthur does bustle in, there's a moment's pause before Lachlan jumps to his feet. I walk over to her and greet her warmly. She looks much older than when I last saw her, with a face that is leathery and brown from the sun. She's also wearing a shapeless dress, shabby and faded, and her boots are deeply scuffed and discoloured.

'Governor and Mrs Macquarie,' she exclaims, looking mortified. 'I'm so sorry about my appearance. I've been so looking forward to seeing you, but I had no idea you were visiting today . . .'

'No, no, Mrs Macarthur,' I reply. 'The fault is all ours for appearing out of the blue like this. We should have sent news of our impending arrival. It's just that I was so keen to meet with you, Mrs Macarthur.'

'Please call me Elizabeth,' she says, smiling at me.

I feel myself flush with pleasure. 'And please do call me Betsey,' I reply.

Lachlan quickly launches into all manner of questions about Parramatta, Elizabeth Farm and the Macarthurs' famed merinos until Elizabeth halts him. 'Governor Macquarie, I'll have my overseer, Mr Herbert, come and speak to you and show you around,' she says. 'Ah, there he is, coming up the path.'

Elizabeth leads Lachlan outside and introduces him to Mr Herbert, before coming back to the drawing room and calling for a servant to bring us some tea. She then gestures me towards a seat at a small table. A moment of awkward silence follows as I struggle to think of something to say. I've looked forward to this moment for so long, but now I'm actually here, I can't think of how to begin the conversation.

'So, you're all alone here?' I ask, looking around.

'Well, not really,' she replies, seeming amused. 'My daughters and their governess Miss Lucas live here with me, and we have Mr Herbert, of course, and the servants and plenty of convict labourers, too. You can't really call that "alone"!'

I nod and smile despite feeling as though I've been subtly ticked off.

'Oh, Elizabeth,' I say. 'I completely forgot! I have several letters for you from home. The Kingdons and the Meyricks have written, and they also asked me to pass on their fondest good wishes to you. They all want to know how you've been—'

I'm interrupted by the appearance of the maid we met on our arrival coming in with tea. Elizabeth smiles at me warmly, though it's clear she's having trouble resisting the desire to look at the bundle of letters I've brought.

She indicates to the maid where to put down the tea tray. 'It's taking us a bit longer to make tea at the moment,' she says. 'A few years ago, a fire destroyed our kitchen, so we're having to do everything over the hearth. I'm having the kitchen rebuilt, although, I must confess, I haven't paid it enough attention. The task is dragging on . . .

'But enough of these domestic details. How have you been, Betsey? It was such a surprise when the Meyricks wrote to say you and Mr Macquarie were betrothed and then to find out you and Lachlan were taking up the position of Governor and First Lady of the colony. I've been so looking forward to seeing you again.'

I notice her use of 'again' and start to relax, reassured that she remembers me.

'I've been very keen to see you again, too,' I say.

'And how are you enjoying Sydney Town?' she asks.

'Well, to be honest, Sydney is very different to what I expected. It's much less . . . less . . .' I search for the right word '. . . advanced?' I offer uncertainly, not wanting to offend her.

There's a moment of silence as Elizabeth gazes out the window, but when she looks back her expression is softer. 'It certainly does take some getting used to,' she says. 'But it's infinitely better than when we first arrived. In fact it's almost unrecognisable, if you can believe that.'

I can't, but smile and nod nevertheless.

'I'm sorry I couldn't come to Governor Macquarie's investiture. I would have loved to be there to welcome you both, but my eldest daughter Lizzie has been unwell and I couldn't leave her. However, I'm sure there'll be plenty more occasions to meet. I often come to town.'

'Yes, I certainly hope so,' I reply. 'We'd love you to visit us at Government House.'

'How are you settling in?' she asks. 'Is Government House comfortable? Are people treating you well? I imagine you must be very busy.'

To my horror, I suddenly feel on the verge of tears, overwhelmed at the prospect of finally unburdening myself and sharing my doubts with someone I know, however slightly. My words come out in a rush. 'Well, Lachlan is so busy with affairs of state I barely see him. He spends his days catching up on affairs and issuing edicts. And while that is all very well, at the moment all I seem to be doing is remaining at Government House entertaining people, which I find hard. I do not *want* to live like that.'

To my disappointment, Elizabeth looks a little nonplussed. Of all the women I've so far met in the colony, I'd felt sure she would understand my frustration. After all, she's almost living a man's life out here, with total control of the running of the Macarthurs' concerns in Mr Macarthur's absence.

'I look around Sydney and there are so many things I want to have done there,' I continue. 'Though naturally Lachlan is taking charge of that, I'd like to contribute, too. I want to be of service—'

'But, my dear,' Elizabeth says, interrupting me, 'it is our role to help our husbands in their endeavours. It is not for us to have ambitions of our own. We sacrifice those the day we marry. And it's only natural Governor Macquarie has many demands on his time so early in his governorship. Is it not right for him to want you to look after domestic affairs? Being of service to him is the greatest contribution you can make.'

I try not to show my dismay. How could I have misjudged her so? But she is making her own way here without her husband. She is running everything without him. How can she now insist a woman's primary role is assisting a husband?

'Do you not think I wouldn't love to have my husband John here to look after?' she continues, as if reading my mind. 'That would be my greatest joy. It is only for him that I tend our flocks and organise for the fleeces to be sent back to Britain. When you can't have what you want, you simply have to get on with the hand God has given you.'

'Yes,' I reply, hiding my disappointment. 'I can see how hard it must be for you. I'm sorry. I wasn't thinking.'

'I do realise times are changing, Betsey,' she says, with what feels like a new note of kindness. 'And this is a different world to the one we knew at home, with so much more freedom to make your own life and draw up your own rules. You don't have to be as restricted by the conventions of polite society here, but you still need to be careful and not too forthright about it.'

I nod, eager for her to continue.

'If you want to forge a path of your own, you must find a way to make your time in New South Wales work for you. No one can tell you what you should do; you need to find that out for yourself. And though there are huge challenges, they come with a rare freedom. If you don't take advantage of that you'll have only yourself to blame.'

It's clear she's telling me, in her own way, that I will have a more satisfying life here if I am wise in how I go about it. These are words I will take away with me, and ponder at my leisure. She does make good sense, and I feel grateful for her thoughts. I'm just about to say something when we both jump as the door behind us opens and Lachlan and Mr Herbert enter the room. I know

Lachlan will be keen to get on and has probably given me as much time with Elizabeth as he can spare.

I rise to my feet and thank her for the tea and conversation, then invite her to dinner at Government House in Sydney whenever she has the time, before bidding her farewell. Although our husbands undoubtedly won't agree on many things and neither of us has any idea what might happen between them in the future, I hope she and I will become friends, allies and confidants.

'Goodbye for now, Elizabeth,' I say. 'Thank you so much for the advice. I will heed it.'

'Goodbye, Betsey. It has been a pleasure seeing you again,' she replies.

Lachlan looks at the pair of us curiously but says nothing, and for once I am grateful. It's only on the journey back to Sydney the following day that I realise I didn't even ask Elizabeth how her daughter Lizzie was.

Chapter 3

FINE PALACES AND FOOTMEN

Elizabeth Macarthur

8TH JANUARY 1810, PARRAMATTA

Elizabeth Macarthur gazes at her departing visitors in wonderment—and not a little irritation. Sydney not advanced enough? What on earth did Mrs Macquarie expect from such a new colony? Fine palaces and footmen?

And by God, how could she go on so about how hard her life is in the colony? After only a few days, she's already finding it tough-going? She'd mentioned Lizzie to Betsey too, and how sick she is, yet Betsey hadn't even enquired after her!

Elizabeth had tried to be as sympathetic and understanding as she could, aware the colony might be a shock for someone of Mrs Macquarie's privileged and sheltered background. But she feels annoyed as she goes back over their conversation. She'd been looking forward to meeting up with both Mrs Macquarie and the

Governor, though she'd never expected them to simply drop in unannounced.

She had been only too aware of her shabby work clothing as Betsey smiled at her, the surprise in her eyes plain as daylight. By the time Mr Macquarie greeted her, it was too late. She knows she has somehow failed this glamorous couple, and it's hard to swallow her anger at the injustice of being put in such an awkward situation.

She's lucky to have a husband on the same side of the world! she muses as she clears the cups on the table away. And if she wants to help and be of service, why doesn't she just get on with it instead of bleating about it to people like me who have too much to do already?

As Elizabeth picks up the letters the Macquaries brought, to see who's written to her, she tries to force herself to calm down and focus on what's important. Lizzie is lying ill in bed at the moment, and though she's always been sickly, Elizabeth's never known her to be like this. Her prayers have become increasingly fervent in the week since Lizzie's legs collapsed under her as she tried to get out of bed. Since then Lizzie's been completely unable to stand. Her legs seem utterly useless.

Elizabeth makes a mental note to contact Dr Redfern again. Despite his dubious past as a convict mutineer, everyone knows what a skilled practitioner he is. He's kind, too; although he's now so busy as the colony's assistant surgeon, since receiving his pardon. He'd ridden all the way to the farm to see Lizzie after Elizabeth originally summoned him. However, after examining her, he'd confessed he had no idea what the problem was. And though he'd promised to consult his medical books back in Sydney, it was clear he didn't hold out much hope.

Elizabeth frowns, annoyed at her visitors. This is the first afternoon she's asked Miss Lucas to take over at Lizzie's bedside for any considerable time. She'd lined up so much work to do, and now she's achieved nothing. The fleeces from some of their five-thousand-odd sheep that were sheared before lambing in spring were full of dirt, twigs, burrs and grass seeds, which she knows will reduce their value considerably when they arrive in London. So she's started experimenting with running the sheep into streams to try to clean their fleeces a little before the late shearing in early autumn.

This very morning, she ordered the convicts to try dipping the sheep in tubs of soapy water before rubbing them down, hoping that would make a difference. She'd wanted to supervise them to make sure only the most skilful convicts were allowed near the sheep. The thought of all the washing of sheep still to be done, as well as making sure the lambs have plenty of feed to keep growing and the dams are full enough to keep them watered, exacerbates her bad mood. And Lizzie, too, is such a worry.

As if on cue, Miss Lucas puts her head around the door and reports that Lizzie is sleeping peacefully and asks who the visitors were.

'The new Governor and his wife,' Elizabeth replies.

Miss Lucas raises her eyebrows in surprise. 'Really?' she asks. 'Were you expecting them?'

'No.'

'Do you know them?' asks Miss Lucas, looking perplexed.

'I've never met the Governor before, though I did meet Mrs Macquarie once when she was a young girl,' says Elizabeth.

'But how discourteous of them!' says Miss Lucas. 'The very least they could have done was send word they were going to drop by.'

'Yes, it was plain rude!' Elizabeth replies. 'If the Governor hadn't finished his tour, I suspect Mrs Macquarie would have been quite content to sit around and drink tea all afternoon.'

'But they brought letters for you?' Miss Lucas asks, seeing the bundle in Elizabeth's hands. 'That was kind of them.'

'I suppose so,' Elizabeth says grudgingly. 'But as soon as she gave them to me they were all I could think of. I wanted to tear them open right there and then. Instead, I had to sit and listen patiently while she told me how hard her life is here.'

'Really?' Miss Lucas replies. 'Her life, hard? How does she reckon that? She's living at Government House surrounded by servants. How can her life be anything but comfortable?'

Elizabeth can't help smiling at that. She and Miss Lucas are of a similar age, Elizabeth now forty-three and Miss Lucas forty-two, but sometimes the younger woman seems such an innocent in the ways of the world. But yes, they all work hard around here, Miss Lucas included, and this is the last place the Governor's wife should have come expecting sympathy.

'Well, Mrs Macquarie wants to do more to improve Sydney,' she says. 'She believes her husband isn't giving her the chance to play a role. I told her she needs to find a way to make her time in New South Wales work for her.'

'And what did she say to that?' Miss Lucas asks.

'She seemed to be inordinately grateful for such banal advice,' Elizabeth replies. 'Oh dear, perhaps I should try to be more understanding. She's led a fairly sheltered life in England and coming here would be confronting for her.'

Without much of a family to call her own, Elizabeth had learned early on to be self-sufficient, and when she and John had arrived in New South Wales twenty years before, she'd had to steel herself against some of the terrible things she'd seen in those early days. Betsey's journey would have been much easier, and her living conditions much more pleasant than those Elizabeth had endured on her arrival.

Miss Lucas interrupts her thoughts. 'Did she mention Mr Macarthur at all?'

At her husband's name, Elizabeth is silent. She's been feeling guilty, knowing John wouldn't have approved of her summoning a former convict to treat Lizzie, no matter Dr Redfern's good reputation. Eventually, she shakes her head. 'No, neither of them did,' she says. 'Thank the Lord for small mercies! I actually mentioned him, but Mrs Macquarie left well enough alone.'

That, in fact, was what she'd been most nervous about. John is on his way to England to defend himself and his friend Major George Johnston for their role in the mutiny against Governor Bligh, and he's taken their two youngest sons, James and William, with him to join their two brothers already there at school. Elizabeth feels a pang of sorrow and fear every time she thinks of all four of her boys being so far away. She wonders what they're doing and whether any of them miss her half as much as she misses them.

And what of John? Who knows what trouble he might cause in England when his ship finally arrives? He's a good husband to her, affectionate and doting, as well as being well-read and clever—traits that had early on attracted her to him. He'd always had a fierce ambition, drive and pride, too; qualities that she, from a humble background herself, found quite dazzling. But coupled with those was an impulsiveness that she sometimes found a touch disturbing, and a firebrand nature that frequently saw him in trouble with the authorities. Even on their voyage here from England, he'd been involved in a duel with the first master of their ship. Later, he'd actually agreed to another duel, for goodness sake, with the colony's Lieutenant Governor, Colonel William Paterson, and ended up shooting and wounding him, for which he'd been sent back to England the first time in 1801 to face a court martial. He'd been lucky on that occasion, using his time away to make some excellent contacts amongst those in positions of power in London, and returning to New South Wales unscathed.

But by leading the revolt against Bligh, he may have pushed his luck too far. It might not matter to the Government back in England that Bligh had already been subject to a mutiny on the HMS *Bounty* before his time in New South Wales. The authorities responsible for the case against John simply might not care that they had put a monster in charge.

Elizabeth feels that familiar knot of worry in her stomach every time she thinks of John and the boys. He'll look after their physical needs well, she has no doubt, but he's not the kind of man who'll be particularly loving towards them. In turn, they adore and look up to their father, even though she sometimes suspects they are all slightly afraid of him, too. But no, she reminds herself sternly, she is back here with Lizzie, Mary and Emmeline, and it's her job to look after the girls. She also needs to make sure everything remains in good order with the sheep for when John returns home—if he ever does. She shakes her head as if to rid herself of the thought. There's no point dwelling on all the unknowns. Better to focus on the here and now and what needs to be done.

Untying the red ribbon around the bundle of letters, Elizabeth wonders if one of them will be from John. 'I do so hope things are going well,' she says. 'Bligh should also be in England by now. John is likely preparing for the court case.'

'It's such a shame he had to go all the way to England to defend himself,' Miss Lucas says. 'Why couldn't he have been tried here?'

Elizabeth sighs. When she'd argued with John about going home to England, he'd said he could only be sure of a fair hearing if he was in London in person, able to look Bligh in the eye and present his case. He'd wanted to argue as forcefully as possible against every point that Bligh might make against him.

Indeed, Bligh had only been permitted to board the HMS *Porpoise* on the promise he would sail directly to England, so John and the boys had left immediately. John had insisted that if he stayed in New South Wales he might be arrested for treason, and even swing from the gallows.

Elizabeth had half considered the Macquaries might shun her because of John. After all, no Governor since Arthur Phillip had socialised with her, being wary of John's behaviour and reputation. So, she'd thought it possible the Macquaries might avoid her company as well, and possibly even worse, make sure that she'd be barred from polite society. That prospect had been too terrible even to contemplate. It was tough enough being so far out of town, but to be socially isolated as well whenever she went into Sydney would have been almost unbearable. Instead, it seems as though they've embraced her as an old friend of friends, and presumably don't hold her accountable for all the trouble John has caused. She knows she could be a great ally for them. She knows who's who, who'd like to be who, who's done what, and why.

But then again, what will John think of her spending time with the new Governor and his wife? He'd come to view himself as a kind of de facto administrator of the colony after Bligh's ousting. Would he see any friendship she might have with Betsey as a betrayal?

After Miss Lucas says she's going back to check on Lizzie, Elizabeth riffles through the letters absent-mindedly. There's one from the Kingdons, another from the Meyricks and a third from her dear friend Captain John Piper. Currently the Acting Commandant at Norfolk Island, she's been told he's due back in Sydney soon. But her heart thuds as she glimpses a much-thumbed envelope . . . from John! She pulls it from the pack and starts to tear the envelope open, wondering how she'll reply to his letter and what she'll tell him about the new Governor and his wife. It's clear that Betsey seems to have picked her out as a possible confidant. She's inexperienced and lonely, and doesn't seem to realise the politics involved in such an unlikely friendship. But maybe it won't do any harm to have such an influential friend, Elizabeth muses, especially one in such an exalted position in the colony. She hopes Betsey might think her manner in their first encounter in New South Wales was much more genuinely friendly than it really, in truth, was.

With John in London, and no sign of when he might return, pursuing a friendship with the Macquaries might even be critical to the long-term success of the farm and any other business ventures. She smooths the pages on the table and begins to read.

Chapter 4

A HOT-HEAD AND TROUBLE-MAKER

Betsey Macquarie

10TH JANUARY 1810, SYDNEY

On our way back to Sydney I feel thrilled to have made a friend of the colony's most prominent and admired woman, and pleased that she might end up a valued advisor. Despite John Macarthur having not been a great supporter of successive Governors, she obviously keeps her own counsel. I decide to write her a letter to thank her for her hospitality, and to build on what we've already begun. I wonder if she's found the letter from her husband yet in the bundle I handed her. Lachlan hadn't noticed it, and I'd decided not to mention it.

But back in Sydney, my good mood doesn't last for long. Just as we're settling in and I'm finally getting used to the terrible heat and humidity, the weather breaks and an horrendous thunderstorm strikes in the middle of the day. I've never seen anything so ferocious in my life. Though we had some terrible storms in the

West Highlands, with the wind blowing a freezing gale from the North Sea, here everything always seems on a much bigger scale. One moment, the sky is brightest blue, with not a cloud to be seen; the next it's as pitch black as night, with the loudest thunderclaps you've ever heard. They're accompanied by lightning streaks across the sky, one of them even smashing into the offices of the *Sydney Gazette*, where Lachlan publishes his official pronouncements. It knocks George Howe, the *Gazette*'s owner and editor, to the floor and sets alight parts of the building. Everyone rushes over with buckets of water to put the flames out and to rescue Mr Howe, but it leaves me with a real sense of foreboding which I find difficult to shrug off.

I don't dare tell Lachlan about my superstitions, so instead I confide in Ellis Bent when he comes to visit. My friendship with the young Judge Advocate has continued after our voyage out.

'It feels like a bad omen,' I tell him. 'I don't like it at all. That storm came from absolutely nowhere. And of all the places for lightning to strike! Lachlan depends on that newspaper.'

Mr Bent grins. 'It was an accident, Mrs Macquarie,' he says. 'Don't make more of it than it deserves. This country is a place of extremes of weather events as much as of temperatures, and it will not do to place too much importance, or meaning, on them.'

'But it's hard . . .' I protest weakly. 'How could that happen just as Lachlan tells George he will be using his newspaper regularly? And poor man! He's badly shaken by the incident.'

'Mrs Macquarie, George is a tough old nut. He'll recover.'

'I suppose so,' I reply, trying to shake off my dark mood. 'And how is everything with you? I hear you don't much like your predecessor's house. I even heard that you called it a pigsty.'

Mr Bent has the good grace to laugh, and I realise that it's something I've rarely heard him do before.

'Yes, it was a pigsty,' he says. 'I couldn't bear to subject my wife and son to such squalor. But Lachlan has kindly agreed to have another house built for me, allowing me a special contract to sell spirits to help fund it.' He stops and smiles suddenly. 'And yes, I'll be sure to show you the plans for our new house. I know that's your area of interest.'

It's now my turn to smile. Mr Bent has a real knack for helping me forget my worries and build up my confidence. I'm always very grateful to him for that, especially when Lachlan is so busy meeting and greeting people while he tries to master the detail of everything he has to manage.

'So, how did your trip to Parramatta go?' Mr Bent asks. 'Did you meet Mrs Macarthur?'

'Yes, what an amazing woman!' I reply. 'Just think, she lives all that way out, looking after so much on her own. How brave!'

He raises his eyebrows. 'Her husband isn't really any friend of the Government,' he says. 'He's a hot-head and a trouble-maker. Be careful there. Make sure you don't confide in her or tell her anything your husband plans to do. Information can be powerful in the wrong hands . . .'

'You misjudge her,' I say. 'She barely mentioned Mr Macarthur. Don't worry, dear Mr Bent. If I can try to forget the omen of the lightning strike, you must cast any fear of Mrs Macarthur out of your mind.'

'Who's afraid of Mrs Macarthur?' says Lachlan as he enters the room.

'Lachlan!' I exclaim. 'I didn't hear you come in. You're home early. I was just telling Mr Bent what a pleasant time I had with Mrs Macarthur the other day. No one's afraid of her!'

Lachlan grins and I realise he's toying with me. I find myself wondering what's really going on in his mind. Our marriage is still comparatively new and most of our two-and-a-half-year engagement was spent on opposite sides of the world, with Lachlan serving in India while I stayed in England, allowing us little opportunity to get to know each other. Our voyage over was the most time we've ever spent in each other's company, but now we've arrived in Sydney we hardly seem to see each other again.

'Excuse us, my dear,' says Lachlan, drawing Mr Bent aside. I pull out my writing paper and take a chair by the window.

I think about what I should write, and wonder how much Elizabeth Macarthur knows about me and Lachlan. Our relationships with our husbands seem so different. Her and John's sounds like it was a real meeting of passion, with her pregnant even before her wedding day. In stark contrast, no one could ever call my relationship with Lachlan romantic. We are distant cousins and we actually met at the deathbed of Murdoch Maclaine, Lachlan's uncle, who happened to be married to my sister Jane. Lachlan had admired a path I'd designed and had laid on their estate. Though Jane had been thirty-five years younger than Murdoch, they had a very happy relationship. When Lachlan began courting me, I'd worried about the sixteen-year gap in our ages, and the difference in our temperaments and life experience.

'Betsey, don't be silly,' Jane had told me when I'd expressed my concerns to her. 'Look at the difference in ages between Murdoch and me, and we've been very happy. Besides, Lachlan's a fine catch. We've known him for a long time now, since Murdoch was the father he never had, and Lachlan's made him so proud with all his achievements. I think the two of you will work well together.'

'But we're more like friends than lovers,' I said.

Jane shrugged. 'That's not such a bad way to begin,' she said. 'Passion can fade while friendship can develop into something far deeper.'

I was never under any illusion that Lachlan felt a new wife would be of benefit to his future career. I don't mean to sound harsh, but he's such a rational man. And before we met he'd bought land on the Isle of Mull, over the water from the Isle of Ulva, where he's from. It's only natural that once a man has land of his own he'll start thinking about the need for a wife and heir.

As for myself, well, I'm not perfect, either. I did think carefully about Lachlan's offer of marriage. Most women in the Scottish Highlands are married by their late teens and start having children almost immediately, whereas I was twenty-six years old when I met Lachlan. I'd had a few suitors but most had been pretty half-hearted, and I couldn't really blame them.

I've never been what you'd call a beauty. My nose is too long and my hair too unruly. Although as a Campbell I'm well born, with both parents cousins of the most powerful family in Scotland, we had little money and few meaningful connections, and most matches are made for either contacts or wealth.

'I don't know, I don't think I'm good marriage material,' I'd told Jane. 'You and Margaret are much more feminine and sweet, and courteous to all the men you encounter. But I always like to be *doing* things. Do you remember how Father would always scold me for trailing around after the staff on the estate, watching them as they worked, and then for the rest of the time having my nose buried in a book?'

Jane laughed. 'And how dismayed Mother was when you returned from school in London even more independent and outspoken than when you'd left!' she said. 'She s always despaired of your wilful, stubborn streak.'

I smile at the memory. I didn't remember much of my father, who died when I was nine, but I'd been twenty-two when my mother died, and I can summon up an image of her, and her warmth and her admonitions, at will. I understand why she seemed so afraid about my future, too, being convinced I would forever remain a spinster.

Before I met Lachlan my future had seemed mapped out for me. As the youngest child in my family, I spent half my time at my family's estate of Airds at Port Appin on the west coast of Scotland, keeping house for my brother John and his wife, particularly when he was away with the army. The rest of the time I oversaw the housekeeping for Jane and her family at Lochbuie on the Isle of Mull nearby. Though, occasionally, I took time out for trips to London to see friends and visit galleries, I had no doubt my life would be dominated by service to my family.

I love my nieces and nephews, don't mistake me, and enjoy spending time with them, but there's a certain drudgery in looking after someone else's children. Whether I was at John's or Jane's, every time I sat down with a book or tried to have a little quiet time to myself, one of their children would be asking me to join them for a game of hide'n'seek or to play some other game with them. I seemed destined to live in the shadows of others.

After Lachlan came into my life, my world opened up. As well as being a kind, decent, honourable man, he had a proud military record in wars overseas where he'd shown great courage. He'd also been married once before in India, and was a widower. And while we may not have experienced love at first sight, our relationship suited us both.

This was especially due to the fact that Lachlan was planning to retire from the army and settle down, and build a bigger, grander home on Mull, something I was looking forward to helping him with, since I do love architecture and landscaping so. But then, much to his surprise—and not a little annoyance—he was asked to come to Sydney as the commanding officer of his regiment, which would be accompanying the new Governor to New South Wales. When the appointee for Governor fell ill and pulled out, however, I encouraged Lachlan to apply for the governorship instead.

It would be one last adventure for us both, I told him, an experience we could share and an exciting chance to help shape a part of the world we were hearing so much about. It would be a fine legacy for him, a fitting finale to his long career of service to his country and a great opportunity for me to see something of the world.

But now we are here, life is rather different to how I'd pictured it. I'd hoped this time in the colony would draw us closer, but so far it hasn't. I put down my pen, the paper still blank, distracted by the conversation between Lachlan and Mr Bent. Even if I'm not being included, at least I can make sure I'm well informed.

'Bligh promised to set sail directly for England after the rebellion,' I hear Lachlan say, 'but as soon as he was out of sight of The Heads, he insisted that the captain of HMS *Porpoise* turn south and sail to Van Diemen's Land.'

I clap my hand over my mouth in shock. Elizabeth Macarthur had been so sure he'd already set sail for London, where her husband was going to face him in court. How horrified would she be to hear this latest news! I listen for Lachlan to continue.

'He's been lurking there ever since, hoping for an order from London to restore him to power here,' he says.

'That was never going to happen!' Mr Bent responds.

'No,' Lachlan agrees. 'Our arrival in Sydney sealed that. Bligh has to accept his time as New South Wales Governor is well and truly over.'

I'm unable to stop myself breaking into their conversation. 'Mrs Macarthur seemed to be under the impression he might already be back in London,' I say. 'As he's still here, maybe we should try to ease his passage back instead. I don't know much about what went on during his time as Governor, but I can't help feeling sorry for a man with such a long list of past achievements, who undoubtedly tried to do his best here.'

Lachlan and Bent turn towards me as I continue. 'It might smooth the transition to treat him with kindness and compassion since he must be finding it hard to come to terms with his sudden loss of power. Could we invite him to dinner when he arrives back in Sydney from Van Diemen's Land?'

Lachlan nods. 'That's an excellent idea,' he says. 'Could you make the arrangements, my dear?'

'Yes, of course,' I reply. 'But in the meantime, we need to make this house suitable for entertaining. It's Sydney's most important building, a lovely structure, beautifully symmetrical, but look at how dilapidated it is now . . .' I add, gesturing around the drawing room.

'With not too much work we could easily recreate the splendour it once had,' I continue, emboldened. 'I'll hire some men to replace some of the rotten timbers, have the place repainted and the cracked glass in some of the windows replaced. We have a beautiful view of the harbour, but you can't really appreciate it when you can't even see through the windows. Then, when we've put some of our own furniture in, it will feel a lot more like home. And I can't wait to start work on that garden!'

Lachlan smiles to hear me say that, no doubt also thinking of the path I built that initially brought us together. 'That sounds wonderful,' he says. 'Let me know if you need any help.'

'No, I'll be fine,' I say. 'I'll get started tomorrow, just as soon as I finish this letter.'

Over the following weeks the convicts, overseers and servants all pitch in to help renovate Government House and its gardens. I want to find some way of thanking them, and showing how much I appreciate their industry. I broach the subject with Lachlan, who thinks it a splendid idea.

So I invite our helpers to a celebration on the 17th of March and organise for a marquee to be erected in the grounds of Government House and a magnificent St Patrick's Day feast served, with ale. When Lachlan and I walk into the room, everyone stops talking and stands up. Then Lachlan gives a funny little speech of welcome while I beam at all the happy faces around us. After he's finished, he bids everyone to start eating, and the band I've organised starts to play popular songs, which most of the crowd sing along to. Our guests are plainly delighted. I imagine many have never seen such a feast before, if ever, and some are completely overwhelmed.

At the end of the evening, tears of joy well in my eyes as a man stands and delivers a speech of thanks to us. For the first time, it's beginning to feel like we are actually making a difference here. Because we are treating people with respect and gratitude, we are receiving the same back.

It heartens me that we're preparing to treat Bligh with respect too, and when he finally sails back through The Heads, Lachlan sends Captain Antill out to greet him on his ship, with an invitation to dinner that evening. But it soon seems clear Bligh has no intention of disembarking without a salute of guns and a full military escort to Government House. I'm amazed at his gall, though I can't help admiring it. He obviously wants to go out in a blaze of glory.

Lachlan complies with Bligh's requests and invites him to dinner the next evening. I instruct the cooks at Government House to make a special dinner of soup, wild duck, roast beef, jellies and tarts, to show Bligh respect by making the occasion as grand as possible. He arrives with his eldest daughter Mary Putland, who served as his First Lady when her mother didn't want to make the long voyage from England.

After it's all over, however, I wish I hadn't bothered. From the moment Bligh steps into Government House, he barely acknowledges me and then treats me with ill-disguised disdain. Even worse, he greets Lachlan with such an over-exaggerated formal courtesy, I know his regard is in no way genuine. Though he's had a terrible time, after spending a few hours in his company I am not at all surprised that he's met with such misfortune.

He talks endlessly about how the colony is going to the dogs, how it's corrupt and drunken and how there's no hope for its future. He doesn't acknowledge that we are new here, and wouldn't welcome such an uncompromisingly negative tirade. Instead, he appears to have no respect for us or our position, and makes no attempt to hide his belief that we will make absolutely no difference, and our time will end in similar ignominy. He then switches to the subject of John Macarthur, whom he seems to blame for every aspect of his misfortune.

'He is a schemer, a power-hungry martinet, a man who believes he knows better than everyone and is entitled to more land and favours than anyone else alive,' Bligh declares. 'Yet he's little more than a common soldier with a crude tongue and a grasping manner.'

I can't wait for the dinner to end and am appalled when Lachlan invites Bligh to stay with us at Government House for the rest of the time he's in Sydney. Thankfully, Bligh refuses. I find him a wholly disagreeable, bitter, bad-tempered man who makes me think that Elizabeth's husband is perhaps not such a shocking rabble-rouser after all.

The next day I write another letter to Elizabeth telling her about the things we've been doing in Sydney, including our renovations to Government House, how we've tidied up the gardens with the help of our convict labourers and how we treated them to a thank-you dinner. I also write about Bligh's visit, omitting all the terrible things he said about John, but saying how terribly disagreeable we found him. Captain Antill kindly says he'll deliver it for me as I'm not sure when we'll be free to go out to Parramatta again to visit Elizabeth, or when she'll be able to come into town.

I feel little doubt she'll be delighted to hear our news, and amused to learn how difficult Bligh's visit proved for us.

Chapter 5

BACK TO BUSINESS

Elizabeth Macarthur

12TH JANUARY 1810, PARRAMATTA

Elizabeth Macarthur has been at the Cowpastures, her family's second big landholding in the remote south-west of Sydney, for the last three days and, dressed in her oldest working clothes, is relieved no one but the convict labourers and Mr Herbert are around to observe her. She's thinking about whether she'll ride the thirty miles back to Elizabeth Farm tomorrow as she stands outside the sheep yard, watching one of the workers try to separate out a ewe from the rest of the flock. As the young man lopes over towards the animals in one corner of the holding pen, they scatter in all directions. Diving to catch one as it races past him, the man lands face-first in the dirt. Swearing, he gets up, dusts himself off and follows the sheep, which are now bunched in the opposite corner looking warily at him.

Yelling and waving his arms, he sets off another tumultuous stampede. Flailing wildly at one of the scattering sheep to try to snatch at its fleece, he misses and it runs past him to safety.

Elizabeth can't help but laugh along with the other men watching, though she's anxious about the smaller, weaker sheep getting injured in the rush. She also doesn't want the bigger sheep becoming bruised or stressed by some idiot grabbing at them by their wool.

'Leave them be now, Matthew,' she calls over. 'I'll see to it.'

Once the worker has left the yard, Elizabeth goes through the gate and walks slowly and quietly towards the sheep, standing still when they start to shuffle. She whispers to them in a low, soft voice, and by the time she begins her approach again, they seem almost soothed by her presence. Suddenly, she grabs one large ewe by the head, pulls it towards her and firmly straddles it, pressing her knees against its flanks.

The sheep tries to struggle, but Elizabeth puts a hand on its head and talks to it gently until it is calm. Then in one smooth motion, she pulls a knife from the pocket of her apron, leans over and slashes the animal's throat. It struggles for a second, then slumps forward, sending a river of red blood gushing into the earth.

'Take this back to the hut and we'll butcher it later,' she says to the men. 'Hopefully, it will provide enough mutton for everyone for the next three days.'

The men stand looking at her, transfixed. They've all become used to the sight of this formidable woman doing anything and everything around the place, but this is the first time they've seen her actually slaughter an animal.

'Come on,' she urges. 'What are you waiting for? Christmas?'

'No, ma'am,' they chime in unison, then scurry over to pick up the carcass.

Heading off to check on the length and quality of the merinos' fleeces, Elizabeth's mind wanders to Lizzie. The bag of potions Dr Redfern brought back to Parramatta have led to a recovery that appears almost miraculous, thank goodness! With Lizzie now sitting up in bed and eating properly, Elizabeth felt comfortable leaving her in the capable hands of Miss Lucas while she came here to the Cowpastures to supervise operations.

Yet again, she marvels at what her life has become. As a young woman growing up with the vicar's family in Devon, she'd never imagined she'd venture far, let alone to the other side of the world, or do anything like this. But John has always been enormously persuasive, and with he and the boys now over in England, it's been up to Elizabeth to hold the fort. To her surprise, Elizabeth has found she quite enjoys taking charge despite the myriad weighty responsibilities. Looking after the sheep, and making sure they're not stolen by marauding natives or dingoes, is perhaps the most pleasant and rewarding task, besides giving the children lessons on their letters, numbers and the Bible. It's harder having to constantly check their cattle, dairy cows, horses, hogs and chickens, while supervising the growing labour force necessary to sow and harvest the crops, bring in the vegetables and pick the fruit from the orchards. That's been trickier since the severe drought of last year continued into this year, and the seedlings needed more care and the produce grew meaner. Then there's the onerous task of making sure it's all properly stored, preserved and prepared by the kitchen. Even worse, though, is the interminable bookwork she has to do, with accounts and chasing up debts, which she's found she absolutely hates. Approaching John's male friends to remind them of what they owe, especially when the contracts are all in his name, and they don't readily respond to her requests to pay, always makes her feel as if she's bitten off far more than she can chew; it feels like an endless tide of errands, duties and obligations. But out here on the land with the animals, life feels far less complicated and confronting.

She spends her final morning riding over their lands with Mr Herbert, counting the sheep to make sure they haven't had too many losses, checking on the lambs and taking notes on the state of the wool and working out schedules for shearing and baling fleeces. At midday, they take a short break for a hurried meal of bread and cheese before they start riding back to Elizabeth Farm in a companionable silence.

Elizabeth has developed a deep respect for Mr Herbert, even though he was transported as a convict a year after she arrived. She's never asked him why, nor expected him to volunteer any information. She's heard the others gossiping about a theft, and about him receiving a death sentence which was commuted to transportation for life, but she's avoided paying too much attention. When John decided to take him on as their resident overseer, she was surprised since he's always had such strong antipathy towards convicts, but he never mentioned Mr Herbert's status, so his crime couldn't have been anything too worrisome. John would never put his family in danger. As the pair trudge along the muddy track towards Parramatta, Mr Herbert breaks into her thoughts to ask how Mr Macarthur is doing in London.

Elizabeth shrugs. 'I'm not even sure if he's had his day in court yet.' She likes talking to Mr Herbert because he listens, but rarely offers her advice, as most men would.

'Mrs Macquarie delivered a letter from him when she visited the other day,' she continues. 'He said how expensive London's become and asked me to try to collect some of the three thousand pounds owed to him around town. He needs the money to fund himself and the boys while he's waiting for his case to be heard.'

She sighs heavily and Mr Herbert nods. 'That's a difficult task,' he says. 'But if anyone can do it, Mrs Macarthur, you can.'

'Thank you,' says Elizabeth, who's still routinely taken aback by how well she's managing everything in John's absence. 'Oh,' she adds, 'and he wrote about how pleased everyone is with the quality of our wool, especially when compared against that of the Reverend Marsden.'

At her words, Mr Herbert sits straighter in his saddle and smiles with satisfaction. 'Yes, ma'am. That's good to hear. It helps too that we've kept the numbers up. The natives have mostly so far left us alone, even though the drought must have reduced their food supplies, and I shot a dog last week that had been prowling around, looking for lambs. The sheep look healthy and the fleeces are in excellent condition.'

The first lot of Spanish merino sheep to arrive in the colony was divided amongst John, Reverend Marsden and a few other farmers. When John first went back to England in 1804, he bought more top-class merinos, including some from King George III himself. From those, he'd managed to breed their several flocks, and three years ago had started exporting the first wool from the colony back to England.

Before he left, John had impressed upon Elizabeth how important it was that they keep their merino strain pure, with no opportunity for any cross-breeding. Even though she doesn't agree with John about everything, she trusts his instincts on the merinos and has been following his instructions to the letter. Meanwhile, the Reverend Marsden has been cross-breeding his merinos with sturdier varieties, trying to create heavier sheep for their meat rather than keeping them pure for the fineness of their fleece.

'And the Governor seemed impressed by Elizabeth Farm,' Mr Herbert says.

Elizabeth nods thoughtfully. 'His wife hasn't been so impressed by Sydney Town, though,' she says. 'But they do seem a very civil couple.'

The pair ride on as Elizabeth casts her mind back to the Sydney she and John landed in—wracked by famine, with shortages of food and fuel, and convicts living in tents and working in the brick and saw pits, many sick and dying. John saw to it the family lived in a wattle-and-daub home, which had looked luxurious compared to most others' living conditions, but was nothing like the comfort she'd known at home.

The town of those days had little in common with today's Sydney that Betsey finds so appalling. Still, at least the new Governor doesn't seem to be holding any great grudge against her and John. While he'd been extremely civil towards her, Betsey was almost gushing. She'd even invited her to dinner at Government House whenever she was free to come along!

The number of white-washed houses with their distinctive red roofs grow steadily more numerous amongst the rolling green hills, woods and pastures, and Elizabeth knows they're now back in the settlement of Parramatta. So much of the land here has been cleared of trees to make way for the planting of corn, wheat and barley, with the Parramatta River providing fresh water for the settlers and their farms. The centre of the township is gradually taking shape, too, with the military barracks there first, then the Town Hall, Parramatta Gaol, St Johns Church, the brewery and Government House. The town allotments are much larger than in Sydney, intended to produce enough food to supplement the entire colony's supplies.

From here, Elizabeth knows it's not far to her farm, and she allows herself to take pleasure once more in all they've achieved out here. They employ more than forty labourers these days and have a hundred acres of Elizabeth Farm under cultivation with wheat, corn and potatoes, and they have a garden of about three acres bursting with vegetables. The remaining one hundred and fifty acres have been cleared, ready for planting. And though modest, their single-storey farmhouse is very comfortable, surrounded by a garden, a vineyard, and an orchard with almond, apricot, pear and apple trees that are currently in full bloom, even with the lack of rainfall. If only John were here to share these bountiful days with her, she would be truly happy.

As they approach, Elizabeth turns to Mr Herbert. 'Doesn't it look wonderful?' she says.

'Yes, indeed, ma'am,' he replies.

'So often this country reminds me of an English park,' she says suddenly. 'Despite all the native plants growing in wild abandon everywhere.' She pulls her horse up to a stop and sniffs the air. Yes, she can smell the perfume of the shrubs in flower, too.

Elizabeth catches sight of one of the labourers working in the paddocks near the dairy. The man straightens up just at that moment and waves to her. She returns his wave and eases her horse into a trot, asking Mr Herbert, 'Shouldn't he be churning butter by now?'

'Yes, he should,' Mr Herbert replies, as he kicks his horse into a canter towards the man.

Elizabeth veers off the path towards the front of the house and heads for the stables around the back, where she slides off her saddle and grabs the reins in one smooth movement. No sooner has she started to walk to the house than she hears her name being called, and looks up to see Miss Lucas rushing towards her with a letter in her hand. 'Welcome back, ma'am,' she says. 'This arrived for you earlier today. It has the Government House seal on it.'

Ripping the envelope open, she finds a note on perfumed note-paper, written in a woman's handwriting. 'Ah,' she says, smiling, 'it's from Mrs Macquarie.' She pulls off her riding gloves to read it. Then her face crumples.

'Mrs Macarthur! What's the matter? Is it bad news? Is it Mr Macarthur?' asks Miss Lucas.

Elizabeth stops reading and tries to compose herself. 'Yes, it is bad news,' she replies. 'Bligh didn't go back to England as he was supposed to. That evil man obviously had no intention of following orders and facing up to his accusers back home. So, John has taken the boys over to England on a fool's mission. And who knows when we'll all be together again!'

Adding to Elizabeth's dismay is the realisation that the Governor and Betsey have been wining and dining Bligh. How could they? she wonders. It's about time she paid a visit to Government House, she decides. She needs to tell Betsey a few home truths.

Chapter 6

HAUNTED BY PAST LOVE

Betsey Macquarie

1ST MARCH 1810, SYDNEY

The Reverend Samuel Marsden and his wife Elizabeth have just arrived for dinner and I'm anticipating a very pleasant evening. He's a prominent figure in the colony, as its only Church of England cleric, a magistrate in Parramatta and a leader in the wool industry, so I'm keen to make a good impression. He's recently returned to Sydney after a three-year trip to England and I'm also keen to hear news from home. Lachlan and I are, furthermore, looking forward to his responses to a number of changes Lachlan has introduced that he should welcome, including imposing earlier closing times on drinking houses, outlawing work on Sundays, declaring church compulsory for all convicts and encouraging couples who've been living in sin to marry.

Before dinner, Lachlan and I chat to Reverend Marsden and Lachlan outlines his reasons for the new proclamations. Though the mood is serious, when Lachlan tells the clergyman he sees it as his duty to improve marital relations and intends to persuade couples to marry as the first step to making New South Wales society more respectable, I can't help laughing aloud.

Lachlan and Reverend Marsden both look at me quizzically.

I stifle my mirth and say, 'Ah, the convicts complain about their sentences. Will not the settlers now protest that they too have a sentence—and theirs is for life?'

Lachlan looks a little shocked, but Reverend Marsden is plainly outraged. I quickly change the subject to how appalled I am by the number of children wandering the streets with little to do but make mischief. At that, the Reverend nods enthusiastically and I breathe a sigh of relief.

When we finally take our seats at the table to dine, I bring up the subject of Parramatta, where the Marsdens live. I've been looking forward to discussing it with them, since they will know it so much better than we do.

When I start to share my enthusiasm about the area, however, and tell them how picturesque I found it, things take a decidedly murky turn.

'I think it's charming you see only the positives there,' Reverend Marsden says, though it's clear he finds it anything but. 'But, Mrs Macquarie, I think you are a little, if you don't mind me saying, naïve.'

Lachlan's face tightens at this and I touch his hand lightly under the table to warn him not to rise to the bait.

'Really, Reverend?' I reply. 'Please do tell me how I'm being naïve. When we were out in Parramatta, we found everyone very friendly and the landscape beautiful, with all that lush pasture down by the river. In fact it looked to me like a veritable paradise. And Mrs Macarthur only confirmed my impression, saying everything planted there grows in abundance.'

As soon as the words come out of my mouth, I realise I've blundered. Reverend Marsden's face darkens and he looks at Lachlan and me with outright disgust.

'You visited Mrs Macarthur?' he booms. 'Why on earth would you see fit to call on *her* on one of your first official visits to Parramatta? Are you not aware of what her husband did? Mr Macarthur . . . Mr Macarthur . . .' he exclaims, his ruddy complexion now so flushed I truly worry he might be ready to explode.

'Of course, we're well aware of the actions of Mr Macarthur,' Lachlan interjects. 'But he'll be dealt with in London by people much more qualified than us to judge. In any case, Mrs Macarthur has done nothing wrong, and will continue to enjoy my protection for as long as she wishes to stay in the colony. Now, tell us, why are we so wrong in our assessment of Parramatta?'

'As you know, I served as a magistrate in Parramatta for many years, and regularly saw the kind of felons who live in the area,' Reverend Marsden says. I notice Elizabeth Marsden tensing and looking down demurely at her empty plate as he draws breath and puffs out his chest. She's obviously heard this little speech before.

'Absolutely nothing would surprise me about the place anymore,' he continues. 'There is thievery, depravity, immorality . . . all far too base to describe around a dinner table such as this.'

He stops talking as two of the servants bring in a platter piled high with smoked prime cuts of pork along with a tureen of vegetables.

After they've gone I force myself to smile at him and say, as sweetly as possible, 'But you are a man of the cloth. Isn't there always hope that even the worst criminals can be rehabilitated? Have you been able to persuade many to repent and return to the path of righteousness?'

Reverend Marsden seems unsure about whether I'm mocking him, and says, 'Swift and harsh punishment is the only way many of them will ever learn. Sin is always abominable and it's up to magistrates to make sure it never goes unpunished.'

I bite my tongue, thinking how unlike he is to any other churchman I've encountered, particularly the Reverends Meyrick and John Kingdon, God rest his soul. Surely meting out such severe retribution is totally at odds with his calling as a Christian clergyman? I suddenly understand why people refer to him as the 'flogging parson'. Though I'm horrified, I try to give away nothing of what I'm feeling, and certainly nothing about having just received a letter from Elizabeth Macarthur, telling me she will be in town in a fortnight for business and will drop in to see me. Since there are many well-regarded people in the colony who think highly of Reverend Marsden, I don't want to annoy him any more than I've managed to do already.

I spend the rest of the evening asking the Marsdens about their time in England. Mrs Marsden barely says anything, and even when she does, her husband continually talks over her.

As the evening draws to a close and they take their leave, Lachlan and I both breathe a sigh of relief.

'That was hard work,' I say. 'Elizabeth seemed so timid and quiet, but I think I'd retreat into my own world too if I had such a pompous, overbearing husband!'

Lachlan laughs aloud. 'Then thank goodness you don't,' he replies. 'Or, I don't think you do . . .'

'Well . . .' I tease him, and he laughs again.

Then his face clouds over. 'I'm sorry, Betsey, but I have to go into the study to do an hour's work, catching up on my papers. I'll come up to bed as soon as I can.'

He kisses me gently on the forehead and leaves, and I move over to my violoncello and play for a full half-hour to calm myself down, knowing I won't sleep a wink otherwise. Unlike the piano, which I play with gritted teeth, I always find the violoncello soothing.

The Marsdens aren't our only difficult dinner guests, however, even if they stand out as the worst so far. In fact, the flow of visitors barely stops.

Much to my consternation, Bligh has become something of a regular caller. Lachlan and I were both enormously relieved a fortnight ago when he told us he'd decided to leave for England soon. We were actually so quick to congratulate him on his decision that he looked annoyed, as if we were supposed to try to dissuade him from leaving us so soon. We hosted a series of dinner parties—at his insistence—to farewell him. Then, just two evenings ago, he told us he'd changed his mind and has to visit more friends before he's ready to go. I'm exhausted and I know Lachlan is close to running out of patience, but we smiled and waved him farewell, knowing he'll be back in another week or so before making another date for his voyage.

His daughter Mary Putland is a much more welcome guest. I wondered aloud to Lachlan yesterday whether her mother refused to come to the colony to avoid spending so much time with such a disagreeable husband. Mary's own husband came over with them to serve as Bligh's aide-de-camp, but tragically died two years ago. Yet despite her no doubt difficult time, Mary is bright, friendly and very amiable, so I've quickly warmed to her.

She's a similar age to me, maybe just a few years younger, and she's plucky, too. Apparently, when the mutineers appeared at Government House to depose her father, she tried to fight them off with her parasol! I would have loved to have seen that. She's also charming, so much so it's as if she's been practising her whole life to be a pleasant diversion from her father. But when I expressed that thought to Lachlan, he chided me for being crabbit, and told me to be more generous. I felt embarrassed and, to be honest, not a little irritated.

Yes, Mary can also be flighty and vain, but she is great fun. Her mother sends her all the latest fashions from Europe, and Mary loves the stir she sometimes causes when she wears a new outfit. At one function, she turned up in a frock so diaphanous and translucent, a little gasp of shock rippled around the room.

'Mary!' I said. 'What on earth are you wearing—or not wearing? I hope you've remembered your undergarments!'

Mary had the grace to blush. 'Don't worry,' she replied. 'I'm wearing pantaloons underneath, so I'm perfectly respectable. Now tell me, is Reverend Marsden here?'

I looked at her aghast until she started giggling and I couldn't help joining in, glancing over my shoulder to check that Lachlan hadn't heard. Then it was my turn. 'You do look stunning,' I told her. 'Do you think I could borrow that ensemble one day to liven up an official occasion?'

Mary stared back at me in amazement before realising I was joking and we both dissolved into more laughter.

I noticed my good friend Ellis Bent looking over at us with a frown of disapproval, and when our paths crossed, I asked him why. He looked at his hands and was silent for so long I wondered if he hadn't heard the question. But then finally, choosing his words very carefully, he said, 'I find Mary conceited and affected to a greater degree than any woman I ever saw before.'

I laughed at that. 'But my dear Mr Bent, just how many women have you paid much attention to before?' I asked him. 'You're so devoted to your wife and your job, you barely have time for anything else! Frankly, I'm amazed you've even noticed Mary.'

He had the good grace to smile. 'She is very hard to miss,' he said.

He was right, of course, and I have recently observed that Mary also seems to have caught the eye of Maurice O'Connell, our Lieutenant Governor who's in charge of Lachlan's 73rd. Sometimes he looks as if he doesn't quite know what to make of her, but at other times he seems quite entranced.

Maurice has always been a very serious young man so I've enjoyed watching him start to come out of his shell and laugh and joke whenever she's around. As a result, a few times when Mary's arranged to visit I've sent word to Maurice as I feel they would make an excellent couple. Mary hasn't had an easy life and I feel she deserves some pleasures. Lachlan smiles when I tell him of my plans to play match-maker for the pair but warns me to be careful not to come between Mary and her father as Bligh's wrath would be terrible.

'And Betsey, remember that we really don't want to give him any reason to stay longer!' he chides me. But Mary seems more than capable of running her own life and I ask her if she'd like to stay at Government House for a while as an alternative to being with her father. I mean it as a favour to her, but it won't hurt either that it'll present her and Maurice even more opportunities to get together. With Elizabeth Macarthur coming to visit, I store up the delicious gossip as fodder to pick over with her. I want to talk to her some more about Parramatta, too. One day, if we're blessed with more children, it might be a wonderful place to bring them up—much nicer than Sydney Town—and I want to ask her what it is truly like, as I don't place much store in Reverend Marsden's opinion.

I'm impatient to see Elizabeth once again, so it's with real pleasure I receive another note to say she'll be calling the next afternoon if I have time to see her. Of course I do! It's not without a sense of guilt that I realise she's now given me two notices of her forthcoming arrival, when Lachlan and I turned up on her doorstep completely unannounced.

By the time Elizabeth arrives at Government House, I'm all ready for her. I've had the cook bake a fresh batch of scones and cakes for afternoon tea, have filled the house with fresh flowers and left the windows of the drawing room open to air the place. While our Sydney residence is obviously much grander than Elizabeth's home, it's nowhere near as elegant, and nothing like as imposing as the Government Houses I saw in Madeira and Rio during our voyage. Despite being two storeys instead of one, it's not terribly big either, with only six rooms in the main house. Admittedly there are a number of small outbuildings, including the kitchen, a bakery, offices, workrooms and stables, but the Macarthurs also have a number of other buildings behind their main residence.

I hear the bell chime, followed by the sound of our butler Robert Fopp walking up to open the front door. I hurry ahead of him, wanting to welcome such an important guest myself.

'Elizabeth! Please come in. It is so lovely to see you!' I say, leaning forward to kiss her on the cheek. Just as I do she steps in, and we bump foreheads awkwardly. 'Oh! I'm so sorry. How clumsy of me!' I exclaim, blushing with embarrassment, while cursing my complexion, which is so pale that it never allows me to hide any discomfort.

'No, no,' she replies. 'You must forgive *me*. I spend so much time in the countryside in the company of men, I've quite forgotten how to behave properly in society.'

'Not at all. Please come into the drawing room,' I say, gesturing towards the door Mr Fopp is now holding open for us. 'I've had the room made ready for you.'

As she enters the room before me, I see she's dressed in a fine silk gown of deep plum with an intricately beaded matching bonnet. I would hardly have recognised her as the woman I saw last month in Parramatta.

She turns around before I can glance away and I blush again.

'Oh, don't worry,' she says. 'I'm sure I look very different today. I don't usually meet the dignitaries of the colony in my work clothes!'

'Yes, I am so sorry about us turning up without warning, my dear Elizabeth,' I stumble. 'On reflection—'

'Please don't worry, it's forgotten,' she replies before changing the subject. 'I see we have a delicious tea ready here.'

We both take a seat at the table. 'How are you?' I ask, thinking how radiant she looks. 'Is your business going well in town? And how are the sheep? And . . . Lizzie?'

At her daughter's name, Elizabeth brightens. 'I thought at one stage we were going to lose her, but Dr Redfern has done amazing things,' she says. 'I don't know how we can ever repay him. When he first saw her he had no idea what ailed her and returned to Sydney to study her symptoms in his books. A few days later he returned with some potions to try out on her. Since then she's been growing stronger every day.'

'That is such good news,' I say. 'How wonderful! I look forward to meeting your daughters, when Lizzie is quite recovered, as well as this Dr Redfern.'

'He is a former convict,' Elizabeth says. 'But he has proved himself a very respectable member of the colony since. He is both a very good doctor and a very kind man.'

I nod, and decide I shall invite Dr Redfern to Government House. If Elizabeth has chosen to praise him so, despite his having been a convict, then he must be worthy of notice. He might be someone I can talk to about improving Sydney Hospital, too.

'And thank you very much for delivering those letters to me,' Elizabeth says. 'I don't know if you've also heard from the Meyricks, but they are well, and have asked me to keep an eye out for you, and John Kingdon, the Reverend Kingdon's son, sends his regards, too.'

There's a note of melancholy in her voice, and I realise she is probably still grieving the deaths in the only real family she'd ever known. 'I was very sorry to hear of the Reverend's death, especially coming so soon after his wife passed,' I say. 'And, of course, their daughter Bridget, to whom you would have been very close.'

'Thank you,' Elizabeth says. 'I now correspond with her youngest sister Eliza, but it's not the same as someone you've grown up with . . .'

I hesitate before speaking. 'I think there was also a letter from Mr Macarthur, wasn't there? I hope his news was all good.'

Elizabeth starts at the mention of her husband and for a split second I wonder if I should have said anything. She may not have known I'd seen his letter in the bundle.

'Yes, thank you for asking,' she says. 'He is well.'

The tea arrives and we fall silent as I pour her a cup.

'And have you heard any news of your sons?' I ask. 'You must miss them so very much.'

She bows her head over her cup, and is silent for a moment. When she looks back up, her eyes are glistening. 'I know the first part of their journey went well, and John spent his time on the ship making preparations for the court case,' she says. 'I don't know what will happen now. I didn't know until I received your note that Bligh hadn't departed for England, which is the whole reason

John and the boys left. And now . . .' She spreads her hands in a gesture of despair. She pauses and I can see she's making an effort to compose herself. Then she changes tack. 'I understand from your letter to me that you didn't much like him?'

'Yes,' I reply. 'I found him most objectionable.'

'So, will you be inviting him here for dinner again?' Elizabeth asks me pointedly.

I feel myself stiffen. I certainly sympathise with her dislike for Bligh now that I've met him, but it's not up to her to grill me on what guests we entertain at Government House.

'It's up to Lachlan, really,' I reply. 'He mightn't have much choice in the matter. We both have to treat Commodore Bligh as befits a former Governor, however little we might personally enjoy it.'

Elizabeth smiles tightly then changes the subject. 'John also said in his letter that our sons are prospering,' she says. 'Although they miss me. That's the hardest thing about remaining here to hold the fort, so to speak.'

I nod sympathetically. I can only imagine how hard it must be for her, with her husband and sons so many thousands of miles away and having no idea when she'll see them again—or even if she ever will.

'Still, this country offers many opportunities,' she continues. 'It has one of the finest climates in the world, we have all the necessities of life and the soil is fruitful. The main difficulty lies in educating our children and being so far from the rest of the world. That remoteness can be an advantage but it can also be a curse. Still, no point fretting about it. We just have to get on with it, and do our best.'

'From what everyone says, your husband adores you,' I say. 'He obviously writes to you often, and maybe it's good for your sons to have their father over there while they are at school . . .'

She sighs. 'Yes, it is good for them,' she says. 'But our daughters miss him, and of course I do too. He is my first love and will always be my only love.'

It's a surprise, somehow, to hear such an obviously down-to-earth and no-nonsense woman opening up about her love for her husband. I'm deeply touched.

'And you are lucky, being your husband's first love too,' I say. 'There's nothing so wonderful as first love . . .'

I break off and she looks at me quizzically.

I take a deep breath and say, 'You probably know that Lachlan was married before? Sometimes I wonder if he will ever recover from the grief of losing his first wife.'

Elizabeth nods and suddenly my words come out in a rush. 'Of course we're very happy together, but sometimes it feels like I will never escape the shadow Jane Jarvis casts over our lives. His estate back on Mull is called Jarvisfield after her, did you know that? And he named his valet, a former slave boy he bought in Cochin, George Jarvis after Jane's younger brother. Whenever he talks about Jane a certain light comes into his eyes and he has this faraway expression.' I swallow and try hard to stifle a sob, but tears run down my cheeks.

'He met her while he was serving on his first posting in Bombay,' I continue. 'She was the daughter of the Chief Justice of Antigua, young and beautiful and rich. Theirs was a real love affair in the true meaning of the word, and they married when she was just twenty. But then she contracted consumption. He was beside himself and organised for her to be taken to Macau, hoping the climate there might cure her. But she grew weaker and weaker, and died when she was twenty-three. How can I possibly compete with her?'

There's a long silence. I feel exhausted after such a long speech. I've thought about Lachlan's deep love for Jane ever since he first made overtures to me. But it's not something I've shared with a living soul, apart from my sister Jane. I have no idea what Elizabeth will think of me now. She's so tough and resolute, she probably sees me as some pathetic, whining creature.

I look up and see her gazing at me with kindness in her eyes.

'I understand what you're saying,' she says, 'but I don't think a man like Mr Macquarie would ever marry a woman he doesn't deeply care for. He strikes me as much too honourable for that. Yes, I can see it could be hard being his second wife after such a significant first love, but he didn't choose to pine alone for the rest of his life; he chose to marry you. And I saw the way he looked at you at Elizabeth Farm. He obviously holds you in extremely high regard.'

I smile at this and she continues, with a chuckle, 'I hear you didn't make the courtship particularly easy for him either.'

I join in her laughter. She is right. After Lachlan and I became engaged he had to leave for India, promising to be back as soon as he could. A year later, he was appointed to the command of the 73rd regiment so was free to return to Scotland. But he wrote to say he was extending his stay in India instead, and that I should wait for another year or two. He even advised me to spend the time taking lessons in music, French and drawing, expecting me to meekly accept his instructions.

But while that might have been Jane Jarvis, it wasn't me at all. I stopped writing to him so regularly and took a position as governess to the Meyrick children in Devon. That shocked him and it wasn't long before he wrote back saying he was coming home. When he returned, he wanted us to have a formal Highland wedding, but I was having none of that either, and we were married quickly in a quiet ceremony in Devon. I like to think he was scared of losing me.

'How did you know about what happened?' I ask Elizabeth, wide-eyed. 'Ah!' I add as it suddenly dawns on me. And then we both say, at exactly the same time, 'The Meyricks!'

It feels suddenly as though we've formed an even stronger bond now, and she laughs and laughs as I tell her about another romance I hope is brewing—and indeed am stirring—between Bligh's daughter Mary and Lieutenant Governor O'Connell.

'Well, that would serve the old tyrant right, to lose his last ally to another man,' Elizabeth says between chortles. 'I'd just love to see that happen! Tell me, what can I do to help?'

Chapter 7

A WOMAN'S PLACE

Elizabeth Macarthur

20TH MARCH 1810, SYDNEY

On Elizabeth Macarthur's ride home, the broad rutted tracks are boggy after a sudden unseasonal downpour and she has to watch carefully where her horse is stepping. As she brushes past the branches of gum trees along the sides of the carriageway to avoid the furrows, she can feel the water soaking her skirt and slowing her pace even further. Still, the journey gives her plenty of time to think.

She's dismayed at how upset she became when talking about missing John and the boys. The intensity of her sadness and her unbidden show of emotion had been unexpected. She'd thought she had it all under control. She doesn't like displaying vulnerability, especially to someone she doesn't know very well. Even on the few occasions she's struggled, Elizabeth has always been careful never to reveal any sign that she isn't handling everything with complete ease. And she's also tried to hide her annoyance at people telling her a woman's place is in the home with her children, rather than out in the paddocks with sheep and horses, or in the fields tending to the vegetables, fruit and herbs. Of course it is, as she'd told Betsey, but she had no choice under her circumstances.

At the same time, Betsey's qualms about Lachlan's first wife had surprised her. In one way, she'd felt for her and her insecurities, but she also felt rather impatient. He'd married her, after all. What greater sign did she need of his commitment? And Betsey was lucky to have her husband by her side, and the most powerful man in the colony at that! Elizabeth sighs. If only her life were that straightforward, and she had so much free time to brood.

She glances ahead, beyond the glistening wattle leaves and myrtle, listening to the gum leaves rustle as they dry in the breeze. After crossing the last bridge on the road, she feels a sense of relief when Elizabeth Farm comes into sight, and looks around for Mr Herbert. He's nowhere to be seen, so she makes straight for the cottage, sends a servant out to look for him, then goes to her bedroom and takes off her finery before slipping back into a work smock.

Feeling calmer and more comfortable, Elizabeth goes into the drawing room to find Mr Herbert waiting for her. He updates her on what's happened in her absence, and then she briefs him on the business she conducted in Sydney and mentions her visit to Government House.

'They seem good people,' Mr Herbert says. 'Mr Macquarie is a very civil man, and Mrs Macquarie pleasant.'

'Yes, though I think she will take a while to settle in,' Elizabeth replies. 'She does seem a good and forthright woman, but I don't know if she will become a force to be reckoned with . . .'

Mr Herbert nods politely. 'But you know, when you first came here, there might have been some who said that about you,' he remarks mildly. 'And look at you now!'

It's rare that Mr Herbert offers an opinion on anything other than the farm and livestock, so it takes Elizabeth by surprise. 'Well, I suppose you are right there,' she says, with a good-natured grin. And then the moment passes. 'Now, I've been thinking about when the rams should be introduced to the ewes,' she continues, 'and wondering how many of the good Spanish rams we should take to the Cowpastures to improve the quality of the stock.'

The rest of their discussion is strictly business: the sheep, how often the horses need to be watered, the behaviour of the convict crew tending the crops, and the many chores to be completed before nightfall.

As they plan the next few days, and pore over the figures Elizabeth meticulously records in her notebooks, she thinks again about how little she knows of Mr Herbert. John had merely told her that he'd worked with horses in London until his employer died, and was then cast out to find his own way. She wondered if that had proved his undoing; if he'd stolen something to put a roof over his head. But whatever, he certainly had a way with horses and all the other animals she'd seen him work with, including sheep and dogs. He is firm but fair with them, the same as he is to the workers beneath him. While John's been away, Mr Herbert has never given any indication of resenting working for a woman, and has always been polite and kind, for which she will always be grateful. Elizabeth wonders if there's some kind of favour she can do for him, and makes a mental note to request a land grant from the Governor on his behalf, if the opportunity presents itself.

With a start, she realises Mr Herbert has stood up and is looking at her. 'Sorry,' she says. 'I was lost in my thoughts. Do go off about your business. Thank you so much, Mr Herbert.'

He touches his cap, and strides away.

She walks back out too, and up the path to the main outbuilding, stepping around the ruins of the kitchen. She's finally having a new kitchen built after the original wooden one caught fire on a hot summer's day in 1805. The wind fanned the flames until they were licking at the main house, but thankfully the military detachment on duty in Parramatta had arrived just in time to put the fire out. The kitchen building, however, was completely burned to the ground and they've spent the years since having to heat food over the fire in the sitting room. Somehow, John never seemed to get around to having a new one built and now finally, in his absence, she's having it done. But before she left for Sydney, the head workman had even tried to insist on building a wooden lintel over the stove in the new kitchen.

'No,' she'd said firmly. 'I've told you I want a *stone* lintel.'

The workman had sighed and shaken his head as if he were dealing with a stupid child. 'A timber lintel would be so much cheaper and quicker,' he'd replied. 'That would make much more sense.'

'A timber lintel is exactly why my last kitchen burned down!' Elizabeth said. 'I'm not having another timber kitchen. I want a kitchen, a scullery and a cellar built entirely of stone.'

'I know Mr Macarthur would want a timber kitchen,' the workman insisted. 'He's a sensible man.'

'But Mr Macarthur isn't here,' Elizabeth had replied, an edge creeping into her voice. 'You're dealing with me now.'

'Yes, yes, I know that, but I'm telling you what he'd favour. It doesn't make sense to go to all the expense and difficulty of stone.'

At that point, Elizabeth had smiled genially and saw the man begin to relax. 'I know you're the expert,' she told him. 'And I know you're trying to help me.' He nodded. 'So slice yourself some bread on the table there, pour yourself some water for your journey, and when you get back to Sydney, let them know I'm looking for another builder—perhaps one who is less certain they are always right.'

The look on his face as Elizabeth had left the room had been priceless. But now she needs to find another workman and it's hard enough making do without a proper kitchen. While the servants never complain, she knows it's awkward making meals for so many over the main hearth. She thinks wistfully of Betsey, who has a husband, a working kitchen and a dozen servants to do everything.

But dinner is ready, and Elizabeth sits down with Miss Lucas and the children for a meal of broth, leg of lamb and fresh vegetables from the gardens, followed by a milk pudding. They talk about the day, and Elizabeth makes them laugh as she describes how shocked Betsey had looked to see her in her grand clothes. She's pleased to see Lizzie's face looking rosy and her eyes bright in the halo of candlelight.

When dinner is over, she helps Miss Lucas put the girls to bed and then comes back down the stairs alone.

After talking with Betsey about John and the boys, she wants to feel their presence again and takes John's letter back out of its envelope. It's dated the 22nd of July 1809, and marked 'Rio Janeiro' so John must have written it during the voyage and given it to someone bound for the Cape of Good Hope to be shipped on to Sydney.

Elizabeth notices her hands trembling as she puts the pages in order. She takes a moment to savour the familiar affectionate start: '*My dearest Elizabeth . . .*' There are many who say John is headstrong, wilful and obstinate, and she doesn't disagree with them, but he is also a very good husband and father. As a commissioned army officer, he'd managed to first secure land grants and a great deal of convict labour to work them, and then important positions in the colony, like inspector of public works, providing for his family very well. He was most affectionate with their children, and solicitous to her, but he always did love playing politics so! If only his family and farm were enough for him . . . She feels her vision blur as she reads on, but her spirits lift at his words: '*The boys and myself have been perfectly well, and were as comfortable while we were on board the* Admiral Gambier *as could be expected.*' It is always too easy when you're so far away from your loved ones to imagine the worst.

John also mentions encountering someone who met their eldest son Edward in Plymouth after he arrived safely back from fighting in Spain with the 60th Regiment. Edward had just been to visit his grandmother—Elizabeth's mother—and reported to his friend that she was well, too. Elizabeth's pleased but is hungry for more news of her boys. Sadly, John passes on nothing more of them. If only he'd told her how James, now eleven, and nine-year-old William had managed the long voyage, whether they'd been seasick or crying at night for home. Needless to say that if either were true, John would want to shield it from her, unless it simply didn't occur to him to share such news. She hopes she'll receive another letter later, telling her how their other sons are faring at school.

John says he's heard the New South Wales Corps are to be recalled and that Macquarie, whom he's heard is 'a Gentlemanly Man' is to be appointed Governor of New South Wales.

At that, Elizabeth smiles. Quite right, but just a little late with the news. Otherwise, John sounds immensely frustrated with the Government in London. Everyone who speaks of Bligh has condemned his conduct, but no one will say whether or not he'll be arrested.

She won't be writing back, however, to tell him Bligh is being entertained by members of the establishment in Sydney, including the Macquaries. Even though Betsey told her she disliked Bligh, she clearly has a misplaced sense of duty and lacks the will to stop inviting him. It seems to Elizabeth that it's most unlikely Bligh will go home to face the music. She frowns at the thought that it might be John, in fact, who'll be heading straight to gaol . . .

Her heart goes out to him. It's clear he's already missing them: '*What would I give to know how you all do, particularly our poor Elizabeth, but tis vain to wish upon such a subject*,' he writes. '*Remember me to the few friends who may enquire about me, and most affectionately to all under our own roof. God bless and preserve my Dearest Wife. Prays her ever affectionate John Macarthur.*'

Elizabeth holds the letter to her cheek and sits for a moment, lost in thought. Then a sudden clattering from the back part of the house has her almost jumping out of her skin. Everyone is in bed so who on earth could it be? She stands up stealthily and reaches for the musket near the cupboard. Tucking it under her arm, she calls sharply, 'Who's there? Show yourself!'

'Mistress! You won't want to be using that!' a man's voice answers as footsteps approach.

Elizabeth snatches up the nearest candle and sees a thin man dressed in hessian rags hunched in front of her holding an empty sack over one shoulder.

'Who are you?' she demands. 'And what on earth are you doing in my house?'

'What do you think?' he replies with a strange grin. 'But mistress, I don't want trouble and you probably don't even know how to use that musket. Please put it down.'

Elizabeth feels the blood rush to her face. She lifts the musket, points it straight at the man, cocks the hammer and puts her finger on the trigger. 'I might know how to use this, I might not,' she says. 'But do you really want to risk finding out?'

No longer grinning, the intruder looks like he doesn't know what to do. Then he drops his sack and holds out his hands to show he has nothing concealed.

'I'm sorry, mistress,' he says, his voice breaking. 'I haven't eaten for three days and my family is starving and I was just hoping to find something to eat . . . I didn't mean to frighten you. I thought everyone would be asleep. Please let me go. I promise I won't be back.'

Elizabeth hesitates as he starts to back away from her, not taking his eyes from her face. She's not quite sure what to do. He looks in genuine distress, but then again, her three daughters are sleeping in their bedroom. If she had been asleep too, what might have happened?

Elizabeth sighs with relief at the sound of footsteps running towards her. Two of the servants run through the doorway and go straight up to the man, who becomes motionless at the noise, seemingly paralysed with fear.

'What would you like done with him, ma'am?' the male servant asks.

'Tie his hands and feet,' she barks, 'and throw him into the cellar. Then send a rider to the barracks to tell them what's happened.'

Her visitor doesn't resist as the pair tie him up and lead him, shuffling, away. When they return, Elizabeth is sitting back at the table, trembling. 'My husband taught me how to fire a gun just in case of trouble like this,' she tells them. 'But next time, I'll make sure it's loaded.'

Chapter 8

CELEBRATIONS AND COMMISERATIONS

Betsey Macquarie

15TH APRIL 1810, SYDNEY

I couldn't be more intrigued. This morning I just received a note from Mary Putland that she's invited Lieutenant Governor Maurice O'Connell over to Government House today, and the pair would like to see me and Lachlan, if we have time.

I guess what they want to talk to us about as soon as they are ushered into the drawing room, O'Connell in his uniform and Mary dressed most conservatively in a pretty pale blue frock. Glancing at Lachlan, I see he looks mystified and I wonder, not for the first time, how he can be wise on so many important matters, then fail to see what is happening right before his eyes.

Mary is nervous and insists Lachlan and I sit down while she stands formally with O'Connell before us. 'The past two years haven't been easy for me,' she says. 'Since my husband passed, I've often thought I would never find happiness again. I believed it was my duty in life to look after my father in his time of need. But then I met Lieutenant O'Connell . . .' she hesitates and looks up at him. My heart melts to see the tenderness in his expression as he smiles back at her encouragingly.

I turn towards Lachlan, who's still looking puzzled. Honestly, sometimes I despair of him.

'We wanted to see you,' Mary continues, 'as both our head of state and dear friends, to ask your permission to marry . . .'

There's a moment of silence as they wait anxiously for our reaction. Seeing Lachlan looking absolutely stunned, I stand up and take Mary's hands in mine.

'That is wonderful news!' I say, beaming at the pair. 'Many congratulations!'

'Yes . . . What a surprise!' says Lachlan finally. 'I join my wife in offering our congratulations and wishing you both every happiness.' He stands too to shake O'Connell's hand and then kiss Mary on the cheek, asking her, 'What does your father say?'

At that, Mary's face clouds over, and her usual air of insouciance is replaced by an expression of anxiety I've never seen on her before. O'Connell takes her hand as if to steady her and she says, 'Father's in the Hawkesbury seeing friends so I haven't had the chance to share our news. I am not sure he will be pleased.'

I notice suddenly how pale she looks.

'So will you both be leaving for England with your father later this month?' I ask her.

She shakes her head and says, 'No, we plan to stay here. This feels like my home now and I know I will be happy here with

Maurice. My father won't like it, but he has his life and I have mine. He will just have to accept it.'

I feel a mischievous thrill that Bligh is going to be extremely put out. I can't wait to tell Elizabeth Macarthur.

Lachlan nods at Mary's words. 'Yes, I very much hope you're right and he will accept our engagement,' he says, smiling at her reassuringly, though I can see doubt in his eyes.

The next two days at Government House are very tense as we await Bligh's return. But as he finally sails in and demands yet another formal welcome to mark the occasion, he seems almost jolly.

As the days pass, I keep asking Mary, 'Have you told him yet?' Her reply is always that she's waiting for the right moment. I send a note to Elizabeth Farm with Captain Antill, so keen am I to let Elizabeth in on the unfolding drama.

Captain Antill arrives back with a note from Elizabeth saying: *'This is a turn up for the books! I don't think Bligh will take this well at all. He demands blind obedience from everyone and won't stand for any independent thought. The more his ego is pandered to, the worse he behaves.'*

I wonder if that's a little dig at me about entertaining him at Government House, but I let it go. It feels good to relish Bligh's discomfort with someone.

Each day, Mary looks a little more wan, and it's clear she's finding it all a huge strain. Eventually, I counsel her to act, saying, 'You realise the right moment may never come, don't you? And the longer you leave it, the harder it will be.'

Tears run down her cheeks as she replies, 'He's always been able to rely on me even as others have betrayed him. I fear he will see my engagement to Governor Macquarie's Commander of Forces and Lieutenant Governor, and my decision to stay in New South Wales rather than remain by his side as a devoted daughter, as the ultimate treachery.'

I confide in my friend Mr Bent that I really do fear for her and would not like to be in her position. No doubt her father has long been as domineering with her as he is with the men under his command, and it would take rare courage to stand up to that.

Mr Bent agrees. While he doesn't have as much time for Mary as I do, he doesn't wish her ill.

With Mary growing more and more uneasy, I offer her the use of Government House for their wedding to try to cheer her up.

But even as our official reception to farewell Bligh starts, Mary has still not told him she is engaged and plans to stay in Australia. Elizabeth, whom I've made sure to invite despite how annoyed Bligh will be to see her there, looks immensely amused all evening at the thought of Bligh's rage. Mary still doesn't tell him, however, and it's only as she's preparing to be rowed across to the *Hindostan* with Bligh's party for the night, that she vows she will. I hug her and wish her well.

The next day, Mary arrives back at Government House with red, bloodshot eyes and a face so ashen she looks like a ghost. Before I can embrace her, Bligh marches in, his expression like thunder.

Mary tells us later that he was outraged when she told him of her plans and refused to give permission for the marriage. Yet Mary remained resolute, saying she was marrying Lieutenant Governor O'Connell and they would be staying in Sydney. Father and daughter had argued for a full two hours, Bligh yelling at the top of his voice, Mary speaking quietly and earnestly. By the following morning Bligh had been forced to concede yet another defeat. His most steadfast ally had deserted him.

I expect him to set sail with all haste, but unfortunately his departure continues to be the most drawn-out saga anyone has ever had the misfortune to experience. Instead, he decides—to Mary's joy—to stay for the wedding and leave shortly afterwards.

We invite every dignitary in the colony, including Elizabeth, to the wedding. Though Mary protests her attendance, given that Mr Macarthur was one of the ringleaders of the plot against her father, I overrule her. It would be ridiculous, I tell her, to exclude one of the most notable members of Sydney society.

So it is that on the 8th of May 1810, Mary becomes Mrs Mary O'Connell, with the ceremony conducted by the Reverend Marsden. Lachlan presents the couple with two and a half thousand acres of farmland between Parramatta and Richmond as a wedding gift, which the O'Connells name 'Riverston' after his Irish birthplace.

At the evening ball that follows, I keenly await Elizabeth's arrival. When she walks in, she's looking quite brilliant in a beautiful emerald velvet gown, fringed with gold lace.

I greet her warmly. 'Thank you so much for coming!' I say.

'I wouldn't have missed it for the world!' she replies, her face more animated than I've ever seen it before. 'How is the old devil? Suffering, I hope.'

After glancing around to make sure Lachlan isn't within earshot I smile conspiratorially and say, 'It's clearly the last thing he ever expected. But in the end, what could he do? He seems to be finding it very difficult to stomach, though.'

'As we did him,' Elizabeth says. 'I hope he chokes on the toasts!'

After swapping recent news and agreeing we'll catch up later, Elizabeth circulates around the room, carrying herself with dignity and conversing equally with both the men and women, always leaving the people she's been speaking to charmed and smiling. I can see why everyone speaks so well of her, regardless of the enmity and discord her husband so readily provokes. I have heard that the Governor before Bligh, Captain Philip Gidley King, as well as his second-in-command Lieutenant-General William Paterson—whom John injured in the duel—both hated John with a passion. Elizabeth had for a while, however, managed to remain friends with both their wives, Anna Josepha King and Elizabeth Paterson. It seems to be the same too with the Reverend Marsden. He glowers at her when their paths near, but his wife gives a friendly little wave, and Elizabeth simply smiles graciously back at them both.

Mary similarly appears to be avoiding her all evening, and Bligh makes a point of scowling at her before he looks away in distaste. I'm sure Elizabeth is aware of them, but she does an excellent job of not showing it. Whenever our eyes meet, we exchange a smile and I am pleased I insisted on inviting her.

Mr Bent, I'm happy to note, looks as relaxed and happy as ever I've seen him, dancing with his shy wife Elizabeth. Like Mrs Marsden, she says so little in my company, I feel I barely know her. Mr Bent takes my hand at one point for a dance, and asks me if I've heard the latest about how Mrs Macarthur recently arrested a burglar at her house. He recounts what happened and I'm amazed at her pluck. At the first opportunity I draw her aside.

'Elizabeth! I hear you had a burglar!' I exclaim. 'What happened?'

'How did you hear about that?' she asks. 'Who told you?' She looks around the room and her eyes rest on one gentleman. 'Ah! Mr Bent!' she says.

'Yes, but what happened?' I ask impatiently.

'Oh, nothing much,' she replies.

I'm starting to feel frustrated. 'But I heard it happened at night, and you had to defend yourself with a firearm?'

'Yes, but I think he was harmless. It was really nothing.'

Elizabeth is approached by a young officer who wants to dance, and she looks almost relieved to be off the hook. 'Please excuse me,' she says, as she allows herself to be swept off to the dance floor, leaving me speechless at both her courage and her modesty. The wedding feasting and dancing go on well into the night and I decide that, aside from our St Patrick's Day Feast, it's one of the loveliest celebrations we've had during our time in Sydney.

Two days later, to everyone's great relief, and with us now having been in New South Wales for four and a half months, the bride's father makes his final departure. Lachlan obligingly has his men of the 73rd line the road from Government House to the wharf and accompanies Bligh to the Governor's barge, then doubles back in the carriage so we can go to South Head to watch his flotilla clear The Heads.

'I won't be able to really believe he's gone until I see his ship pass through The Heads and into the open ocean,' says Lachlan.

'I don't think his time as Governor justified anything like that violent mutiny, but I can see how unpopular his administration was. Personally, I find him very unreliable.'

We both watch with great satisfaction as Bligh's flotilla of ships is carried out into the open sea by a strong wind. As we turn towards the carriage again, Lachlan reaches for my hand. Suddenly, life feels infinitely easier.

Lachlan is in a much better frame of mind now Bligh has finally gone. He's been working tirelessly on a range of projects to improve the colony and is continually issuing new laws and proclamations. One of the most pressing problems of late has been the shortage of wheat, corn and other grains after damaging floods last year, so Lachlan starts buying grain from ships arriving in Sydney from India and America.

I'm particularly thrilled that he's asked for my opinion about several things. Emboldened by Elizabeth's excellent advice on taking the most of opportunities to carve out a role for myself, I suggest ways in which I can help. We both agree on the importance of starting a program of building new schools, and he raises the duty on spirits to pay for it. I've spoken to him before, too, about the filthy rags in which many of the convicts are clothed, and he also buys fabric to distribute to them. It's an expensive exercise but I believe it is essential. Again, I feel profoundly grateful to Elizabeth for showing me a way forward, and giving me the confidence to summon the courage and patience to start out on the path I want to follow.

One of the issues that Lachlan and I have discussed the most, however, is the position of those convicts after their terms have been served. It's something we both feel strongly about. 'When someone has served their time, they deserve a second chance,' I say to him one day. 'There's always a chance of redemption. In England, a felon at the end of their prison sentence would be automatically freed to go about their life with full civic rights. Why should life in the colony be any different?'

'I couldn't agree more with you, Betsey,' he replies. 'There are plenty who don't, and wouldn't. But we now have more convicts in New South Wales than free settlers so I believe it is time to act. We'll need to draw on the skills of those convicts whose sentences have expired or who've been given pardons. Then those emancipists should be allowed the same rights to hold land and positions as the settlers. To deny them would be to hold the whole colony back. I do realise this will be a move, however, that will be very unpopular amongst some of the settlers and naval and army officers, who want to safeguard privileges for themselves.'

'I'm sure you're right, Lachlan,' I reply. 'But those exclusives shouldn't be allowed to obstruct progress, or deny the former convicts the chance they deserve to lead a fulfilling life in the future.'

Many Catholics believe that you carry original sin with you until the final Judgement Day—even though you can confess. But Lachlan and I share the Protestant beliefs we were brought up with in Scotland and both very much believe that you can repent and make amends for wrongdoing while you're still alive.

There are so many different types of wrongdoing, too, and some of them, like political agitation, are punished much more harshly than others. I grew up on stories about the 'Scottish Martyrs' who were arrested for calling for reforms to the economic and political system. They were tried for sedition and sentenced to transportation to New South Wales. Four are now dead. Even though such brazen challenges to authority can't be accepted, political prisoners do seem to have suffered far out of proportion to their offence.

I remember Mr Bent asking me one day why we have many Scottish free settlers here, but very few convicts. 'Easy,' I replied. 'The Scottish penal code contains far fewer capital offences than England's. And mitigating circumstances like poverty, losing a job or being orphaned are taken into account more willingly by magistrates and judges.'

Mr Bent looked surprised to hear this and I told him how petty crimes, such as the theft of food or clothes, are punished a great deal less severely in Scotland too.

'They're seen as more a result of the environment in which the person was brought up than as a symptom of some innate criminality,' I explained. 'Sometimes, I can't help feeling the settlers who argue "Once a criminal, always a criminal" are just wanting to keep a ready supply of free labour.'

Mr Bent is far too cautious to offer an opinion on this—although I do note to myself that he didn't argue when he was offered room at former convict Andrew Thompson's house while his new one is being built. But it's becoming my firm belief that the current assignment system, under which the Government 'lends' convicts to people to work for them in return for their keep, is condemning many of the convicts to conditions of dire poverty for long periods of their lives. This cuts both me and Lachlan to the quick because we've grown up seeing the results of real hardship. Though Lachlan doesn't talk about his childhood much, I know he came from very humble beginnings on the small, windswept Isle of Ulva, off the coast of Mull. He moved to Mull at the age of thirteen, and his father died soon afterwards. I think the memories of the poverty and difficulties his family faced still pain him. He knows what it's like to have nothing; he has felt that pain and seen first-hand the desperation that can cause, and as a result has real sympathy with those who struggle. In the end, it was only the patronage of his wealthy uncle, my sister Jane's husband, that rescued Lachlan and allowed him to get an education and the means to embark on a military career.

My childhood was much more comfortable by comparison, though we were still far from well-off. My grandfather built our grand home, Airds House, but after the death of my father, we faced an uncertain future. My sister Jane had only recently married Lachlan's uncle, Margaret was still unmarried at twenty-four, John was twenty-one, and I was nine. We had very little income to spread between so many of us.

Naturally, we worked hard to keep up appearances, but it wasn't always easy. While I didn't experience privation anything like the intensity of Lachlan's, I never felt entirely safe from the threat of it.

Over here, our sympathy with the downtrodden puts us very much in the camp of those emancipists in favour of giving convicts their rights after their time is served. In opposition, the exclusives shun their company and believe convicts should always be regarded, and treated, as third- or fourth-class citizens. John Macarthur is a celebrated exclusive, so I'm far too wary to bring up the subject with Elizabeth in case we fall out over it. I dearly want her as a trusted friend and don't want our husbands' differences to come between us.

Nevertheless, I'm pleased when Lachlan finally takes the step of proclaiming that the convicts whose sentence terms have expired can apply for certificates stating this, and can then be declared free men and women.

'I think that's a wonderful move forward,' I tell him, even as we both brace for the backlash.

Of course, I understand, and share, his impatience with the exclusives' arguments. Often the convicts they despise so have the kind of skills the colony really needs and are much more useful than many of the free settlers. Look at Dr Redfern, for example. I've looked into his case and found that he was tried and convicted for sedition, but he is now doing invaluable work as our assistant surgeon.

Another former convict, Andrew Thompson, has become one of Lachlan's greatest friends and confidants. Found guilty of the theft of cloth and transported to New South Wales, he's an extraordinary fellow and now the colony's wealthiest man. Despite his past, he was later allowed to join the police force in the Hawkesbury, where he served with incredible distinction and courage, ultimately becoming chief constable. Lachlan tells me he's heard legions of stories about Andrew's courage as a policeman: tackling crime, hunting down felons and heroically rescuing settlers from terrible floods. He's also had considerable success mediating disagreements between settlers and natives.

Andrew now owns a number of thriving farms, not to mention a salt business, a tannery, a brewery and a ship-builders, as well as a store and inn on the Hawkesbury. He even constructed a toll bridge over the Hawkesbury River. Lachlan is so impressed by Andrew he's taken the unprecedented step of appointing him a magistrate. He's also told me he intends to make Andrew one of the three trustees of the new turnpike road he plans to have built to the Hawkesbury. Along with Andrew and the Reverend Marsden, Lachlan is also intending to appoint another former convict, Simeon Lord, who is now one of our most successful merchants.

Ironically, given the number of times Lachlan urged me to be patient when we arrived, it's now my turn to worry that Lachlan might be moving too far in relation to the emancipation of convicts, and it's me who's warning *him* to slow down so we don't make too many enemies.

As if on cue, Reverend Marsden comes to see us the day the three men are announced as trustees in the *Sydney Gazette*. Rather than expressing gratitude for his appointment, he says he refuses to 'sink to the level of serving with two convicts' because it will lower his standing and raise theirs to unacceptable levels.

'He even said that emancipating convicts and giving them prominent roles is destroying the right and proper social structure of civilised society,' Lachlan tells me.

'Is he serious?' I exclaim. 'What a pompous ass! He is as far from a Christian as I have ever seen.'

'I told him I consider his refusal to be a trustee as an act of hostility to the Government and of disrespect to me personally,' Lachlan says. 'It's just as well he changed his commission from military to civil while he was in England, otherwise I would have seen him court-martialled for disobedience. He also objects to Andrew being a magistrate because he's a bachelor, and Marsden believes all magistrates should be married men.'

I roll my eyes at that one. How petty can this man be?

Lachlan is furious. 'What's more, he criticised me for our St Patrick's Day event. He considers it most improper to invite convicts to a social occasion at the home of the Governor and to mingle freely with them in such a way. He claims he would never dream of inviting the convict servants working his land into his home. He's now threatening to write to the Colonial Officer and to the Archbishop of Canterbury to complain about our behaviour. How dare he!'

I suddenly feel faint and my knees start to buckle.

Lachlan catches me in his arms. 'Betsey! Are you unwell? What's the matter?'

I wait a moment for the dizziness to subside and then I smile up into his concerned face. 'Yes,' I tell him. 'Both myself and our child are well.'

Chapter 9

CRUEL PUNISHMENT

Elizabeth Macarthur

4TH JUNE 1810, PARRAMATTA

When Miss Lucas walks into the dining room she's startled to see Elizabeth Macarthur sitting at the table with her head in her hands, sobbing. She's known her mistress for five years now, and has never seen her shed a tear, despite all the troubles caused by her husband, her sons leaving for England and Lizzie's illness.

'Mrs Macarthur, what's wrong?' she exclaims in alarm, rushing over to comfort her. 'Has something happened to Mr Macarthur or one of the boys?' She puts a hand on her employer's shoulders and kneels down to look at her mistress properly. 'Oh, Mrs Macarthur, tell me what is wrong!'

Elizabeth's sobs slowly subside and she raises her head, revealing eyes which are red-rimmed with tears. 'Not, it's not John,' she says. 'It's that convict. Remember? The one I caught in our house that night . . .'

'Yes, yes,' says Lizzie. 'But what of him?'

Elizabeth wipes her eyes with a handkerchief and blows her nose. 'He appeared in court and has been sentenced to death by hanging,' she says. 'But I believe he only intended to steal a loaf of bread. And he had children to feed. Why did I not give him some bread and let him go?'

The news of the intruder's sentence has come as a terrible shock to Elizabeth. She'd been feeling so cheerful after Mary Putland's wedding and the subsequent annoyance of Bligh, followed by his final departure. To top it off, she'd had a whole week without the loss of any sheep after instructing the men to take turns watching over the flocks by night. She'd even written to John about both the sheep and Bligh, knowing how much both pieces of news would please him. But now everything feels trivial beside the loss of a man's life.

As Elizabeth starts to weep again, Miss Lucas kneels by her chair.

'Please, Mrs Macarthur,' she says. 'You weren't to know this would happen. You couldn't have known the court would pronounce such a sentence. You are not to blame. The day he decided to break into your home was the day he set in train his own fate. If you hadn't seized that gun, who knows what he might have done? You weren't to know if he intended to murder us all in our beds.'

'Except the gun wasn't loaded,' Elizabeth replies, flatly.

'Well, yes,' says Miss Lucas. 'But you weren't to know that. And if you'd let him go, he might have thought you a soft touch, and worth another try. You had to have him arrested for breaking the law as an example to him and other would-be intruders.'

'I suppose so,' says Elizabeth, wiping her eyes. 'But hanged for a loaf of bread!'

'Yes, but these are difficult times for everyone,' Miss Lucas says. 'People are going hungry every day with the drought causing food shortages and soaring prices. Yet most simply work hard, store as much as they can, and eke out their rations for as long as possible. Decent folk don't resort to creeping into other people's homes to steal food. The rule of law and order is critical in a place like this. And, I ask you, would Mr Macarthur have done any different?'

At that, Elizabeth forces a smile. 'You're right,' she says. 'I dread to think what he might have done. Thank you. I do feel a little better. Now, I had better get on . . . Mrs Macquarie has invited me to Government House this evening for the King's birthday celebrations. Captain John Piper is back from Norfolk Island and he's sending his carriage for me as my escort. I'm so looking forward to seeing him after all this time. We have so much to catch up on. I need to decide what to wear so I look my best!'

'Then you shall!' Miss Lucas declares. 'You shall be the belle of the ball! Maybe I could help you get ready?'

By the time Captain Piper's carriage arrives at Elizabeth Farm, Elizabeth has undergone a complete transformation. Smiling and excited after her earlier despair, she's wearing a soft lilac, full-length silk Empire-line gown, its folds cascading down and twisted into a series of silk roses. Around her shoulders, she has a shawl of the same material, embroidered with matching roses. The beautiful amethyst drop earrings her husband gave her for her fortieth birthday glint in the last pale rays of sunlight as she walks to the waiting coach.

'Mrs Macarthur!' Captain Piper exclaims and holds out his hand to help her mount the carriage step. 'You look ravishing! If only you were a free woman!'

Elizabeth laughs, relaxed and happy in the company of her dear friend who's always the life and soul of any gathering. There are few others in Sydney whose company she prefers, and the thought of arriving at the Governor's Ball on his arm pleases her no end. She's so missed him since he was transferred to Norfolk Island all those years ago, and she'll be forever grateful to him for being such a faithful ally of her husband when he'd returned to Sydney. Back then, he'd sided with John in his row with William Paterson, even acting as John's second in their duel. As a result, he'd narrowly escaped a court martial and been returned to Norfolk Island for six years as Acting Commandant. Now, with the settlement there winding down, he's back in Sydney, and with his land grant in Parramatta she hopes they'll see each other much more regularly.

'So how is everything with you, my dear?' Captain Piper asks, looping her hand through his arm. 'And how are John and the boys enjoying London? And your girls?'

Elizabeth laughs. 'Slow down!' she scolds. 'One thing at a time! I am very well. I believe the boys are also well in England. And as for John . . . who really knows what's going on over there! You may well have heard more than me. I sometimes think he doesn't tell me everything so as not to worry me. The girls are good, too, though Lizzie was seriously ill for some time.'

'She's better now, I trust?' he asks.

'Yes, she has fully recovered, happily.'

'And how are you finding our new Governor and his young wife?' Captain Piper asks.

Elizabeth smiles. 'They both seem very nice and fair people on a personal level, and they have been nothing but good to me,' she replies. 'Mrs Macquarie in particular seems to have attached herself to me. I met her many years ago in England, though she was but a girl at the time.'

Captain Piper raises an eyebrow. 'Well, that's an association that will do you no harm. However did you manage to carry that one off?'

Elizabeth has the grace to look embarrassed. 'I suppose it is an unusual friendship, given our husbands,' she says. 'I think it's surprised a few people in the colony, and I'm sure there are many who don't approve of the Governor's wife socialising with the wife of . . .'

'The man who felt *he* should have been in charge,' Captain Piper breaks in, laughing. 'So, what's been the general response to Governor Macquarie?'

'Some people think he's making too many changes in haste, some of them ill thought out,' Elizabeth says. 'For instance, he entertained convicts for dinner at Government House a few months ago. Can you imagine?'

Seeing the look of surprise on Captain Piper's face, she continues. 'Yes, they invited them for a St Patrick's Day feast. I also hear talk the Governor recently appointed two of them, Simeon Lord and Andrew Thompson, as turnpike commissioners, alongside Reverend Marsden no less. As you know, I don't have much time for Marsden, but still. He was very affronted, and I, for one, don't blame him. I've written to John to tell him all about it, and I think he'll find it hard to believe.'

'Well, well, Macquarie is clearly going to govern very differently to Bligh,' says Captain Piper. 'He's bound to upset a lot of people with behaviour like that. But then again, maybe it's time for a fresh look at how this place is run. Many of the convicts have turned out to be very good citizens once they've been given a chance.'

'Yes, that's undoubtedly true,' Elizabeth admits. 'It was Dr Redfern who saved my Lizzie's life. But the convicts have been sent out because they've broken the law, so I'm not convinced they really deserve to be permitted to live as the rest of us do. After all, we're the ones who came over of our own accord and struggled to build a decent life for ourselves, often paying a heavy price for the privilege. And men like Lord and Thompson have much more comfortable lives here than they would have had in England!'

Captain Piper nods thoughtfully and Elizabeth is encouraged.

'You look at their fine mansions and their good clothes and it's as if they've been rewarded rather than punished for their criminal deeds. And now they're being invited to Government House and are dining with the Governor and his wife. Who's to know where it will all end? The rest of us decent, upright, honest citizens are being excluded.'

'Oh, my dear,' Captain Piper says. 'I hardly think you're being excluded! You have a very nice house, a good life here and it sounds as if you're also now friends with the Governor's wife.'

Elizabeth shrugs and says, 'It wouldn't surprise me if Mrs Macquarie has never thought about the morality of mixing with convicts. She's never mentioned anything like that to me, and she's never even asked me about John and what he stands for.'

'Well, maybe she is wiser than you think, not mentioning such affairs to you,' Captain Piper says. 'But I have yet to meet her, so I shall hold my judgement in reserve. I do think you underestimate her, though. I understand she's been through some very tough times.'

'What do you mean?' Elizabeth asks.

Captain Piper pauses, seemingly unwilling to be drawn, and changes the subject. 'Do you know who's going to be at the ball this evening?'

'I think everyone of any note will be there,' Elizabeth says with a smile, 'as well, no doubt, as others of little note at all.'

'You mean there might well be some former convicts there, too?'

'Quite possibly,' Elizabeth says. 'But let's not talk of them anymore. What have you been up to?'

The rest of the journey is taken up with the pair catching up on gossip until the carriage draws up at Government House, which is an absolutely stunning sight, ablaze with candles and festooned with garlands of paper flowers.

Captain Piper springs out of the carriage and rushes around to the other side to help Elizabeth out. A parade of finely dressed guests are mingling and chatting as they wait to go in, and Elizabeth notes the envious glances from a couple of officers' wives when they see who her escort is. She smiles graciously and nods her head in greeting. The pair are soon swept into the ballroom of Government House, where the Governor and Mrs Macquarie stand arm-in-arm, greeting their guests. The Governor looks almost regal in his scarlet dress uniform, and Betsey is radiant in a long, elegant ivory gown, her glossy dark hair wound into a loose bun, with wispy ringlets at the temple, and a beautiful pearl necklace at her throat.

'Elizabeth!' Betsey exclaims. 'It's wonderful of you to come. So lovely to see you!'

'And so nice to see you, too,' Elizabeth replies, a little stiffly.

'And who is this gentleman?' Betsey asks, smiling towards Captain Piper. 'I don't think I've had the pleasure . . .'

Captain Piper steps forward and snaps his heels together. 'Captain Piper, madam. And the pleasure is all mine,' he says, bending to kiss her hand.

'Ah, Captain Piper,' says the Governor, reaching out to shake his hand. 'Good to see you again.'

'Thank you, sir,' Captain Piper replies. 'And thank you for inviting me. It's a great honour to be here.'

The evening passes in a whirl of drinking, eating, music and conversation. At one stage Elizabeth goes in search of Ellis Bent and, after exchanging pleasantries, mentions to him her distress at finding out that her convict intruder was sentenced to hang.

'But surely that is a good thing?' he replies, puzzled. 'The justice system these days is running much more efficiently, and quickly.'

Elizabeth grimaces. 'Yes, that is wonderful to see,' she replies. 'It's just that I do not want to be responsible for a man losing his life. He did not seem a huge danger. And he has a family to look after.'

Mr Bent is about to say something else when Betsey arrives, apologises for interrupting their conversation and draws Elizabeth aside. Elizabeth is annoyed; she'd wanted to continue the conversation with Mr Bent, to see if anything could be done about her intruder. But the moment has passed.

Betsey leans in close and whispers, 'Oh, Elizabeth, I have something wonderful to tell you. Since you have always been so kind and welcoming to me, I feel I want you to be one of the first to know. I'm with child!'

Despite everything, Elizabeth is genuinely pleased for Betsey. 'Oh, my dear,' she says. 'That is such welcome news. Many congratulations.'

'What are you two women being so conspiratorial about?' asks Captain Piper, who has sidled up, unnoticed.

'Oh, nothing!' Betsey replies gaily. 'Nothing at all.'

'Then,' says Captain Piper, 'Mrs Macquarie, you must dance with me. You look so ravishing. If only you were a free woman!'

Elizabeth smiles. Captain Piper simply can't help trying to charm every woman he meets. She loves him dearly but knows him for exactly what he is: wonderfully smart and entertaining to spend time with, but nothing like as fearsomely intelligent and solid and dependable as her husband.

Suddenly, she misses John terribly and wishes he were here so they could dance together and talk. His mood in his last letter was very low, his tone quite defeated. He sounded awfully homesick for her and the girls, as well as for his farm and the sheep. He was clearly frustrated that things were moving so slowly in London and it was proving such an effort to be granted audiences with the people who might be in a position to help. He'd even suggested that maybe she and the girls should return to England so the family could all be together. But although she hates being apart, she knows going back to England will never do. Everything they have now is out here, as well as their hopes and dreams for the future.

Tomorrow she will write him an entertaining letter to cheer him up. She'll tell him all about Lizzie's continually improving health, Captain Piper's return and the Macquaries, including their scandalous socialising with the convicts. But she won't mention Betsey's pregnancy, which feels more like a secret between women.

She'll describe the scene at Government House, and how Simeon Lord looked such a dandy as he made his grand entrance, dressed to the nines. She'll need to take special care to write about it all in a way that will make him laugh. And she'll put in how charming Captain Piper turned women and men alike into putty in his hands. He'll find that amusing, too. Hopefully, that will keep his spirits up.

Elizabeth realises with a start that this is the first time she's admitted to herself how worried she really is about her husband. She's known times in the past when he's sunk into a darkness of his own imagining and now, so far away, she knows if that happens again, she will be too distant to save him.

Chapter 10

MRS MACQUARIE'S CHAIR

Betsey Macquarie

2ND AUGUST 1810, SYDNEY

I am in such a good mood today that nothing and no one can upset me!

I'm sitting in my favourite spot in Sydney, on one of the steps of a sandstone rock on the promontory of the harbour. I love it here, taking in the fresh sea breeze and looking out over the vast waters, the various small islands, right across to the long fingers of land reaching out to The Heads. It's the one place in this strange foreign land where I can truly lose myself and dream, make plans, and think about my hopes for the future. I also often come here to write in my journal, sketch in my pad, sew or just sit and savour the view. Lachlan jokes that it's my 'special chair', and he was kind enough to have the steps cut into it to make it more comfortable for me to sit here.

Whenever I feel homesick I find it strangely comforting to come here because looking out over the harbour somehow reminds me of gazing out of my bedroom window as a child, taking in the vista of Loch Linnhe, the myriad small islands off Lismore all the way down to the Firth of Lorn and the open ocean beyond.

Occasionally, a ship will enter the harbour, raising hopes of mail, fresh provisions, new arrivals or returning friends. Today I've brought the treasured wedding gift the Meyricks gave me and Lachlan—a 1793 edition of James Boswell's biography of Samuel Johnson. I love his description of a visit they made to Ulva, where they stayed in the humble home of the last chieftain of the Macquarie, a distant cousin of Lachlan's family. Dr Johnson describes rain pouring into his room through broken windows, writing: '*I undressed myself and felt my feet in the mire. The bed stood upon the bare earth, which rain had softened to a puddle.*'

I smile to myself as I contemplate how even winter in Sydney Town feels so much more comfortable than gloomy wet summers back home. When I arrived seven months ago, I was filled with nostalgia for Scotland but now . . . I feel so much more warmly towards Sydney. The prospect of a little one has changed everything for me, and I put my hand on my belly, thinking wistfully of the son or daughter I will bring down here to play and point out the boats.

I look up with a start at the sound of Lachlan calling, 'Betsey! BETSEY!' Turning around, I see him striding through the tall grasses towards me.

'What are you doing?' he asks as he draws near. 'Is everything all right?'

'Yes, I just wanted some air,' I reply. 'I saw you were busy in your study and didn't want to disturb you.'

He takes my hand and we both gaze out over the harbour. 'It can be so beautiful on days like this,' he says after a moment of shared silence. These times when we're alone with each other feel very precious.

'You know, I'd love to draw up plans for some paths around here,' I say. 'It's such a tangle of trees and shrubs and it would be good to introduce a little more order. We could have a pathway built from here to the point so more people could come to this spot and enjoy the splendid view of the harbour.'

'That's a good idea,' Lachlan says. 'But you shouldn't be taking on too much with the baby coming . . .'

'I'm absolutely fine with all the help we have,' I reply with a laugh. 'And I'm so enjoying having the gardens landscaped at Government House. I've been working on some ideas for the gardens around Government House in Parramatta, too. Everything grows so well in Elizabeth's garden, so she might be able to give me some advice.'

Lachlan smiles and squeezes my hand, saying, 'I'm so proud of you, Betsey. And I'm delighted you're taking the lead with all your plans. I'm sorry I can't be of more help to you. I'm so busy at the moment with this scheme.' Lachlan had recently introduced a system by which people could buy cattle and sheep in exchange for grain.

'I'm pleased it's proving so popular, but the administration . . . Sometimes I despair! And the turnpike road to Parramatta is almost finished and the plans for a church at Richmond . . . but I feel as though I'm neglecting you . . .'

'No, no,' I say. 'I know how busy you are. And I'm proud of all the changes you're introducing. They're already making a big difference. It feels like Sydney is a much more pleasant, respectable place. The streets are less muddy with the new drains, and I think people aren't throwing so much rubbish into public spaces because they're taking more pride in their surroundings. Mary O'Connell told me that people she's spoken to have enthused about the naming and signposting of the streets. She also said how much safer everyone she knows feels with your soldiers on patrol at night.'

'Thank you, my dear,' Lachlan says, squeezing my hand. 'Despite the griping here and there, I do think we're making headway. And I don't know how I could do what I'm attempting without you here by my side.'

As I smile up at him he encircles me in his arms and kisses me tenderly on the lips. I melt into his embrace. It feels like Lachlan and I are growing closer and closer all the time. He's definitely much more affectionate and our relationship is changing from good companions to more like true partners. And, of course, we're both looking forward to becoming a real family.

Happily, we've reached a stage where Lachlan feels happy confiding his ideas and involving me in his plans, and he takes heed of my opinions, even if he can't always act on them. That said, it's not always easy, because we don't always agree and he doesn't take dissent very well. Sometimes he sees it as almost a personal affront and betrayal. I suppose his years in the military led him to expect people to obey him without question. As Governor, he's not exactly imperious, but when he issues orders he assumes they'll be fulfilled as quickly as possible. I'm trying to teach him, as best I can, that negotiation and compromise are signs of strength rather than weakness. I like to think it's gradually having an effect.

Lachlan is a good, kind, wise man but, at the end of the day, he's still a man. And as a woman, you learn very quickly that you'll achieve nothing if you demand things of men. You have to ease your way around them, subtly giving them ideas that they come to believe were really theirs in the first place. At least he now understands that while I'll support him publicly in everything he does, in our private domain I won't always go along with what he thinks if I don't agree.

Lachlan's pride sometimes prevents him from getting things done. When he likes someone, like Mr Bent, Mr Thompson or even Elizabeth Macarthur, he's loyal to a fault and will do anything for them. But when he sees people treating him without the respect he feels he deserves, he can lash out far too quickly. That's one of the reasons I'm trying to be so nice to Reverend Marsden, although he's an insufferable prig at times. I know Lachlan is going to have to work closely with him for our term here, and it's important that I smooth the way as much as possible. It's far easier for women to swallow their pride than it is for men.

Despite all the improvements Lachlan's been making, conditions here are still hard for many people. With Lachlan issuing so many new edicts, passing so many laws and introducing so much change, it's ironic that I'm now the one warning him to be more patient and careful to carry the people with him, and not to get important people offside. It's not enough to rule from above; he needs to win their hearts and minds, too. I've talked to him a little about this and, to his credit, when he was approached by a group of businessmen who had a plan to hold the colony's first horse race meeting, I encouraged him to agree. When he announced the event would go ahead, it proved so immediately popular, we both knew it had been the right decision. The races are now to be held in Hyde Park in the middle of October.

People here seem to love to gamble on horses more than anything else. No doubt it will involve a lot of drinking, too, but everyone has their own way of letting off steam. There probably haven't been enough public events since we've been here, so when I'm invited to become the patroness of the races, I agree.

More exciting for me, however, was that I recently accompanied Lachlan to visit two of the sites he's earmarked for schools. I'd drawn his attention to the number of children wandering the streets and suggested building a network of parish schools offering free education, like the ones we have at home. I was delighted when, soon after that conversation, he'd drawn up legislation to establish free schools. We've been inspecting the various plots of land for the schools, and Lachlan has spoken to the foremen in charge of construction.

A week later, we visit the Female Orphan School in Sydney Cove, which can now cater for up to a hundred children. The matron tells us that Reverend Marsden has been the driving force behind the school's establishment, and they are now teaching the girls reading and writing, needlework, cookery, spinning, good manners and all the skills they'll need to be good domestic servants, wives and mothers.

After our tour, the matron asks if I would be patroness of the school as well, and I tell her I would consider it a great honour. I know what it's like to lose both parents, although I was considerably older than these girls when it happened to me, and in a far more privileged position. Besides, on our voyage over to New South Wales, during a stop in Madeira, I had seen a terrible sight that haunts me to this day: a young girl, weeping, being received into an order of nuns, an order that was described to me as one of the strictest known. To me, and doubtless to the girl herself, it looked as if this was a premature end to her life. If I'd been able, I would have dragged her away with us, for whatever awaited us at the end of our journey could not possibly be worse than what awaited her in that nunnery.

So if I can lend any of these poor orphans a hand, and give them the chance of a better life, I will be more than happy. I express my concern, however, to the matron about the orphanage being right next door to the colony's main lumber yard where so many men loiter after work, not to mention opposite the guard house where dozens of soldiers are based. It worries me that the presence of so many men close by could be a corrupting influence on young, impressionable and doubtless needy girls.

The matron assures me that the girls are not allowed out on their own but, unfortunately, they seem not always to heed that rule. As we are preparing to leave in our carriage, I see a workman grab the arm of a little girl playing by herself in the street outside.

She squeals in terror and I spring from the carriage and shout at the man.

He looks up in shock as I race towards him and bellow, 'Get away! Let her go!'

Thankfully, the man is so startled by my sudden appearance that he releases his grip on the girl and scuttles off.

I take the child's hand and say, 'Don't be afraid. You're safe now.'

By then our coachman and Lachlan had sprinted up and together we walk the girl back to the orphan school, where I renew my concerns about the location of the orphanage to the matron.

On the way home in the carriage, I suggest to Lachlan that he should have the orphanage moved somewhere safer.

'But where?' he asks.

'Maybe we could have another orphanage built out in the fresh air and greenery of Parramatta, where there are fewer men to threaten the girls,' I reply, adding, 'We saw plenty of spare land along the river when we visited Elizabeth.'

Lachlan nodded, thoughtfully. 'That's a very good idea. And who do you think should take charge of such a project?' he asks with a grin. 'But I think I already know the answer to that question.'

'I'd love to do something like that,' I reply, hopefully. 'It would be so worthwhile, and would make such a difference to those girls' lives.' It feels very gratifying to have the power to give a helping hand to the poorest young girls in such desperate circumstances.

Lachlan immediately turns to the practicalities, saying, 'We shall find you some good people to help. Maybe you could talk to the matron and Reverend Marsden and then we could draw up a list of possible trustees and get the process started.'

I am so excited, I write immediately to Elizabeth telling her of the scheme. Perhaps there will be an opportunity to visit the site of the school together, given she's so close to the proposed site. And when it's built, maybe we could both talk to the older girls. Elizabeth would make an excellent example to them of how much a woman can achieve . . .

But, sadly, when I meet with Reverend Marsden to talk about my plans it doesn't go well. I show him my sketches of how the orphanage could be built, which I'd based on Airds House, looking down to the river rather than the loch at home, but he regards them with ill-disguised scorn. I am enormously affronted by his reaction but he is oblivious to—or just doesn't care about—how upset I am.

'Yes, yes,' he says. 'We'll see when the time comes.'

I take a deep breath and ask, 'And when will that be? These girls are in danger now. We need a safe place for them to live as soon as we can provide it.'

'I appreciate that,' he replies. 'But these girls are very low in the ranks of society, they are children of the State. We don't want them to grow up as immoral and as depraved as their parents and then start propagating themselves. They could even end up outnumbering the convicts, and what a fine population we would have then!'

I force myself to stay silent. He has a terrible way of twisting everything to his own grim view of the world, and he never fails to see the depravity of our convict population. And we are talking about children, for goodness sake. But I know I need his support. As the man appointed trustee of the orphanage, with all his connections, he could be a powerful ally—and an equally formidable enemy.

'Yes, of course,' I say. 'It will be wonderful if you can see a way forward to start . . .'

'We'll know when the time is right,' he interrupts. 'Until then I have a lot of work to do in preparation.'

Inwardly, I am seething, but there is little I can do.

I decide not to mention it to Lachlan when I get home. He has enough to worry about. But when he comes into the drawing room, I'm practising my violoncello with fierce concentration.

'Ah! I'm assuming your meeting with Reverend Marsden didn't go so well?' he asks.

I have the good grace to laugh, and decide I will occupy myself with other schemes that don't need to involve the Reverend.

By the time night falls, I've regained my good mood, and Lachlan and I lie in bed laughing over names we'd like to call the baby—Lachlan for a boy and Margaret after my eldest sister for a girl. But suddenly I feel a sharp pain.

'Lachlan! Oh my God!' I cry as I curl up in agony.

'What is it?' he asks. 'Are you in pain? Where is it?'

I can't reply as wave after wave of agony wracks my body.

Lachlan lights a candle and puts his arms around my shoulders, trying to keep me steady. 'It's all right, it's all right,' he says, trying to comfort me, even though we both know it isn't. 'Just relax, my darling. Try to relax.'

I whisper a prayer to God that our unborn baby isn't in danger. Not now. Not here. Not again.

'Betsey, I'm going to call for Dr Redfern,' he says. 'Just to be sure . . .'

I manage to struggle into a sitting position, and gingerly touch myself between my legs. When I draw my hand up it is covered in blood.

'Oh, darling,' says Lachlan, drawing me closer to him, his voice breaking. 'I am so sorry. So sorry.'

There is nothing I can say. I feel completely empty. I suddenly wish Elizabeth were here with me. She'd understand. It's at times like this, with your family so far away, that you really need a close woman friend.

When Dr Redfern arrives, he comes straight to my bedside, almost completely ignoring Lachlan. I'm surprised at his lack of formality, but grateful that he seems far more concerned about me than the need to swap niceties with the Governor.

'Oh, Mrs Macquarie, I came as soon as I could,' he says somewhat breathlessly. 'Now, could you please lie back and permit me to examine you? This won't hurt. I'll be as gentle as I can.'

I close my eyes as Dr Redfern presses down on my abdomen and listens for a heartbeat. Eventually, he covers me and stands. I can see Lachlan standing behind him, looking worried.

'I am so sorry, Mrs Macquarie . . . Governor,' Dr Redfern says, looking at both of us in turn. 'Your baby has been lost. But I can see no reason for this to have happened. Otherwise, you seem healthy and well, Mrs Macquarie. I can't see that you've sustained any damage. I know it is so hard, but you mustn't give up hope. Next time, you might not be so unlucky.'

He is being so ineffably kind, my eyes fill with tears. His brow furrows even more deeply with concern, and I understand why Elizabeth speaks so highly of him. He puts his hand over mind. 'You are strong and you are young,' he says. 'There will be plenty more chances for you to have children. You have time. Do not let this unfortunate occurrence make you lose hope. Now please rest and regain your strength.'

I stay in bed for a day and send a note to Elizabeth, asking if she can call on me when she is next in town. Lachlan and I are both in mourning, but few others would have any idea. I know that the more he sees me in bed, pale and wan and listless, the worse he feels. So it is up to me to shake off the sorrow and get on with life.

As Dr Redfern says, we have plenty of time in front of us.

I just hope he is right.

Chapter 11

A SHARED HORROR

Elizabeth Macarthur

4TH AUGUST 1810, SYDNEY

After a thoroughly hellish day, Elizabeth Macarthur is almost asleep on her feet. She got up before dawn to supervise the loading of several hundred washed fleeces onto a barge at Parramatta, ready to be taken to the docks in Sydney. The foreman of the barge complained about the tide, and said it would take at least twelve hours to reach the port.

Elizabeth told him that if the barge reached Sydney earlier she would pay each oarsman a bonus. When the foreman touched his cap and smiled as he accepted her offer, she realised that's all he'd been waiting for. But they'll still arrive after dark so they'll have to load the ship the next day.

At least the ship due to sail to England with the fleeces is in dock and the captain is expecting the load, she thinks, as she rides ahead to Sydney, anticipating another early start the next morning.

But just as she reaches her lodgings in town and is ordering something to eat, she receives a note from Betsey Macquarie.

'I would be most grateful if you wouldn't mind calling on me,' she's written in her familiar looped writing. 'I very much need to see you.'

Elizabeth is surprised. Betsey's notes to her are usually much more formal and a great deal less direct than this one. Only a few days ago, she received a primly worded letter from Betsey regarding a plan to move the Female Orphan School to Parramatta and saying that, once it was finished, she'd be most obliged if Elizabeth would visit the students in her spare time.

She'd been a bit indignant at Betsey's assumption she had any time left over from all her duties, but when she'd mentioned the request to Captain Piper, who'd called in the next day, to her surprise he suggested that she really should think about it.

'I don't believe you give Mrs Macquarie enough credit,' he said. 'There aren't many women who'd push so hard for relocating the orphanage to avoid the girls being placed in danger.'

Elizabeth reads the note again and wonders if there's some kind of problem, then writes back saying she'd be delighted to visit the next morning.

Entering the drawing room, Elizabeth is shocked by Betsey's appearance. She looks pale and exhausted and her eyes are red-rimmed.

'Betsey, are you alright?' Elizabeth says. 'I hope you're not overdoing things . . . You must think of the baby.'

At that, Betsey's face crumples and Elizabeth realises what must have happened. 'Oh, my dear, I am so sorry!' she exclaims, feeling mortified. 'I didn't think . . . I didn't know . . . I should never have brought it up.'

Betsey shakes her head and says, 'No, no, it's perfectly all right. I'm coming to terms with it now, and Dr Redfern seemed to think there's no physical reason why I can't carry a baby in the future.'

She stops, and her eyes fill with tears. She looks so desolate and frail that Elizabeth's heart goes out to her.

'I'm sure he's right,' Elizabeth says firmly, pressing the cup of hot tea that has just arrived into the other woman's hands. 'Do not worry. You have plenty of time.' She pauses, and then says, 'I had a child on our voyage over, a daughter. She was premature and died within the hour. There was nothing I could do but commit her tiny body to the waves and watch them carry her off. During that hellish voyage—they say it was the worst vessel in the worst fleet, battered by storms and gales—I nearly lost my son Edward, too, as well as John when he contracted rheumatic fever. And four years after we arrived, my second son James died only a few months after his birth.'

She hesitates, then adds, 'Now look at me. I have four healthy sons and three daughters, far more children than any woman could reasonably manage! Your time will come; I have no doubt of it.'

Betsey smiles weakly and Elizabeth takes her hand and gently strokes it.

'Do you want to talk about it, my dear?' she asks softly. 'Events like this are such a shock!'

'But this hasn't been the first . . .' Betsey whispers.

She pauses, and Elizabeth asks tentatively. 'You've been through this before?'

'Yes. This is my second miscarriage,' Betsey replies. 'But the worst . . . the worst . . . experience I've ever been through . . .' She looks as though she's about to break down, but manages to compose herself. 'Lachlan and I were blessed with a daughter ten months after our wedding. She was a gorgeous, smiling, happy baby, and we both doted on her. But . . . but . . . she was cruelly snatched away from us when she was ten weeks old. We both took it very hard.'

The two women are both silent for a few minutes, then Elizabeth asks, 'What was her name?'

'Jane Jarvis Macquarie,' Betsey replies.

'Jane Jarvis?' Elizabeth remarks, startled. 'Wasn't that . . . ?'

Betsey says nothing, clearly not wanting to bring up the memory of Lachlan's first wife.

After a pause, Betsey says, 'So when this chance arrived for us to come to the other side of the world, I thought it would be a new start. I was overjoyed when I discovered I was again with child before we left England. But just twenty days before we left, I started bleeding. I was inconsolable and Lachlan was as crushed as me. He longs for a family, as do I. I only hope that . . . but sometimes I wonder if ever . . . I despair . . .

'This latest one . . .' Betsey whispers, still obviously in her own world of pain. 'It's been twice now and I wonder whether it will ever happen. Perhaps there's something wrong with me.'

Elizabeth puts her arm around her shoulders this time. 'No, no, you must never think of it like that,' she says. 'I'm sure the good Dr Redfern would have informed you if he'd found anything amiss. It will happen in its own good time, and fretting about it will only make things worse. You must have faith. The Lord will look after you.'

Betsey nods her head, though she looks unconvinced and tears brim in her eyes again. 'You are right,' she says, finally. 'But I long to give Lachlan a son or daughter. It doesn't seem fair that he's had two wives and yet . . . and yet—'

'I'm sure the Governor doesn't think like that,' Elizabeth breaks in.

'He loved Jane so much,' says Betsey. 'And I thought the one thing I could give him that she hadn't was some bonny children, but it seems to be beyond me.'

They both drink their tea, deep in thought.

Elizabeth wonders if the loss of those babies may have been what Captain Piper meant when he said Betsey had been through tough times.

'How terribly rude of me,' Betsey says suddenly. 'Elizabeth, I didn't even thank you for coming over so quickly. And I didn't ask, how is Lizzie now? And Mary and Emmeline? And have you had any more news of Mr Macarthur and the boys?'

In that moment, Elizabeth's attitude to the Governor's wife softens. She's always been wary of her, seeing her as a gentlewoman living in the lap of luxury in Government House. But now, so grief-stricken at the loss of her baby but still asking after Lizzie and the family, Elizabeth feels a whole new respect. This young woman is turning out to be quite a surprise, Elizabeth thinks to herself. Perhaps she was wrong to dismiss her so quickly, and take such a set against her from the beginning. She's obviously going through some real personal difficulties, and yet she still seems so determined to make her own mark on the colony with her buildings and landscaping and the Female Orphan School.

And goodness knows, it's not as if Elizabeth has many other women friends. She'd been friends with Elizabeth Paterson until John had fought her husband in their duel. She'd also finally lost her friendship with the third Governor's wife, Anna King, after John had regaled him with complaints. Maybe Betsey could fill the gap they'd left in her life? She decides to be a great deal more gracious and understanding from now on.

'It's very kind of you to ask,' Elizabeth replies. 'Thankfully Lizzie is much, much improved. She's still a little weak, but growing stronger by the day. Mary and Emmeline are both well, and I'm hoping to receive more letters from John and the boys soon.'

'You must miss them so much,' Betsey says.

'Yes, but I try not to think about it,' says Elizabeth, a little taken aback by her own candour. 'If I think about them too often I feel too pained. So I keep busy and don't dwell on their absence. Sometimes I wonder what they're doing when I'm by myself in the quiet of the evenings. The rest of the time, there is too much to do.'

'Yes, I like to keep busy, too,' says Betsey. 'As I wrote to you, I'm determined to have the Female Orphan School moved to a better site in Parramatta. I couldn't do anything for our dear baby daughter, but I still want to improve the lives of young girls.'

'And how is that project coming along?' Elizabeth asks.

'Ah!' sighs Betsey. 'I'd hoped we'd be started by now, but Reverend Marsden seems determined to hold everything up.'

'Then we must put our heads together and find a way of persuading him to behave more to our liking,' says Elizabeth. 'After all, we have our methods . . .'

Chapter 12

STICKING TOGETHER

Betsey Macquarie

24TH SEPTEMBER 1810

I feel so much better after spending the morning with Elizabeth Macarthur. It was such a relief to talk to someone I admire who's been through the same experience as me. If she can be so brave after losing two children, I need to have more faith that I'll be luckier next time. I sometimes think that maybe it's my fault, and there's something wrong with me. But I need to get on with life, as Elizabeth so wisely counselled me when I went to Elizabeth Farm that first time.

To distract myself from the melancholy I'm feeling, I throw myself whole-heartedly into the arrangements for the horse racing meet. Here again, Elizabeth provides me with salvation in the form of her good friend Captain Piper's help. This proves a blessing since he knows a great deal about horses, as both a breeder and lover of horse racing. He also very well connected and is an excellent organiser.

When I tell Lachlan how much Captain Piper is helping me with the coming meet he says, 'Be careful, Betsey. John is a very nice man, but you need to watch what you say to him.'

'Well, he's been nothing but good and helpful to me. He knows so many people, too. They can't all be wrong about his character!'

'No, I didn't mean that,' Lachlan replies. 'It's just that he's a close friend of John Macarthur. It may well be that he's reporting everything we do to him. We can't afford to give Captain Piper any ammunition he can pass on.'

'Yes, of course, I'll be discreet,' I reassure him. But every time I'm back in the captain's company, I somehow can't help myself. He's so much fun, I find him a great joy to be around, and it's hard to keep up any attempt at formality and wariness. After all I've been through, I'm enjoying being able to relax and be myself.

Yet even with an event as happily anticipated as this race meeting, Lachlan seems unable to avoid controversy. When he attends a pre-race ball party at Simeon Lord's mansion, his critics decry it as the first time a Governor has ever visited the home of a former convict. It's simply ridiculous, and I tell Lachlan to ignore it. We will only make such people matter if we pay them too much heed.

Besides, the people in general seem happy. Lachlan has declared the three days of races as public holidays to give everyone the chance to attend, which has, predictably, proved very popular. We attend balls in the evenings of two of the race days, and as patroness, I present the Ladies Cup to the winner on the final day.

Sadly, on the eve of the final day we receive news that Lachlan's good friend Andrew Thompson is poorly again. He has never totally regained his health since wading into a swollen river last year to save people and their livestock. Though he didn't talk about it to us at all, many others spoke of his heroism. Lachlan and I are both distraught when he dies a week after the races. It is all so sudden, neither of us can believe the news when it arrives. Soon after, Lachlan goes into our bedroom, telling the servants he doesn't want to be disturbed. When he eventually emerges, his eyes are red and his hands are shaking.

'We've lost a good friend there, Betsey,' he tells me. 'We do not have many here, which makes it even harder. He was a good man, one of the best. He gave his life to save others, settlers and convicts alike. Seeing what a splendid, selfless citizen he became . . . makes it all the more difficult to abide those who would condemn the men transported here as hopeless cases.'

A few days after the news of Andrew's death, Lachlan tells me that neither of us have seen enough of the colony and we both need to have a break from Sydney Town. He's decided it's time to undertake our first official tour of the colony.

I clap my hands with excitement. 'Yes, I'd love that!' I say.

And so we set out in the Governor's carriage, with our servants, tents, campaign beds and baggage going before us. Accompanying us are Lachlan's aide-de-camp, Captain Antill; pardoned convict James Meehan, who's now the acting surveyor of lands; Dr Redfern; our guards; and my nephew John Maclaine, the son of my sister

Jane, who came over to New South Wales with us as a member of Lachlan's regiment, the 73rd. I'm thrilled at the thought of spending every day with my husband and having real time to explore, to talk and to mull over plans. I'm also relishing the chance to get away from Sydney and its rank odour, crowds and other problems, and to venture into the quiet, fresh air of the countryside. I'm also hoping it'll be an opportunity to visit Elizabeth at her farm again, and this time I send a note to warn her of our impending arrival.

We stay at Government House in Parramatta for a few days, making plans about how we can improve and extend it so it's a more fitting emblem of the Government and a more suitable home, and we decide to use it as a base on this excursion. Our first evening there, however, a note arrives back from Elizabeth Farm.

I open it eagerly. 'Oh no!' I say to Lachlan. 'It says the mistress of the house is away.'

'Is she in Sydney?' Lachlan asks.

I read further down the page. 'No, it says she is in the Cowpastures, their other farmlands. '

'Well, we shall visit her there instead,' Lachlan says, smiling to see my face brighten at his words. 'I will be interested to see that land and the state of her sheep.'

From Government House, we make day trips throughout the district, going to Georges River, the Nepean, the Hawkesbury, Richmond and Windsor. Lachlan discusses his plans for new towns on elevated spots, including one he's decided to call Liverpool after Lord Liverpool, who is currently the Secretary of State for War and the Colonies. These will all, in time, be officially gazetted, and Lachlan will grant land to encourage people to settle there. It feels as though our early plans for new model villages, as we had planned to create in Scotland, are finally coming to fruition.

After we leave Parramatta and venture further, we sometimes stay on settlers' farms or camp in tents. It's wonderful to receive the kind hospitality of people, though it's not always easy. One evening, while we're staying in a family's home, we have just finished dining when a noise comes from the garden. The man of the house immediately snuffs out all the candles, saying, 'It could be a native raiding party. We've been expecting some trouble.'

I'm appalled as I watch him take out his musket and start firing indiscriminately in the direction of the sound. I protest, saying, 'But it could be anybody, a servant or a native woman or child.' I ignore Lachlan's warning look and add, 'Should you not find out who it is? Lachlan can send some soldiers . . .'

'No, m'lady,' says the settler firmly. 'If it is a servant, then they have no business being there. But it is much more likely to be natives, and you can neither reason with them, nor show any weakness. They only understand one thing—firepower.' The next morning we go out to find the bodies of several kangaroos.

After that, I tell Lachlan I'd prefer to camp. I love watching the bright stars come out at night. They are so different to those we have at home. And the draped cotton canopy we sleep beneath allows the bright dawn light to filter through each morning.

I'm delighted when Ellis Bent joins us for a time because I so enjoy his company. Less so John Maclaine, who drinks heavily and tends to become noisy and raucous when he's in his cups. My other nephew, Duncan Campbell, my sister Margaret's boy who also accompanied us from England with the 73rd, isn't much better. He has turned out to be a conceited, spoiled young man. Lachlan decides to post him to Van Diemen's Land to see if that might knock him into shape. We want the two of them to reflect well on us.

One day, we finally ride into the Cowpastures, thirty miles to the south-west of Parramatta on the outer fringes of the settlement. One of our military escorts tells us that it received its name after a herd of over fifty wild cattle was found there about fifteen years ago, descendants of the four cows and two bulls brought over with Captain Arthur Phillip's First Fleet, which strayed from their enclosure in Sydney Cove. Mr Macarthur was later granted five thousand acres of land in the area for the grazing of his merino sheep.

We know we're getting closer to Elizabeth when we see a huge number of sheep, and so we stop a couple of times so our coachman can ask the shepherds tending the flocks where we might find the Macarthurs' farmhouse. The shepherds are always cordial and helpful, and most are astonished to see the Governor and his wife so far from Sydney Town. Finally, we're directed to a small, rough, miserable bark hut in the middle of nowhere. Just as we're thinking this can't possibly be the Macarthurs' base, Elizabeth walks out of the hut and is as startled to see us as we are to see her.

'Elizabeth!' I exclaim. 'I'm so sorry to arrive unexpectedly again. We are on a tour of the area and I didn't expect you to be here . . .'

She accepts my apology, but I can see she's not terribly happy that we are seeing her looking so unkempt. Her hair is tied roughly back, her outer smock is smeared with dirt and streaked with what looks like blood, and her boots are caked in mud.

Elizabeth shakes her head, laughs and says, 'Oh well, at least you'll be able to see how life truly is out here for us sheep farmers! I've just been lambing, which is why I'm covered in dirt and dried blood, and stinking of sheep and horse sweat.'

'Well, nothing would surprise me about you, Mrs Macarthur,' Lachlan says, kindly. 'Now, would Mr Herbert be here to show me around this area, too?'

Elizabeth summons Mr Herbert and soon he and Lachlan ride off, deep in conversation. Elizabeth then tucks her arm through mine and asks me how I've been since my miscarriage, and we have a brief conversation before she leads me into the hut. 'Now prepare yourself,' she warns me. 'This is hardly Government House!'

The inside of the shack is tiny, with only enough space for a couple of people, and very few furnishings or comforts. Still, there's a roaring fire at one end, a table and four chairs, as well as a single bed. Elizabeth asks me if I'd like some tea as she fills a blackened kettle with water. 'There's not much need for the finer things in life here,' she says with a wry smile. 'I only come to the Cowpastures for work. Since John left for England, I just have to get on with it.'

'So it's just you and your overseer and your convict labour out here?' I ask, thinking what a brave woman she is to work in such a remote place. 'Surely it must be dangerous for a woman. . .'

She smiles and says, 'I don't think about it. I suppose the convicts could turn on me or try to escape, but we're on the edge of the settlement here, and no one knows what lies beyond. There're certainly plenty of natives who sometimes steal our sheep. There are also bolters passing through and a lot of dingoes and other wild animals. Oh, and bushfires, which are probably the biggest danger.'

Elizabeth brings the tea to the table in a chipped pot and lays out two cups without saucers. 'What brings you this way?' she asks.

I tell her about our tour of the colony and the various people we've stayed with, including the settler who fired into the dark. Then, I remember my manners and ask, 'But Elizabeth, any word from England?'

She smiles. 'Yes, happily I've had another letter from John just this week,' she replies. 'He says the boys are thriving, growing up big and strong. They're both at school now in England and, although he doesn't say much, apparently they're settling down in their classes.'

'Oh, I am so glad! Though I imagine they're longing to come back here and help you with all this,' I say, gesturing outside.

'Yes, I think you're right,' she says. 'No doubt they will be finding it hard amongst the bustling crowds and huddled buildings after growing up on such wide open lands.'

'So what do you do here?' I ask. 'What is your daily routine? I'd love to know.'

I listen, spellbound, as she talks, and tells me what good sheep country it could prove to be here. She's just describing the fleeces she's recently sent to England when the door creaks open and I turn to see Lachlan standing there, clearly ready to leave. Though I'd loved to have stayed longer, Elizabeth is obviously busy, so I rise to my feet and say, 'Thank you so much for the tea and conversation. It's always so wonderful to see you. I greatly value our friendship.'

Elizabeth comes forward and hugs me. 'We women must stick together,' she whispers, 'otherwise where would we be?'

The next weeks pass in a whirl of visits. We call on Gregory Blaxland in Evan on the Nepean River, twenty-five miles north of the Cowpastures and twenty miles west of Parramatta, who entertains us with his tales of exploring the lands all around the river. He also mentions that he wants to mount an expedition to cross the Blue Mountains. Though Lachlan later tells me Mr Blaxland is simply in search of more grazing land for his sheep and cattle, we're both excited at the prospect of expanding the settlement further.

I force myself to be pleasant when we call in at the home of Reverend Marsden in Parramatta and try to ignore his obvious astonished disapproval that someone of my status is travelling in this manner. We endure an afternoon of excruciatingly polite small talk in the hope of re-establishing good relations with him. I am much more patient with his wife's silences, too. Elizabeth told me how her three-year-old son Charles died in her arms after her carriage overturned, and then not long afterwards she lost her baby in an accident in the kitchen. Now I understand a little more why she's so quiet and withdrawn.

All along the way, we're visited by delegations of natives and there's often an exchange of gifts. One group we encounter near the Macarthurs' land is made up of nine adults and five children. The man who seems to be in charge is called Koggie, and Lachlan tells me he's the Native Chief of the Cowpasture Tribe. He introduces us to his two wives and his children, and it's all very friendly and civil.

Yet my favourite times on the tour are when Lachlan and I ride alone together through the countryside. We alight from our horses and climb hills to enjoy the views, take long walks and throw down a blanket to have picnic lunches. I don't care if Reverend Marsden and his ilk are scandalised by this.

Still, I'm conscious of Lachlan watching me like a hawk when I've been on a horse for more than six or seven hours, or after I've walked up a particularly steep hill, and he occasionally expresses concern about the possible strain on my health from how far I ride, but I assure him that I am fitter and healthier—and happier—than I've ever been in my life before. He seems relieved and impressed at the same time, and I'm glad. I may not yet have been able to give him the child he longs for, but at least I'm proving myself to him in other ways.

One day, however, he looks at me seriously as we sit down together on a patch of green above the Hawkesbury River. 'Betsey, there's something I must talk to you about,' he begins. 'The one-year anniversary of our arrival here approaches. I already feel we've achieved much but we still have more to do, and sometimes that will involve upsetting some of our fellow citizens.'

'Yes,' I say. 'Well, we're already unpopular with some!'

Lachlan laughs and grows sombre again. 'We're at a crossroads now and face a clear choice. We can continue for the next seven years consolidating our progress, without undertaking any more great changes. That would be by far the easiest route.'

'Or . . . ?' I ask.

'Or we can do everything in our power to advance this place even further. I'd love to embark on a major new building program, introducing various institutions the colony really needs in order to move forward, and laying the ground for many more new settlements away from Sydney. But if we're to undertake such projects, we'll need to use the skills of the convict population. There will be people who won't like that, and many others may well try to hamper our efforts. Reverend Marsden and a number of the settlers have already expressed their opposition to lots of the changes we've made. If we push for more, the clamour will likely grow louder still.'

I nod, serious now myself. What Lachlan is saying is true. I've heard whispers he's making some powerful enemies. I know many people here resent how well some of the former convicts are doing and feel their own privileges are under threat. They consider what they see as Lachlan's patronage of current and former convicts an absolute outrage and mutterings about our St Patrick's Day dinner continue to this day.

We could well be in for a tumultuous time if we choose to go further. Some people are on our side, and some against us, but we're never quite sure who's in which camp. The strain won't help our hopes of starting a family, either.

Lachlan looks at me curiously, then continues, the faintest of tremors in his voice. 'Betsey, there is so much I see we could achieve here, so much we could do. New South Wales could be one of the greatest and most flourishing colonies of the British Empire. But I cannot do this alone. I need you by my side as my most important ally. I need to know you are with me on this; your support is critical. And that's why I want to know . . . What would you like us to do?'

Lachlan takes my hand and looks out over the river, the grim expression on his face betraying his anxiety over my reply. Then a sudden high-pitched cry, not unlike a bugle, makes us both jump and we turn to see a single black swan with white wing tips and a blood-red bill sail into view.

We catch each other's eye and smile. At home, black swans are a sinister omen. Here though, they're very common. I squeeze Lachlan's hand and say, 'By all means, let's go forward! To hell with the doubters.'

Chapter 13

A TERRIBLE SECRET

Elizabeth Macarthur

18TH NOVEMBER 1810, THE COWPASTURES, CAMDEN

As Elizabeth Macarthur checks on the bales of poorer quality wool earmarked for sale to the Government for convict clothing, she reflects on her second out-of-the-blue visit from Betsey Macquarie and the Governor and smiles wryly. She would never have expected to see them out here in the wilds of the Cowpastures, but now that she's become better friends with Betsey, it wasn't so unwelcome or awkward this time. Mr Herbert had expressed surprise at how knowledgeable and interested the Governor had been on their ride around the paddocks, and Betsey had seemed to genuinely relish learning what life was like for the colony's pioneers.

In return, Betsey had entertained her with stories about her travels in the colony: the time she'd looked down to see leeches on her ankles and had no idea what they were; and when a group of natives stopped dead in their tracks to see so many Europeans in a group. 'I don't know who was more startled, them or us,' Betsey had laughed. 'They have such a light way of walking, we hadn't heard them coming and we must have sounded—and looked—like a veritable army to them out there in the middle of nowhere!' Later, the natives danced for their visitors and Betsey and her party repaid the favour with gifts of clothing that seemed to leave their recipients completely baffled.

Elizabeth enjoyed the conversation and is grateful that Betsey made such an effort to disguise her unease at the poverty of their surroundings, which makes Elizabeth feel even more warmly towards her. Accompanying the Governor out here would have involved some hard riding and uncomfortable living, to be sure, and a fair amount of courage. No one would ever have previously imagined a Governor's wife doing this kind of thing; it was simply unthinkable. Elizabeth smiles to herself in delight at the thought of how outrageous the Reverend Marsden is no doubt finding such behaviour from a woman. Governor Bligh's wife hadn't left England to come to New South Wales with her husband because she couldn't face the privations of even the journey out here. Yes, on balance, it is good to have a friend like Betsey.

After she'd consoled Betsey about her miscarriage, Elizabeth had also sent Captain Piper a note saying he was right, and she'd decided to be a great deal kinder to the Governor's wife in future. Just this morning she'd received his response, congratulating her—half banteringly, she feels sure—on her newfound magnanimity.

Now she has a chance to finish the letter, and smooths out the pages on the rough wood of the table. She's coming to depend more and more on Captain Piper. A close friend of John's, he's also a great confidant and support for her. She finds his friendship a real comfort.

She reads all the latest gossip he relays about Sydney society, which feels so distant. But then he strikes a sudden serious note, bringing up the subject of Mrs Macquarie and her miscarriages. He reports that a number of soldiers he served with in the past happened to consort with women on their travels, and contracted syphilis. As a result, they'd been treated with frequent doses of mercury pills and later found their wives unable to carry a child to full term or that they'd given birth to babies who failed to thrive. A couple of Captain Piper's friends who'd served in Mr Macquarie's 73rd regiment had confided that the Governor had been seen taking the same pills. '*I would wager my entire fortune*,' Captain Piper writes with a flourish, '*on this being similarly the cause of Mrs Macquarie's miscarriages*.'

His words hit Elizabeth like a thunderbolt and she sits up straight in her chair. Poor Betsey, fretting so over not being able to give her husband a child. She's been torturing herself with her failure, yet it might have nothing to do with her at all. And everything to do with her husband.

Captain Piper closes his letter by saying he will visit Elizabeth soon and asking her to pass on his best wishes to John and the boys. At this, tears well in her eyes and she pulls her last letter from John from her smock pocket. If only he would write more about how the boys are doing! She misses them all terribly and worries about them constantly, particularly now Edward has joined the military. She wonders how he's faring in Sicily, and how James and John Junior are coping with their studies. It grieves her that she won't be with William for his tenth birthday. She longs to hug them all close. It was a major decision to allow John to take them home to England but she'd wanted them to have a good education so they'd have the best start in life.

There's one line in John's letter, however, she hasn't been able to forget. *'I'm in a very dark place,'* he wrote. What could he mean by that? she wonders. And how dark? She grimaces at the thought. Perhaps the dreadful colds he's been suffering in the grim English winters have affected his moods, as well as those blockages in his lungs and spasms in his side.

She wishes he would slow down and look after himself more, but she knows that is a vain hope. Ever since she met him he's been possessed by enormous ambition and a self-confidence. It comes across to others as arrogance, but she knows it stems from a certain amount of insecurity. If only he didn't have such an appetite for causing trouble! Nevertheless, she believes in him, and always will, even though sometimes she wishes he'd just be content with a quiet life with her and the children, instead of causing so many difficulties for everyone. Naturally, she'd never dream of saying that to him or to anyone else.

Hopefully, he and the boys will come home soon. He predicts in his letter that the case against Major Johnston for leading the mutiny against Bligh will be heard in the courts early next year, and at least that will put an end to the terrible uncertainty he finds so hard to handle. Tomorrow she'll send him the seeds, plants, animal skins and black swans he's requested to give as gifts to people in power who might help him, along with another affectionate and reassuring letter.

At least he acknowledges all the hard work she's been doing and bemoans how little qualified help she has, saying he's going to send his nephew, Hannibal Macarthur, over to assist her. She wonders what use Hannibal will be. Hopefully, he's grown out of being the vain, stupid boy he was when he visited in 1805. Still, if John thinks he might be of use, she's willing to give him the benefit of the doubt. After all, he's twenty-two years old now and boys do grow into men, eventually.

Elizabeth then feels the same stab of excitement as she did on her first reading of the letter, when she comes to the news that Lieutenant John Oxley has been asking about Lizzie. Not only would he be a good match for her, but his land grant at the Cowpastures might mean that if they do marry, Lizzie might not live too far away.

Elizabeth refolds the letter and gets up. She badly needs some air, and it's about time she checked on the lambs. She grabs her cream sun bonnet and leaves the hut, adjusting to the glare of the sun, which is high overhead now. Outside, Mr Herbert is waiting patiently, holding her horse.

'I'm sorry I've kept you so long, Mr Herbert,' she says, as she springs up onto the saddle.

The pair spend the afternoon riding from paddock to paddock, counting the lambs and getting updates from the convict workers. There have been a few attacks on the flocks by wild dogs and local native raiding parties, and at least twenty-five animals have been lost.

As they ride on, Elizabeth asks Mr Herbert whether he thinks she should engage more shepherds to watch the sheep at night, saying, 'It's heartbreaking to lose so many, and now with the lambing there're bound to be more predators around.'

Mr Herbert thinks it's a capital idea, given how many men in town would be thankful for the work, even though they might be nervous about encountering the natives.

When he promises to make some enquiries next time he goes into town, Elizabeth asks, 'How about taking on John Campbell?'

Mr Herbert looks puzzled.

'You know, the man who broke in at Elizabeth Farm,' she says.

Mr Herbert appears even more confused. 'But he's sentenced to hang.'

'Yes, yes,' Elizabeth replies, 'but I had a chat to dear Mr Bent and suggested his death sentence be revoked. He, in turn, spoke to someone and now Mr Campbell's sentence has been commuted to transportation to life. That could mean he'll be sent to Newcastle or Van Diemen's Land . . . but why not to the Cowpastures?'

'Mrs Macarthur, you never fail to surprise me. I'll make some enquiries about him, too,' he exclaims.

Elizabeth laughs. She'd been delighted to hear the man's life would be spared, and is extremely grateful to Mr Bent. She wouldn't have been able to sleep at night with his death on her conscience. She has enough worries as it is.

As they ride on in silence Elizabeth returns to mulling over the dilemma of whether or not she should tell Betsey about her husband's syphilis—as well as the one part of John's letter she's been trying to block from her mind. In that, he'd asked her to report on anything Betsey said about the Governor, and any difficulties he was facing, that could perhaps be of use to him in London. Even further, he wanted Elizabeth to casually suggest to Betsey that it might be 'in the Governor's interests' to give them more land for their sheep and more men to work it, and that such a move wouldn't go unrewarded.

Of course, she only ever wanted the best for her husband and their family, and would be reluctant to defy his wishes, but could she really betray Betsey's trust in such a shameful way?

Part TWO

The years are passing here in both the triumph of achievements and the heartbreak of failures. Despite all our efforts, I am still without child and despair of ever giving Lachlan the family I know he craves. But at least we are doing a great deal to improve this godforsaken place and it now has so many more fine buildings and streets and new settlements. It is never easy, however. Lachlan and I constantly encounter so much opposition to our plans, I find it sometimes terribly disheartening, and I know Lachlan does too. For me, Elizabeth Macarthur is proving a great support, even though I know she—and her husband still back in London—don't like much of what we are doing.

Betsey Macquarie's journal,
5TH MAY 1813

Chapter 14

I HAVE FAILED HIM

Betsey Macquarie

6TH MAY 1813, SYDNEY

Although Elizabeth and I don't agree on so many subjects, she has become a good friend and confidant to me over the past two and a half years. I know she doesn't approve of some of the changes Lachlan has introduced, but I still often ask her opinion of various ideas Lachlan and I have discussed. She doesn't always tell me what she thinks, claiming she has neither the experience nor skills to do so, but she sometimes takes me aside to question the wisdom of some of our more ambitious schemes. I do value her counsel because she has enormous common sense, and I have no doubt she's also speaking on behalf of her vast number of friends and acquaintances, whom I'm sure let her know how they feel about some of Lachlan's more controversial plans.

Our building program is one area where Elizabeth and I simply don't see eye to eye. I'm very proud that over the last two years

Lachlan has commissioned some very fine roads, straight streets and excellent public buildings. I feel particularly pleased about the input I had into the grand new hospital near Hyde Park, which replaced the near-derelict, insanitary old collection of buildings and tents at Sydney Cove. It was built on a site I recommended, to designs I'd adapted from my pattern book, as well as my sketches of the Portsmouth Naval Hospital. Not a penny from the public coffers was used for it either. Instead, Lachlan issued two of our most prominent businessmen and surgeon D'Arcy Wentworth each a three-year import grant for rum in return for the funds for constructing the hospital.

Later, when I showed Elizabeth the plans for the Female Orphan School, she gently warned me that she and various prominent friends of hers were concerned about us erecting so many large new buildings, believing that some of the money used to fund them might be better spent.

'We all know you're raising a lot of money from customs and import duties, but are you sure we can really afford it?' she said. 'The Governor needs to be careful that he's not seen as excessively extravagant and wasteful.'

I guess it's only natural she doesn't always share our views about the desirability of Sydney having an impressive civic presence. Just as she must do with the accounts of running Elizabeth Farm, she pays much more attention to the down-to-earth economics of running the colony.

When I argue that Sydney *deserves* to have the kind of public buildings people can be proud of and inspired by, she refrains from responding. Nevertheless, she doesn't agree with my assertion that if we're to make the powers-that-be in Britain sit up and take notice of us, then we need to show them what we are capable of.

Lately, we've refrained from discussing subjects we disagree about, the most prominent of which is the emancipation of convicts once they've served their sentences. While she is a compassionate woman—which she clearly showed by saving the life of the man who intruded into her house—I know she believes just as strongly that convicts don't deserve the same rights as free settlers. We also steadfastly avoid all talk of John Macarthur and what he's doing in London, beyond me inquiring about his health and that of the boys. We both value our relationship too highly to risk it.

Our friendship frequently reminds me of a beautiful line in my much beloved Boswell's *Life of Johnson* that, '*True happiness consists not in the multitude of friends but in their worth and choice.*'

I'm also very grateful to Elizabeth for introducing me to several people in both Sydney and Parramatta whom I've grown to admire. They've been particularly important to me since Lachlan and I lost Andrew Thompson and then, even more heartbreakingly, the friendship of Ellis Bent. That he turned on us was one of the greatest shocks of my life.

Mr Bent came to Lachlan with plans to make the judiciary totally independent of the Governor, and to introduce a jury system. Though Lachlan was surprised by the suddenness of the request, he was amenable to the idea at first. However, it was blocked in London by the Colonial Office, which was still dealing with the aftermath of the coup against Bligh and uneasy about limiting the Governor's influence. The arguments that followed—with Mr Bent saying he would only follow Lachlan's orders as Governor when he considered them 'lawful', against Lachlan's insistence that he should follow all orders whatever they might be—has led to a complete estrangement.

Elizabeth was very sympathetic, even though I know she also has a soft spot for Mr Bent. 'It's hard to know at times what they're thinking over in London,' she said. 'We have to be careful not to upset the apple cart. After what happened here with the rebellion, they're bound to be nervous, especially with so many convicts gaining their freedom.'

I rolled my eyes and she had the grace to smile. 'But, really,' she continued, 'who knows what they're being told in London about what's happening here?'

'Has John said something in one of his letters?' I asked.

'No,' she replied, just a little too quickly. 'But it's just hard from this distance to know what they're thinking.'

She's always concerned about my welfare, however, and often tells me to slow down a little. I've now suffered four miscarriages since we've been in New South Wales, and Elizabeth has always been quick to my bedside. I'm with child again now, and very fearful of what might happen. She's gently encouraging though, reminding me of her own losses and telling me my time will come.

But it's not to be this one, either. This morning I feel a trickle of liquid down my thigh and the horribly familiar cramps. I take to my bed immediately and send a message for Lachlan to come home. The cramps become steadily more painful, and the bleeding heavier.

Lachlan rushes home and doesn't leave my side, then stays up all night holding me as I sob uncontrollably. He whispers to me over and over again about how much he loves me, and how I mean the world to him and how he's sure we'll have a healthy child one day. When he thinks I've fallen asleep, he sits and stares out of the window. These tragedies have brought us even closer together, but I still wouldn't have wished them for the world.

I'm grateful for Lachlan's ministrations but, in the following days, I just can't seem to gather my wits. I shiver with cold as the sun rises on another day in New South Wales even as darkness seems to cover me.

'Betsey, *please*,' Lachlan implores me. 'What can I do to help you? You know I'd do anything to make you happy.'

I see how profoundly worried he is, but somehow I just can't seem to stir myself.

'Should I ask Elizabeth to come?' he asks. 'Would you like to see her? I'm sure she'd be very happy to call.'

'Yes,' I murmur. 'Yes, I think I would like that.'

'Good,' says Lachlan, looking relieved. 'I'll send a message to her now. Hopefully, she isn't too busy. Just wait here, my dear. I'll be but a moment.'

I know I shouldn't give up, but I just feel as though I want to be left in peace to mourn yet another child lost; this baby would have been my sixth. I slide down beneath the covers and close my eyes. Lachlan comes back in to the bedroom and I sense him looking at me, but I pretend to be asleep. I just need to be left to come to terms with yet another heartbreak.

I doze and wake, doze and wake, as the weak late-autumn light penetrates the muslin curtains. Then I start as someone enters the room. I struggle to open my salt-encrusted eyes, and try to sit up as a figure perches on the side of the bed. It is Elizabeth.

'Oh, my dear,' she says, taking my hand. 'The Governor told me the sad news. I am *so* sorry. It's hard to believe this has happened yet again. I can't fathom how you could be so unlucky.'

I sit up and do my best to smile. 'No, not unlucky,' I sigh. 'This has happened too often for this to be a case of bad luck. There is something wrong with me, I know it. Dr Redfern says there isn't but there can be no other explanation.' My voice breaks and it takes all my strength to keep my composure.

'I just have to accept that I have let Lachlan down. He should never have married me. I can't give him the child I know he longs for,' I say, tears running down my cheeks.

Elizabeth looks stricken, then pensive. Then it's as if she's made a sudden decision as she leans closer to me. 'No, my dear, you haven't failed him,' she says slowly.

I stare back, not understanding.

She takes a breath. 'It's not you, Betsey,' she says, hesitantly, her hands twisting in her lap. 'I think it's the Governor who's at fault.'

'Lachlan?' I say. 'I don't understand . . . How . . . ?'

She looks at me, levelly. 'Has he ever told you he has syphilis?' she asks.

I look at her dumbly.

'Many of our soldiers contract syphilis when serving abroad,' she continues. 'And many treat it with mercury pills. It sometimes makes it difficult for them to father children to full term afterwards . . .'

I'm still struggling to understand. She continues speaking, her voice soft.

'Apparently some of the men under his command saw Lachlan taking mercury pills,' she says. 'So he no doubt has syphilis, too. It means that quite probably it's he who has unintentionally caused your miscarriages rather than any shortcoming of yours.'

Lachlan? I think, shocked. No, he's never told me of any possible illness, and I've never thought to ask. Even now, I don't think I could raise the subject.

'I don't think this is something you should ever ask your husband about,' Elizabeth advises, as if reading my mind. 'Men don't like to talk of such things with women, particularly their wives. But it's something you should know, so you can stop blaming yourself for any failures.'

Somewhere, through the fog in my brain, I rasp, 'So it's not me . . . It's not . . .'

'No, it is most definitely not you,' she says firmly. 'Now, you must get some sleep, recover your strength and keep going. You're far too important to us to give up on life just yet!'

'Thank you, Elizabeth,' I whisper. 'Thank you.'

I spend two more days in bed recuperating before, to Lachlan's obvious relief, I get up, get dressed and throw myself back into life in the colony. I feel liberated to know what the problem might be and enormously grateful to Elizabeth for freeing me from my overwhelming self-doubt and blame. My heart feels so much lighter.

I distract myself with my favourite project—the Female Orphan School—which is finally underway, though it took the Reverend

Marsden no fewer than three years to call for tenders. I know he still doesn't like me, although he's very civil when we encounter each other. In return, I am the very picture of sweetness and light towards him.

I've heard that he's told people privately that he blames me for Lachlan's embrace of the emancipist cause. He thinks this 'ill-conceived policy' was my idea, pointing to my inviting convict workers to our St Patrick's Day lunch as evidence.

Despite the Reverend's lack of enthusiasm for my design for the school, it's being built just as I pictured it, based on Airds. Three storeys high and built of brick, it's the highest building in the colony. And as with the building's design, I intend to landscape it in a similar style to my family home.

There are still many tedious delays, however, what with Reverend Marsden's complaints about 'drunken' workers, his refusal to allow convict labour onto the site and disputes over how the builders should be paid. Then there was his long absence after being shipwrecked in New Zealand on his way back from a missionary expedition to the Maori.

'What a shame it wasn't more serious . . .' I whisper to Elizabeth when the news of his misadventure reaches Sydney. She laughs and I do, too. She is the only person to whom I would ever express such a terrible thought.

Lachlan and I have continued our travels around the colony, as well as further afield. He and his men are gradually opening up this country enormously, establishing new towns all over the settlement. We've visited numerous places in both New South Wales and elsewhere, despite the discomfort. Our voyage to Van

Diemen's Land was one of the worst I've ever experienced, with horrendous gales and terrible storms which left me suffering the most appalling seasickness. I spent much of the nineteen days it took us to reach Hobart Town absolutely terrified, though I tried not to show it. When we finally did arrive, people seemed so excited to see us that it all felt worthwhile. There were many events to greet us, then we travelled by horseback and boat to visit a number of outlying settlements, to the gratitude of the settlers. Thankfully, the voyage back was much calmer.

I have other friends now, too, like Dr Redfern and his wife Sarah, who've become trusted confidants. After Lachlan and Elizabeth, they are the first people I tell when I fall pregnant again. I confide in them soon after they arrive as our honoured guests at the dinner party Lachlan organises to mark our sixth wedding anniversary.

'That is wonderful news, Mrs Macquarie,' Dr Redfern says as Sarah gives me a hug. 'I am so glad to hear it. Can you make an appointment to see me next week? I have a feeling all will be well this time. You look positively blooming!'

When, five months later, I am still with child, I hardly dare to believe it. I spend each day in an agony of waiting, fearful of miscarrying at any moment. Dr Redfern examines me regularly and each time he declares me to be as fit as a fiddle. He encourages me to believe that this time I will be more fortunate. It is all I can do not to ask him about the impact of syphilis on my chances of keeping the baby and it living to a healthy age, although I have no idea whether he would know what I now suspect about Lachlan. Happily, as the weeks and months pass, and I feel the baby start to kick, I begin to have the courage to imagine that this child might survive. Lachlan is as excited as me, and urges me to rest whenever I can.

My waters finally break on the 28th of March 1814, the day we are hosting another dinner party for various dignitaries of the colony.

'I'll postpone it,' Lachlan says when it appears I'm in labour. 'We can't possibly go ahead with the dinner this evening.'

'No, no,' I urge him. 'It's an important gathering and it's too late to put people off. And besides, there's nothing you can do. I'll have Dr Redfern and Elizabeth with me, as well as two nurses assisting as midwives, so I'll be in very good hands. I don't want to hear you pacing up and down outside the bedroom door in any case. Dr Redfern will let you know when there's news.'

While I'm in labour I hear the soft murmur of conversation in the dining room and the tinkling of glasses, and find it strangely comforting. Lachlan sends a maid up every half-hour to find out how things are going.

But the hours drag on, and the agony feels like it will never stop, despite Dr Redfern being so attentive and Elizabeth mopping my brow and calming me each time I have a contraction.

Then, just before midnight, the pain builds up and up until there's a final wrenching agony and a sudden silence that seems to stretch on forever. I hold my breath in terror until I hear the pitiful squalling of my baby.

'Mrs Macquarie!' Dr Redfern says. 'Congratulations! You have a son.'

'And he's absolutely perfect,' says Elizabeth. 'Well done, my dear. I am so very happy for you and the Governor!'

At that, she hands me my baby boy already swaddled in white muslin, and I weep as if a dam has broken somewhere deep inside.

There's a thunder of footsteps outside, and Lachlan bursts into the room. 'Betsey!' he yells in delight. 'My darling girl! Is it true? We have a son?'

'Yes!' I reply joyously, as I hand him the baby. 'Here, meet your son, our little Lachie.'

At that he too bursts into tears and holds us both as though he'll never let us go.

Chapter 15

A DANGEROUS GAME

Elizabeth Macarthur

1ST OCTOBER 1814, PARRAMATTA

The words in John's letter send an icy chill into Elizabeth Macarthur's heart.

She knows she's been treading an increasingly fine line between making him feel he's being informed about everything going on in the colony and avoiding giving him anything he can use against the Macquaries. Following the rebellion against Bligh, John had assumed the newly created role of Colonial Secretary, and had seen himself as almost the de facto ruler of New South Wales. As a result, he resents Governor Macquarie's appointment and is angry that he's not granting him more land for his sheep. His rancour is growing with the failure of a number of his enterprises over in London, to do with seal and whale fisheries and trading in sandalwood, and he patently disapproves of what he sees as the

Governor's leniency towards the convicts. His anger is mounting, and now he's drastically ramping up the pressure on Elizabeth.

He seems resolute to try to discredit both the Governor and his wife, and cause trouble for them in London. But Elizabeth wants no part of it. She loves him, of course she does, and generally trusts his good judgement and commitment to do his best by their family. At the same time, she sees how much the colony has flourished under their leadership—despite the grand buildings of which she still disapproves. She has grown fond of Betsey. And she is extremely grateful to Mr Macquarie for his many kindnesses. He could, had he so chosen, made her life hell in the colony. Instead, he treats her with courtesy, respect and, yes, even gratitude for her friendship with his wife.

She's avoided responding to each of John's suggestions that she spy on them and pass on any potentially damaging information. But he seems determined not to leave it be, and she's well aware of how dangerously obsessive he can be.

In his latest missive, he takes a different tack, saying that since she is now so close to Betsey she should casually broach the subject of their sheep and 'lament that the flocks should remain stationary'. Then she should 'cautiously' hint that they'd been on the point of being granted lots of extra land and servants by Bligh's predecessor, Governor King, and if Mr Macquarie were to abide by the same plan, John is in a position to make them both rich.

John argues there is no reason for the Governor not to agree. One of Mr Macquarie's chief rivals for the New South Wales governorship, the hard-nosed Hugh Elliott, also believes that John should be allowed to have more land for his sheep as a valuable source of revenue for the colony. According to John 'everyone' is in favour of him being given more land so Mr Macquarie has no reason on earth to refuse him.

Elizabeth finishes reading the letter and sighs heavily. In her last letter to John, she'd told him about the birth of the Macquaries' son, and the incredible excitement throughout New South Wales at the news. Yet when he receives that letter, she knows he'll be scanning it for something far darker, though he won't find anything.

She's in an even trickier position now that George Johnston, John's co-conspirator, is back in Sydney after being found guilty of mutiny, but only discharged from the army as punishment. Now settled on his farm between Sydney and Parramatta, Mr Johnston will doubtless also be writing to John, so her husband will receive more news of what's happening here. She doesn't want to risk being caught withholding information.

She racks her brains for anything she can distract him with in her next letter.

Looking out of the window, she catches sight of Hannibal striding towards the stables. Since his return to Sydney, John's nephew has actually proved a huge help with the sheep. He works hard and is doing well, and has recently been appointed a magistrate. Yet though he has excellent connections—his wife, Anna Maria, is actually the eldest daughter of the former Governor King—his pleas to Mr Macquarie for grants of land have proved unsuccessful. He has written to John complaining, but there is nothing John can do. But it's not as if Mr Macquarie is refusing all applications. He recently approved her request that Mr Herbert be given some land, for which she will always be grateful.

Elizabeth picks up her pen, then lays it back down. She was going to tell John that Hannibal and Anna Maria have settled into a nearby farm, as they are now expecting their first child. But she knows that's not the kind of news that would interest him at all.

So, what else has been happening? John Campbell, the burglar she saved from the hangman's noose, has taken many of the unpopular overnight shifts with the sheep, so grateful is he for his life and for the wages to feed his family. Elizabeth has only encountered him once in the paddocks over at the Cowpastures in the early morning. When she rode up to him, he'd coloured and bowed deeply and mumbled his thanks. But no, she's never told John anything about their intruder and she's sure he would never approve of her employing him.

Perhaps she'll let him know about the continuing rift between the Macquaries and Mr Bent? Surely it could do little harm to give him the latest on that? She feels a pang of guilt as she recalls Betsey weeping as she described how coldly formal Mr Bent is towards to her now when they run into each other.

'It's like we never really knew each other,' Betsey said. 'And yet we have been through so much together over the years! The voyage here, those first few years in Sydney when everything was so difficult and we all worked so hard together to effect change. It's like . . . it never really happened.'

'You've got to remember,' Elizabeth had told Betsey, 'he's not a well man. He always looks so pale and I hear he's developed dropsy.

The way Mr Bent shuffles about now, he must be in a lot of pain. That does nothing to improve a man's mood—or keep him rational.'

Betsey had nodded in agreement. 'I also blame his brother,' she'd said. 'He's never been the same since Jeffery Bent came out here to join him. That man has been trouble from the moment he sailed through The Heads. I should have realised we were receiving another Bligh when he refused to land until he'd received a formal salute of gunfire. And even after being sworn in as a judge, he refused to sit in court for the first four months, saying he considered the rooms he'd been assigned in part of the new hospital simply not up to his standards.'

Elizabeth didn't like Jeffery Bent either, though she didn't consider him anything like on par with Bligh. But she tried to hide her irritation. 'Yes, he has always had an exceedingly high opinion of himself,' she'd replied.

Betsey laughed. 'Yes, incredible,' she said, pulling a face, mocking his outrage. 'I am so glad, however, he received such short shrift when he complained about the rooms to London.'

'But didn't that just further fuel his ire?' Elizabeth asked with a chortle. 'It seems like he's become even more determined to egg on Mr Bent in any dispute with the Governor.'

'Yes, and that's been dreadful,' Betsey replied. Then, looking down at her son sleeping peacefully in her arms, she said, wistfully, 'I always thought Mr Bent would be a dear uncle to you, Lachie, but that will never be.'

In the end, Elizabeth decides to tell John about how sour the relationship has become between the Bents and the Macquaries as a way to divert him.

Yet she can't help wondering what life will be like when John returns. For the first time, she feels a flicker of trepidation at the prospect of him coming back and living under the rule of a Governor he obviously despises.

Chapter 16

THE PAIN OF A MOTHER

Betsey Macquarie

6TH OCTOBER 1814, SYDNEY

It's nearly midday on a beautiful bright autumn day, and my heart feels light as I sit beside our coachman Mr Joseph Bigg as he drives down George Street to call on our talented Government architect, Francis Greenway. I relish every chance I get to talk to Mr Greenway about our shared passion for architecture and building design.

He was sent out here as a convicted forger, but when Lachlan discovered he had previously been a professional architect, we both interviewed him and were impressed by his knowledge and obvious skills. He inspected the hospital before it was finished and made some excellent alterations. He also commented very favourably upon a sketch I did for the house of the Governor's secretary. He's certainly a gifted architect and we are very lucky he arrived here at a time when we were most in need of someone with skills like his. At the moment he's drawing up plans for a splendid lighthouse on South Head, which will also be a wonderful place for picnics, and an obelisk in Macquarie Place to indicate the length of all the public roads leading to the interior of the colony. We hope these will all be a part of our proud legacy.

He's also masterminding the new Hyde Park Barracks, where convicts will live until they're assigned to settlers or given a job working for the Government. In fact, Lachlan has decided he will give Mr Greenway his absolute pardon on the opening day for those barracks.

Mind you, I don't always see eye to eye with Mr Greenway on designs, and he can be rather arrogant and dismissive of other people's opinions. But we tolerate his foibles in return for the brilliance of his vision.

Joseph slows down as a cart ahead blocks our way and then calls to one of the guards to go and move it. I take the time to look around and smile as I watch some little children playing by the side of the street, digging and throwing handfuls of sand at each other.

When the cart has finally been moved off to one side, Joseph shouts out a warning to the children, then urges the horses forward. But one of the horses seems unsettled and swerves suddenly. There's a dull thud, a violent jolt and a moment of deathly silence before a high-pitched scream of terror. Then there's a thumping of horses' hooves, a thunderous 'Whoa! Whoa! Whoa!' from Joseph and a dozen male voices shouting, shouting, shouting.

Joseph brings the carriage to a juddering halt and I see, to my absolute horror, a tiny child's body lying motionless in the street by one of the coach's wheels.

Swinging myself down from the platform, I kneel on the ground by the small child. There are marks from the muddy wheel on the back of his jacket; he had no chance. I carefully, so carefully, lift one of his shoulders and then the other to gently turn him over. He's lifeless, like a rag doll.

I gather him up in my arms and shout for someone to dispatch a messenger to Dr Redfern to come quickly. Then, almost blinded by tears, I run all the way to the poor child's home as the men point out the way. When his mother opens the door and sees who I'm nursing in my arms, she faints clean away. After she finally comes to, we both sit at the little table in her modest home and weep together until Dr Redfern arrives, examines the child, pronounces him dead and orders me home.

Back at Government House, I collapse and spend the next few weeks confined to bed. The grief I feel is the most terrible thing I've ever experienced. Lachlan is sympathetic, repeating to me time and time again that it was an accident and that I had done everything I could. But I am devastated. I know what it is to lose a child. I nurse little Lachie fiercely and hold him so tight he cries until the nursemaid prises him from my arms.

I have nightmares over the following weeks, reliving the horror. I dream one night that I turn over the body and see Lachie's face. And then I hear a terrible animal-like screaming which goes on and on and on. I wake with a start, slowly climbing out of terror, panic and misery towards consciousness, and realise it's my own.

'My darling, it's all right,' Lachlan says, holding me tight. 'It's just another bad dream. Come now, all is well.'

'Lachie?' I ask fearfully.

'Lachie is sleeping safely in the nursery,' Lachlan reassures me. 'The nanny is with him. Nothing has happened to him. It was just a nightmare.'

Dr Redfern gives me a sleeping potion and says I am in the midst of a complete nervous breakdown. I spend several weeks in bed, but I still feel overwhelmed with sorrow. We agree Lachlan should write to the Secretary of State for War and the Colonies, Lord Bathurst, in England to tell him about the incident. Mr Greenway calls in one day with his plans in hand, but I send my maid down with a message saying I don't feel well enough to see him. The importance of new buildings has been eclipsed by the death of that poor child.

From reports of the inquest held later on the day of his death, I learn his name was Charles Thomas and, agonisingly, the day he died was his third birthday. Even worse, the guard travelling behind us, by terrible coincidence, was the little boy's father. How dreadful for him! The witnesses all told the inquest the child had run into the path of the carriage, and that they'd heard Joseph calling a warning. Thankfully, he is cleared of all charges of either negligence or reckless driving.

But when I visit Charles's mother some months later to pay my respects and to tell her again how terribly sorry I am, his family relates a different story. Charles's older brother, William, who witnessed the tragedy, says that Joseph was driving too fast, and was drunk. I am shocked. William also says that after I had run to the house with his brother's body, the men who'd seen what had happened had tried to attack Joseph, and it had only been the intervention of the boy's father, William Thomas Senior, that had saved the coachman from being killed.

As William gives his account, my hand flies to my mouth in shock, and my grief only grows when Mrs Thomas tells me Charles's father felt obliged to keep working after his son's death.

'Oh, Mrs Thomas! Your poor husband!' I say, bereft that out of a sense of duty Charles's father hadn't come home to her in their hour of need, instead staying to help Joseph. 'I am so sorry,' I sob. 'If only I hadn't come out that day. If only Joseph had not been driving the carriage. If only I'd stayed home—'

'No, no, Mrs Macquarie,' Mrs Thomas breaks in. 'You must not blame yourself. It wasn't your fault.'

'But how could I not feel guilty?' I ask her. 'I know how precious a child is. To have one taken away in such circumstances is so hard to bear.'

She nods. 'It was a terrible accident,' she says. 'But an accident. We do appreciate you coming to see us. That can't have been easy. We know you have a little one now yourself. When you're a mother, your heart is never your own again.'

Chapter 17

A STARK UNDER-ESTIMATION

Elizabeth Macarthur

9TH OCTOBER 1814, PARRAMATTA

Elizabeth Macarthur picks up the copy of the *Sydney Gazette*, which the maid has put on the table, and is surprised to see Betsey Macquarie's name at the top of an article. She's even more surprised when she sees the article is about an inquest into the death of a three-year-old boy who was hit by a carriage Betsey was travelling in.

Elizabeth shakes her head. She'd read before about the death of the boy but hadn't realised Betsey had been in the carriage that hit him. Poor Betsey! And of course, the poor child and his family. How terrible for all of them. The report says the inquest found it was an accident and no one's fault. The child had run under the horses' hooves then been crushed by one of the wheels of the carriage. What a terrible waste of a life, she thinks. She reads how Betsey had run to the boy, picked him up and carried him home to where she'd been told his family lived. That was a courageous thing to do.

Elizabeth had been wondering why she hadn't heard from Betsey of late. This must be the reason. She feels bad now for having remarked to Miss Lucas that the Governor's wife was probably too busy with her young son to be in contact. Lachie was a sickly baby, who constantly seemed to have colds, but then again, Betsey does mollycoddle him so. Elizabeth has warned her on more than one occasion that she shouldn't fuss over the eight-month-old so, but Betsey has always been instantly defensive.

'He is so precious to us,' Betsey had retorted the last time Elizabeth had said she needed to put him down occasionally. 'I like to keep him in my arms.'

'But he needs to go to his nursemaid at times, otherwise he will always cling to you,' Elizabeth had said gently. 'That isn't good for him, or for you.'

Betsey had nodded, but Elizabeth knew she wouldn't heed her advice. Betsey had a blind spot when it came to her son. It was understandable to a degree, given how much she'd gone through to have him. Elizabeth will say a prayer for Betsey, the young dead boy and his family tonight.

She wonders if she should mention the accident to John in her next letter and, after weighing it up, reasons that it will do no harm. He would have heard of it anyway from one of his myriad informants, and would become suspicious if she omitted to mention it. Elizabeth puts her head in her hands. Deciding what to tell

John is so difficult sometimes. She isn't good at duplicity and she desperately doesn't want to betray her friend.

For as she's come to know Betsey more closely, her respect for the younger woman is growing. She'd too quickly dismissed her as a lightweight, assumed her lack of worldly experience would make her shallow and uninteresting, and taken her sweet demeanour as evidence there was not a lot going on behind it. But gradually, she's even come to admire her. Betsey hasn't had an easy run, and yet she's soldiered on. Without doubt, this tragedy would have hit her hard. A few weeks later, when Elizabeth discovers Betsey even went to visit the grieving family, she's greatly impressed by her courage. Mind you, she finds she isn't really surprised. Courage is something Betsey seems to possess in spades. Unlike other first ladies, she doesn't just content herself with entertaining, or staying at home to pursue feminine pursuits like embroidery. Instead, she is a woman of action and deeds. Sometimes Betsey can be head-strong, impulsive and even reckless, but she has plenty of pluck.

Elizabeth is demonstrating her own fortitude, too. She's made history by exporting a commercial quantity of wool to England, alongside Reverend Marsden and farmer Alexander Riley, and has achieved record prices for the shipment. A number of pastoralists have since begun buying merino rams from her to improve the quality of their own fleeces.

In addition, the future now looks even more promising with the return of Gregory Blaxland, William Charles Wentworth and

William Lawson from their successful expedition across the Blue Mountains in early June 1813, talking in glowing terms about the wealth of good grazing land on the other side. Blaxland declares there to be enough grassland on the other side to support the stock of the colony for thirty years, while Lawson says it's the best watered country he's seen in the colony. Their descriptions raise great optimism about the potential for new grazing lands, farms and more towns.

Eleven months later, Lachlan approves an offer from retired Lieutenant William Cox to build the first road across the Blue Mountains. Everyone in the colony, even Elizabeth, follows Lieutenant Cox's progress, together with his thirty convicts and a guard of eight soldiers, with real excitement. It takes them a mere six months to build a road of over one hundred miles, complete with bridges, out of Sydney Town.

But Elizabeth is still surprised, on a visit to Government House, when Betsey tells her she now intends to accompany Lachlan on the first trip into the inland over the new road.

'Do you really think that's wise?' Elizabeth asks. 'Who knows what's out there?'

'But it's going to be wonderful,' Betsey exclaims. 'Think of it! Travelling across the Blue Mountains! Who'd have thought it would ever be possible! And you are always telling me to leave Lachie with his nursemaid . . .'

Elizabeth smiles, despite herself. 'Well, that's true enough. And I suppose it will result in opening up more land for our farmers,' she says hesitantly, thinking of John's ambition to acquire more land.

'No, no, Elizabeth, don't think of it like that!' Betsey replies. 'Think of it as one more step in solving the mysteries of this great land. Lachlan and I will finally have the opportunity to see for ourselves what lies beyond the mountains.'

'Do you really need to know?' Elizabeth protests, thinking that with the confirmation of good sheep-farming land on the other side, John will probably press her even harder to pursue his desire for more land. That would mean spreading herself even more thinly. And who's to know if there will be even more native raiding parties stealing sheep and possessions from settlers in the hinterland? Thankfully, with her men still watching over their flocks at night she has lost very few sheep. But she still has to be vigilant. And it's bound to be worse over the mountains.

When she sees Betsey is laughing, Elizabeth realises she hasn't heard what she just said. 'Oh, Elizabeth!' Betsey is saying. 'Of course we need to know. Don't tell me you of all people have lost your spirit of adventure!'

True to her word, Betsey and Lachlan leave Sydney on the 25th of April 1815 in a party of ten, including Lieutenant Cox, as well as servants and soldiers, to christen the grand crossing. She tells Elizabeth later that her sole misgiving was leaving behind little Lachie, only a month after celebrating his first birthday, but that she was trying to heed her friend's advice.

On the 7th of May, the party reaches the end of the road which Lachlan earmarks for a new town to be called Bathurst, and they rest before returning to Sydney.

Betsey calls in on Elizabeth on their way back, bubbling over with excitement. Elizabeth smiles to see her so animated.

'Along the way, we slept in a farmhouse, a log cabin, some huts and a number of make-shift camps,' Betsey tells her. 'I loved it all. And the views! They were simply stunning.'

'So did you travel in the carriage?' Elizabeth asks.

'Some of the time, but mostly on horseback.'

'Really?' Elizabeth is amazed. 'But you didn't tire yourself out? Lachlan must have been worried.'

'Yes, I think he was at first. He kept stopping and checking that I was managing. But of course I was. Everything was fine. And all those grassy plains we saw below . . . They look like such good land for our farmers.'

'Just think, you're the first woman from the colony ever to cross the Blue Mountains,' Elizabeth says. 'You've done well, Betsey. I don't think I could have done it.'

'Nonsense!' Betsey replies. But at the same time, she looks very pleased.

Elizabeth realises, however, that such physical feats seem to come more easily to Betsey than some of the political manoeuvring going on around her. Betsey has confided how she is still distressed about the loss of Ellis Bent's friendship and frustrated by the trouble his brother Jeffery continues to stir up. It has culminated in the Governor writing to Lord Bathurst in London, offering to resign unless both Bents are removed from judicial office. Lord Bathurst takes Governor Macquarie's side, and revokes their appointments. But wretchedly, just before the dismissal letter arrives, Ellis Bent dies.

The next time Betsey visits Elizabeth Farm she weeps in the drawing room as she recalls the deterioration of the Macquaries' relationship with Ellis Bent and how much she dreads going to his funeral. Elizabeth does her best to comfort and reassure her.

Reverend Marsden doesn't make it easier. His wife Elizabeth has now had a stroke which has paralysed the left side of her body, and made her even quieter—if that were possible—but it doesn't seem to have softened her husband at all. Instead, he causes a sensation with his eulogy at Mr Bent's funeral, which is less extolling the virtues of the late Judge Advocate than an outright criticism of the Governor. Elizabeth steals a look at Betsey as the Reverend vents his poison and sees she's somehow managing to maintain her composure, with a small, tight smile on her face.

Later, much to everyone's shock, it turns out Mr Bent was virtually penniless on his death and has left his widow and five children destitute. Mr Macquarie asks London to authorise a pension for Mrs Bent, something Elizabeth suspects Betsey suggested he do. She adds generosity and magnanimity to the characteristics she admires about her friend.

But Elizabeth doesn't have much time to mull on politics as she now has fresh troubles of her own. The natives are becoming more daring in their attacks on local farms. Though they are sporadic and not necessarily premeditated—more spur-of-the-moment opportunistic thievery—they're the source of constant concern to Elizabeth and her neighbours. The natives steal maize and rob travellers on the road between settlements, and are now raiding farms and burning down shepherds' huts. And when drought hits the colony and is followed by heavy rains and flooding in some areas, which further decimate crops, it creates food shortages and rising prices, which lead to even greater anxiety, anger and unrest amongst the settlers.

A turning point comes in August 1815 when a group of natives attack Elizabeth's stock keeper and his wife. The stock keeper ends up dying of his injuries.

Then drought continues to decimate crops throughout 1815 and into the following year, and in March natives plunder a farm at Bringelly and kill four workers before turning on their owners. Natives ransack another property the next day, and the situation worsens when they attack a government wagon on the Bathurst Road, as well as a Government depot on the Cox's River at Glenroy, over the Blue Mountains, the same day. Shortly afterwards, another raiding party fights settlers at a farm in the Cowpastures, killing a shepherd. More deaths occur in March, with a female settler and her servant killed on a farm on the junction of the Grose and Nepean rivers in the Blue Mountains.

'We cannot continue like this,' Elizabeth tells Mr Herbert one day as they sit at the table looking over the accounts of their flock numbers. Since he was awarded land by the Governor, he's become even more attentive to the issues the pastoralists face. 'This is a terrible situation. The Governor must protect us.'

Mr Herbert nods. 'Yes, it is time for action. I wonder what he will do?'

He doesn't have to muse long. Two weeks later, the Governor orders troops to arrest some of the native raiders. Two days on, the *Sydney Gazette* reports that a group of natives was rounded up and says that, in the chaos that followed, fourteen of them were killed.

Elizabeth writes to her husband, telling him that the Governor's decisive action has most probably saved their livelihood. She knows John will be both pleased and displeased at the same time.

Chapter 18

BLOOD ON OUR HANDS

Betsey Macquarie

1ST APRIL 1816, SYDNEY

The increasing number of native attacks, including on Elizabeth Macarthur's stock keeper and his wife, is creating enormous pressure on Lachlan to do something to protect settlers. No fewer than five white men have been killed lately, and there looks to be no end to the heightening violence.

It puts us in an invidious position. Generally, Lachlan has always striven to treat the natives with common decency. Early in our time the colony, he'd said to me, 'I think these people could become very useful to society. They are open, friendly and honest, and they've shown themselves willing to help settlers in many cases. I also think they have the capacity to learn. They could become competent in agriculture or mechanics.'

Since then he and I had always tried to maintain a good relationship with the natives. During our travels around New South

Wales, we met many and found them to be friendly and courteous. Lachlan believes strongly in treating them well in return, and has often supplied them with provisions and slops. We have even presented some, like the chief Koggie we met at the Cowpastures, with specially made breastplates as marks of distinction and our good favour.

In fact, one of the projects we're most proud of in the colony is the establishment of the Native Institution at Parramatta, which we set up to civilise native children, and teach them to read and write. Whenever I visit, they're a joy to be with and the manager, trader and missionary William Shelley, says they are doing well at the school. Their parents are permitted to visit them one day each December, and at the annual feast day we initiated for the natives of Parramatta, the children are presented to me, and their achievements are described and celebrated. In fact, it is working so well, Lachlan and I have discussed setting up a similar school at the Cowpastures.

As a result, Lachlan is livid about the attacks on, and killings of, settlers by natives, given he's tried so hard to be fair to them, despite considerable opposition. He's also gone out of his way to urge the settlers to be good to them too, hoping we can all coexist peacefully. But as well as the native attacks on settlers, Lachlan has also received reports of attacks on the natives, with some settlers then attempting to cover up the violence they've afflicted. It's hard. Some settlers are scared of the natives, resenting their poaching of sheep, stealing of fruit and simply being present on their land. I know from our first tour of the colony that some of the settlers fire first and ask questions later.

But, privately, I do wonder at how colossally the natives' lives have changed since Captain Phillip first arrived. So many have died of smallpox and other diseases they had not encountered before, and they are no longer allowed to hunt and fish in many places where they were living before the colony was established. Many have been forced to go elsewhere.

That brought back dark memories to me of our own experiences back in the Highlands of Scotland where landowners, usually clan chiefs, evicted farming families en masse for more profitable sheep grazing. It led to a large-scale uprooting of Highlanders and their scattering to the coast or lowlands of Scotland. They were forced to work in impoverishment, quarrying or fishing or gathering kelp, or to move further afield to America or later to here in New South Wales. It had a devastating impact on people's lives, their communities and the Gaelic culture, and we felt the absolute anguish of people driven off their land.

When I point this out to Lachlan, he's despairing. 'But I have done everything I could for the native blacks,' he says. 'I can't ignore the cruel and barbarous murders of settlers and their workers, nor the killing of cattle and sheep or the robbing of grain and other property. I have to draw the line at these outrages. It's essential I inflict severe punishments and make an example of those guilty of these crimes to deter such things happening again in the future. If I don't secure the Cumberland Plain from these ravages, how can the new discovered country around Bathurst be secure? And if I don't do something to protect the settlers they will construe my lack of action as fear and cowardice.'

My heart sinks. 'What are you going to do?' I ask.

'I want to clear the country of hostile natives,' he replies. 'So I intend to send three separate military detachments of around seventy soldiers to sweep across the Cumberland Plain, with the smallest heading to Elizabeth's farm to reinforce the soldiers there. They'll all be under orders to apprehend any natives who've been found to have committed offences. I'm going to order that as many of the others as possible—who appear not to have been involved in the outrage—be taken prisoner until the guilty surrender or are given up by their tribe. In the event of the natives making the smallest show of resistance, or refusing to surrender when called upon to do so, I will authorise the commanding officers to fire on them to compel them to surrender. If any are killed in such circumstances, their bodies will be hung on trees to strike terror into the survivors.'

On the 19th of April 1816, ten days after Lachlan issued his orders, he returns home more desolate than I've ever seen him before. I am utterly unable to console him. He tells me that Captain Wallis and his troops had encountered a group of natives near Liverpool and fired on them, killing fourteen, including women and children.

'But how did that happen?' I gasp.

'According to Captain Wallis, after they arrived in the field his two native guides ran off,' Lachlan recounts slowly, with a note of despair in his voice. 'That put Wallis and his men at a distinct disadvantage. A week later, Captain Wallis's soldiers crept up to a camp just before dawn and found fires burning but the site deserted. But a child's cry alerted them to the group hiding nearby. At that, the soldiers formed a line and pushed on through thick brush towards the steep escarpment of Cataract River where they saw some of the natives bounding from rock to rock. They opened fire. Some were killed outright and others ran straight over the cliffs.' He puts his head in his hands. 'They hung two of the bodies on the hill to show others how serious we were, and cut off the heads and brought them to Sydney, as well as taking five prisoners, all women and children.'

'So they didn't give the natives a chance to surrender?' I ask.

'I suspect not.' He sighs heavily. 'But I am in charge, and have a duty to my men, so I am responsible.'

Sometimes I think Lachlan's immense faith in his men is misplaced. I can imagine how disconcerted they would have been at the loss of their native guides and how they'd panicked when they came across the natives at Appin. But firing indiscriminately at the natives without warning them or giving them a chance to surrender is barbarous.

I tell Lachlan he needs to sheet some of the blame back to his men, but he is adamant he won't, saying it would be both wrong and a sign of weakness to his enemies.

As a result, he issues a statement to the *Sydney Gazette* admitting that innocent native men, women and children were killed in an ambush, but that the group had failed to surrender and the troops firing on them had been necessary to prevent further hostilities. He hopes the event will '*strike terror amongst the surviving tribes and deter them from the further commission of such sanguinary outrages and barbarities.*'

Though I feel sick at heart about what has happened, a great number of the settlers treat Lachlan like a hero, and Elizabeth tells me she's relieved the Governor acted so swiftly to deter raiders in the future.

Though I know Lachlan didn't intend for this ghastly slaughter to occur, it still pains me that it's happened under our watch. And when Lachlan shows me his report to Lord Bathurst telling him fourteen natives were killed—including two of the 'most ferocious'—and five were taken prisoner, I notice he doesn't mention the five are two women and three children.

But even though he isn't as open and honest as he could be in both the *Gazette* and his letter to Lord Bathurst, can I really blame him? He needed to secure the Sydney area in order to open up new country to the west, and avoid giving any more reason to his detractors amongst the settlers to spread their discontent.

Added to his travails is the widespread criticism over his recently issued proclamation threatening trespassers in the Domain with prosecution in response to the number of felons climbing over the walls to copulate in the shrubbery. Three were caught and given twenty-five lashes. Afterwards, they protested their innocence to Jeffery Bent, who passed on their complaints to Lord Bathurst, saying it was evidence of Lachlan's excessive authoritarianism! Lachlan's enemies then added the details to a ridiculous petition drafted by an old schoolfriend of Reverend Marsden, which the Reverend gave to his assistant chaplain Reverend Benjamin Vale—who'd also been a crony of Ellis Bent—to deliver to London.

Then there was the accursed incident, where Lachlan gave the American schooner *Traveller* permission to enter the harbour but, when he went away to some settlements out west, the same Reverend Vale illegally seized the ship as a prize under the Navigation Act, with the help of the newly arrived Crown solicitor William Moore. As soon as Lachlan found out about it, he released the ship, admonished Vale at Government House in front of his military staff and sacked Moore, which created even more trouble.

This is all so hard. Lachlan constantly has to weigh up everyone's competing interests to make difficult decisions, with malcontents continuing to fester. If he had not ordered a strike on the natives on behalf of the settlers, for instance, he may not have survived his enemies' wrath. And then, if he hadn't stuck up for his men, his adversaries in the military would have pounced. The memory of the last military coup against Bligh is never far from either of our minds when Lachlan is weighing up what to do, always so aware of his circling enemies.

Chapter 19

A BETRAYAL

Elizabeth Macarthur

14TH JULY 1817, PARRAMATTA

It's a fine, surprisingly mild winter evening, and Elizabeth Macarthur is enjoying herself at one of Captain Piper's soirees. As usual, the food and drink are excellent and the company convivial. However, it's at times like this when she most misses her husband. Not only do all her friends enquire after John and her sons, but almost all the other guests are in couples, including now Captain Piper himself. Elizabeth realises it's been nearly eight years that she's been attending events like this on her own. And it doesn't ever seem to get any easier.

Though John has been lobbying hard to be allowed to come back to New South Wales, he refuses to admit any wrongdoing in the mutiny, which is the one condition the British Government is insisting upon for his return. John being John, he refuses to admit he did anything wrong, and while she's pleaded with him in several recent letters to agree to accept some guilt, he has refused point blank. So the future stretches out endlessly before her, alone.

Elizabeth is delighted when she spots Betsey in the corner of the room. Her friend rarely comes to any social events any more—a combination of her reluctance to spend time away from Lachie and her feeling of being under attack from so many sides—and Elizabeth has been missing her company.

'Betsey!' she says as she reaches her. 'How good to see you here. I thought I'd be the lone woman . . . again! I—' Elizabeth stops talking when she sees how pale and ill-at-ease Betsey looks. 'Is everything all right, my dear?' she asks.

'Yes, yes, I'm sorry, but I'd rather not talk about it,' Betsey replies. 'Do you mind?'

'Of course not,' Elizabeth says, trying not to mind, although she really does. She wonders what it is that Betsey doesn't want to talk to her about, but then tries to cheer her up with news about how well the farm is doing, how silky and long the sheep's fleeces are growing, and how her daughters are flourishing.

Not making any inroads there, Elizabeth switches tack and asks how young Lachie is. Betsey briefly lights up.

'He's doing so well,' she says. 'He's not yet three, but is such a bright boy and is growing big and strong. He's the light of our lives.' She stops, and there's a long silence.

Not knowing how to proceed, Elizabeth decides she has a duty to John to bring up their need for more land for their sheep, a subject he mentions in every letter he writes.

'Betsey, if you don't mind, there's something I need to ask you . . .' she begins.

'Oh my goodness!' Betsey exclaims. 'Have you heard? Did you realise? How well you know me!'

'So . . . what's happening?' Elizabeth asks, baffled.

Betsey hesitates, then says, 'Will you promise to keep this to yourself?'

'Of course!' Elizabeth says, crossing her heart in reassurance.

'After nearly eight years here, which is the period Lachlan promised to serve before he started receiving a pension, he's thinking of resigning.'

Elizabeth is stunned. 'But why?' she asks.

'We seem to be making so many enemies and he's just not confident the British Government will continue to back him. It also feels like a good time to return. We'd both love to bring Lachie up in Scotland and for him to get to know his family, too, particularly his young cousins.'

Elizabeth falls silent. If Betsey is planning to go back to England, then Elizabeth is running out of time to pass on John's request. But, much more importantly, she realises her friend's absence will leave a terrible void in her life. John's plotting can wait; her own feelings cannot. Taking Betsey's hand, she says, 'Are you really sure this is something you want to do? I know there's still so much you want to achieve . . .'

'I . . . I . . . don't see any other way,' Betsey whispers, on the verge of tears. 'Life here has become so hard. But yes, I would miss you terribly, too.'

Elizabeth struggles to hold back tears now as well, and is almost grateful when Captain Piper's long-time lover Mary Ann, now his new wife, comes up to greet them, juggling two of their sons in her arms, with two more holding onto her skirts behind her. 'Now why are you both looking so glum?' she asks, looking from one to the other. 'Let me refresh your drinks . . .'

When Elizabeth arrives back at the farm that evening, she feels oddly out of sorts. Even though she knows John will be delighted at the news that Governor Macquarie is thinking of leaving, she is quite the opposite. Without Betsey, she'll have no female confidant left, and she'll greatly miss the close friendship they've forged over the years.

She catches up with Miss Lucas and the girls, sits down and, after hesitating awhile, writes John a letter telling him about the Governor's possible imminent resignation. Even though she swore to secrecy, he is her husband after all, the person to whom she owes her rightful allegiance. When she's finished, she immediately summons a rider to take the letter down to the docks to be sent on the next ship to England.

When she wakes up the next morning, however, she feels a deep sense of shame and regrets sending the letter. She despatches another rider to town to bring it back, but he returns to Elizabeth Farm that afternoon empty-handed. The ship, with the letter, has already sailed. It is too late.

Elizabeth spends the next two weeks brooding about her treachery and avoiding Betsey, knowing she'll be unable to look her straight in the eye. She is wondering if she'll ever be able to face her friend again when she receives an urgent message that John and two of their sons, James and William, are on a ship at anchor in the harbour waiting for Captain Piper to meet them.

She can hardly dare to believe it. It is September 1817 and, after eight long years, they have finally come back! She gathers her daughters to share the glad news, then, to try to fill in the time and calm her nerves, she organises for the house to be cleaned from top to bottom, and rides out to inspect the gardens and paddocks. When she arrives back at the house she paces back and forth impatiently.

Late that afternoon, the moment she's dreamed of for so long finally comes as her sons arrive at Elizabeth Farm—the small boys she'd farewelled now strapping teenagers. She flings herself at them, and they cling to her as if they'll never let go again, telling her John is following in a carriage. When John appears he is limping badly as a result of gout. He is also thinner and greyer, as well as older and less vigorous than she remembers. Then again, she probably looks a great deal more careworn, too.

The family celebrates that night as merrily as Elizabeth ever dared to imagine through her long years of solitude. John and the boys—well, young men now—recount the myriad adventures they had during their time away, and each confess that they feared they might never see her or their sisters again. Lizzie, Mary, and nine-year-old Emmeline listen to their tales wide-eyed, not a little shy in the presence of their father and grown-up brothers.

It is only after the children have gone to bed, and the two of them are sitting alone together in the drawing room, that John tells

Elizabeth more about his time away. In the end, after John consistently refused to admit any wrongdoing in the mutiny, Lord Bathurst said he'd be instead satisfied with an undertaking that he would not interfere in the public affairs of the colony. It was a concession John was happy to make.

Now, as well as catching up on how the sheep and cattle are going, he has numerous new projects he wants to pursue. He's brought grapevines with the intention of making wine, and olive trees to plant, so his hands, he assures Elizabeth, will be full.

'But over the years, I suppose I wrote literally hundreds of letters to people at every level of Government pressing my cause and outlining the appalling state of affairs of Government in the colony,' he tells her. Elizabeth falls silent as her husband details the litany of complaints he made, including a letter saying he'd been told on good authority that, under Governor Macquarie, New South Wales is in an absolute state of fermentation. 'Indeed, I told the British Government that matters have proceeded to such a length that a subscription has been opened by staunch Government men to raise a fund to prosecute the Governor whenever he may return to England,' he says.

Elizabeth reels in shock. Even now, despite his pledge not to meddle in politics, John is still plotting, with others, to have charges laid against Governor Macquarie in England! She sighs. So much for John agreeing to keep out of politics . . . There's bound to be no end of trouble on the horizon.

But throughout his tirade of criticisms and conspiracies, there is one small cause for relief. John had obviously never received her letter about the Governor planning to resign. She glances up to the heavens in gratitude. Her one act of treachery to the Macquaries hasn't been discovered.

And she hopes to God it never will.

Part THREE

Of course, I'm glad for Elizabeth that she has her husband back, but I can only see more trouble ahead. Our enemies seem to be massing and we have to be alert that we do not give anyone any ammunition to use against us. We are progressing the colony far and fast, but maybe too far and too fast for many. I wonder if it would be better for us to leave now for home in Scotland – or should we continue our quest to advance the colony? It is so hard to know, and perhaps only time will tell which would have been the wiser course of action.

Betsey Macquarie's journal,
25TH SEPTEMBER 1819

Chapter 20

THE ARRIVAL

Betsey Macquarie

26TH SEPTEMBER 1819, WINDSOR

With the number of people already plotting against us these days, having John Macarthur back in New South Wales is making Lachlan and I feel even more uneasy. Lachlan has even advised me not to see so much of Elizabeth Macarthur, or to avoid her company altogether. At the very least I must never confide in her. I nod, though I have no intention of complying with his wishes. I know I can trust Elizabeth absolutely.

After nearly ten years here, there still doesn't seem to be any end in sight. By rights we should now be living on a healthy Government pension at Lachlan's estate on Mull, with Lachie at school on the mainland. It worries me that Lachlan is always so tired and drained, and I want him to be able to rest and recover his strength after so many tumultuous years as Governor. We only signed up for eight years, and yet despite Lachlan sending his letter of resignation to Lord Bathurst nearly two years ago now, we've heard nothing.

The sole correspondence Lachlan has received from London contained orders and rebukes. Lord Bathurst dared censure him for the public flogging of the three Domain trespassers, and for admonishing Reverend Marsden's chaplain, Reverend Vale, over the *Traveller* incident. The Secretary of State then had the hide to say Lachlan only had the authority to take action against a chaplain for bad personal behaviour. More recently, he ordered that Lachlan reinstate the sacked Crown solicitor William Moore, too. Lachlan saw red at that, given Moore had been one of the malcontents collecting signatures for a petition to London. I fear all the criticism Lachlan's facing is breaking his spirit. And our troubles are mounting.

The only person I confess my absolute despair to is Elizabeth. We see each other a little less now that John has returned, so I relish the times when we do meet up—either at Government House in Sydney or Government House in Parramatta—all the more. I've been very polite and cordial with John on the handful of times I've met him, but I cannot help being reserved when he is around. I know he is unhappy because he doesn't think Lachlan has given him as much new land as he believes he needs, and has been agitating amongst Lachlan's enemies. Elizabeth and I never discuss it—we both feel our friendship is too important to be contaminated by the views of our husbands.

The last time I saw her, two weeks ago, she tried to cheer me, saying, 'Just stay strong, Betsey! The fact the Governor hasn't heard back from Lord Bathurst is likely because he's having difficulty finding someone of the same calibre as Lachlan to replace him. You should see it as a vote of confidence in his governorship.'

'That's so nice of you to say,' I told her, 'and I thank you for that. But it's hard to believe. There's so much mischief-making and political manoeuvring and scheming going on. People are so consumed by their own self-interest they can't see the very future of the colony is at stake.'

Elizabeth suddenly looks pensive and I kick myself that she might think I was throwing a barb at John, even though he is, indeed, one of the chief schemers. 'But anyway, at least we have our friendship to sustain us,' I say, changing the subject. 'And Lachie can have more time growing up with his favourite aunt!'

I mean that, too. Elizabeth has proved a great support during my darkest days. Just a week ago, I was thrilled to receive a copy of Miss Jane Austen's latest novel, *Northanger Abbey*, and immediately thought of Elizabeth when I read: '*There is nothing I would not do for those who are really my friends. I have no notion of loving people by halves, it is not my nature. My attachments are always excessively strong.*'

Heading back with Lachie to Government House after a walk on the promontory, my heart lurches when I see an envelope that looks like it contains an official communication from London. I call out to Lachlan to come and have a look, hoping it contains an acceptance of his resignation and a date we can leave. To my intense disappointment it mentions neither and instead notifies Lachlan that a Commissioner by the name of John Bigge has been appointed to look into the running of the colony.

I'm instantly anxious, but Lachlan dismisses my concern. 'Don't worry, Betsey. This is purely routine,' he says. 'These kind of inquiries take place all the time in the various colonies. And I'm sure Commissioner Bigge will not find anything untoward. In fact, I think his report on all we've achieved here will show the British Government what an excellent job I've done as Governor.'

I wish I shared his confidence.

Five days later, we're out in the Hawkesbury where a muster—or count—of the convicts and settlers is taking place, when we hear the sound of a horse galloping towards us. We're just outside the Government Cottage in Windsor, which we use when we're in the region, and look up to see a messenger racing into sight.

'Commissioner Bigge has arrived!' he blurts out as he draws close, before he can even hand the paper over to Lachlan. 'He sailed into Sydney this morning and is asking where you are.'

I'm appalled. Lachlan has only just been advised that Mr Bigge is coming to conduct an inspection and we weren't expecting him for a good few months more.

'We should have been in Sydney to greet him,' I say uneasily. 'Maybe we should return immediately? After all, he is an emissary of the British Government and we need to show him as much hospitality as we can.'

'Hush,' says Lachlan, putting a finger to my lips. 'We must not lose our faith in the essential virtue of people—or in their ability to tell the difference between the truth and falsehoods.'

I sigh. I've long since lost faith in people's virtue. The past few years have underlined that lesson again and again. We committed ourselves wholeheartedly to transforming New South Wales and we've achieved so much, yet still we find ourselves battling criticism from those who think they know better or feel they deserve more than they already have. It pains me to see people with malign intent eroding Lachlan's fine reputation with baseless accusations and gossip, and I know the likes of John Macarthur, Reverend Marsden, Reverend Vale and William Moore send carping letters to those in authority in London who have no idea what's really going on here. The trouble with Lachlan is that he is just not a natural political animal. He's so focused on the future and what needs to be done, he doesn't see the jealousies, petty animosities and self-interest of others until they've grown so monstrous that they're impossible to ignore. I go to speak again, but Lachlan nods towards Lachie and gives me a warning look. This is neither the time nor the place to argue.

'I shall send the messenger back to Sydney to arrange for Commissioner Bigge to join us here in Windsor,' Lachlan says. 'I'm sure he'll find the muster fascinating, and we can have a dinner for him tomorrow evening and take him on a tour of some of the settlements we've established here, to show him how well we are opening up the colony.'

I nod reluctantly and we walk with Lachie towards the messenger. Both he and his horse are drinking greedily, and after

Lachlan gives him his instructions, he leaps back into the saddle, wishes us well and gallops off. I try to pick five-year-old Lachie up—he has still not fully recovered from a bout of ill-health over winter—but he struggles and the three of us walk back towards the cottage so I can brief the cook on our guest.

But when Commissioner Bigge arrives in Windsor a day later, he does not seem such a threat. He is a little younger than me, but doesn't carry his years well. He is losing his hair and his skin is so pale that it's almost translucent.

I'm heartened that he turns out to be perfectly friendly and civil, as well as appearing genuinely interested in all we're doing out here. Over the following five days, he accompanies Lachlan on day trips to the Hawkesbury wheat lands and the towns of Richmond, Windsor and Wilberforce, before we all return to Sydney in the carriage. A few days on, his commission is read officially with all due pomp and circumstance, and Mr Bigge gives a beautiful speech in response. I relax. Lachlan was obviously right all along.

The only issue seems to be one not of his making at all. Our principal surgeon, D'Arcy Wentworth, decided to retire and Lachlan had assured our dear friend Dr William Redfern that he'll be assigned to the position. But Mr Bigge travelled here with the naval surgeon Dr James Bowman, who, he informs us, has already been appointed by the British Government to succeed Dr Wentworth. We're devastated. Dr Redfern has done such a wonderful job in the colony generally and been such a good friend to us, yet will not now receive the position he so richly deserves. His wife Sarah has also become one of my closest companions and they christened their son William Macquarie and named their property at Airds 'Campbell Field' in my honour. We tell them that Dr Bowman's appointment is as much a shock to us as it is to them and, as recompense, Lachlan promises that he'll appoint Dr Redfern a magistrate instead.

Unfortunately, when Lachlan informs Mr Bigge of the magistracy role, the Commissioner tells him that Lord Bathurst's rejection of Dr Redfern's appointment as principal surgeon means the Secretary of State doesn't think as highly of him as Lachlan does, and so therefore he can't be sanctioned to that position, either. Lachlan's irate. He brings up the same issue at later meetings, too, and the pair start to clash regularly.

I'm practising on my piano when Lachlan returns home from one of the meetings and I'm alarmed at how pale and exhausted he looks. His health has been delicate for some time, but since Mr Bigge's arrival he's been experiencing terrible bouts of dysentery and general malaise. Having believed the Commissioner would see the progress he's forged in the colony, he is now being disappointed. I've tried to caution Lachlan about expressing his opinions too forcibly, but he still believes being straightforward and open will bring both Mr Bigge and other people in authority around.

'Bigge again refused to entertain the idea of me appointing Dr Redfern as a magistrate,' he says, clearly furious.

'So what did you say?' I ask.

'I said he obviously knows too little of Dr Redfern's character. Even when he was transported, he helped the surgeon on board the ship care for the health of the convicts and also worked hard on Norfolk Island. I told him again that Dr Redfern's work here in Sydney has been exemplary, taking charge of the new hospital while also managing to see patients outside. I also told him about the very valuable report Dr Redfern wrote on the health of convicts during transportation.'

My heart sinks, as I suspect Lachlan gave Mr Bigge very short shrift, but he is in such a bad mood I don't dare say anything to upset him further.

'I then pointed out that Dr Redfern also recommended surgeons be present on all voyages,' adds Lachlan. 'Which is something Dr Bowman has profited from since up until now that work has provided his main income! At that, Bigge said he knows Lord Bathurst well, and since he considers emancipists unfit to act as attorneys, they certainly should not be ruling from the bench.'

I stay silent as Lachlan paces the room, looking like he's ready to explode.

'And then he said that putting Redfern, "*a convicted traitor*", on the bench would be an absolute outrage to the rules of common sense and decency. *How dare he!* I told him I would prefer to surrender the Government into his hands than be seen to be giving in to those who have opposed my policies.'

This is just as I feared. I greatly admire Lachlan's strong views and determination to stick to his principles, but he can be so proud and unyielding that he ends up inviting far more trouble than he deserves. He's always favoured the notion of giving former convicts as much respect as any free man if they prove themselves worthy. But since our great friend Mr Thompson passed, Lachlan's become unswervingly faithful to that principle. The opposition and hostility to the emancipation of convicts he's faced in the intervening years has served only to harden his resolve.

I'm terrified Lachlan's accomplishments over the past ten years will be overshadowed by the politics and self-interest of narrow-minded, parochial and self-absorbed people. That would be so unfair, as he's done so much. Mr Bigge should be treating him with a great deal more respect and humility.

After all, Lachlan's extended the colony over many hundreds of miles, founding new towns all over the settlement, and now even on the other side of the Blue Mountains. He's also pushing the Colonial Office to officially change the name of the colony from New Holland and New South Wales to Australia after seeing the word on some charts made by the late navigator Captain Matthew Flinders. Since then, we've used the word often, and encouraged others to use it too, as it feels like marking a new beginning, free of the convict associations of 'New South Wales'. The new name is being readily embraced by the population. Mr Bigge doesn't seem to be giving Lachlan any credit for such imaginative changes.

Yet even though we're facing so much opposition and antagonism, and receiving so little support from Mr Bigge, we're determined to keep having a positive influence, and would be thrilled to see some kind of patriotism being born here.

On the 26th of January last year, for instance, we had thirty guns fire and I hosted a magnificent ball to mark the thirtieth anniversary of Captain Arthur Phillip's arrival in the colony. That proved very special. It would be wonderful, I muse to myself, if we could turn that anniversary into some kind of annual event.

Chapter 21

A WARNING

Elizabeth Macarthur

26TH SEPTEMBER 1819, PARRAMATTA

Elizabeth Macarthur is out walking to clear her mind of the maelstrom of confused emotions scrambling her thoughts. Everything seems to have changed over the past few months and she's feeling terribly frustrated.

In the weeks following the return of John and the boys, the family had been extraordinarily happy. Elizabeth had taken great delight in showing John her new kitchen at Elizabeth Farm, the extensive array of vegetables she'd been growing, the well-kept gardens she'd overseen so carefully and the many paddocks that had been cleared. And when she'd had one of the workers round up a flock of sheep in the home paddock, she'd been gratified by John's positive reaction to their long, fine wool.

As they rode over to the Cowpastures the following week, Elizabeth was filled with joy at finally being relieved of the heavy burden of making all the decisions about their land. While John's health and strength is no longer what it was, he's keen to take back control from her and Hannibal, and is drilling their sons hard to learn about the wool industry. Elizabeth is happy to be handing the administration and accounts back to John. And though Hannibal has been a great help, he's also pleased to have the opportunity to concentrate more on his own farm, store and business interests.

But lately John's mood has soured and he's full of rumblings about Sydney politics. She's walking through the green pasture fringed by the Nepean River, close to Nepean Crossing, trying to work out what she can do to improve the situation, when a cacophony of plaintive bleating comes from the direction of the water.

Elizabeth immediately snaps into action, running full pelt towards the river, then slowing as she sees the source of all the noise. A ewe has sunk down to her knees into the mud of the riverbank and is crying despondently, while her tiny lamb runs frantically around her, mewing.

'Hush, hush,' Elizabeth croons as she advances slowly towards the pair. 'Come on now, I'm here to help.' The lamb darts off and stops a safe distance away, while the stuck ewe stands and trembles, regarding her with absolute terror.

'It's all right, it's all right,' Elizabeth whispers. 'Stay still now, stay still.'

As the ewe calms down, Elizabeth lunges for it and grabs two thick handfuls of its wool. Then, pulling with all her might as the ewe struggles and scrambles to get away, she manages to lift the front half of the sheep out of the mud and, with a deafening bleating, the animal makes its way towards its lamb. As Elizabeth staggers away she falls and lands bottom-first in the mud, but laughs as she sees the pair race off together.

Ah, if only all problems were so easily solved by swift action and resolve! she thinks as she heads back to the house.

These days, Elizabeth can never be sure what awaits her with John. His moods careen erratically from deep depression to wild elation, sometimes within a single hour. He's obsessed with trying to undermine the Macquaries, and continually expresses his disgust at their emancipist policies and the fact that former convicts are serving in positions of such enormous responsibility in the colony. Elizabeth is aware he's been staying in touch with his vast network of contacts in London, updating them constantly on what he believes are the follies of the Governor, and here in Parramatta he spends much of his time in shadowy meetings with other men with the same goal of discrediting him.

Elizabeth always deliberately avoided politics, seeing it as men's business and, besides, she has much more important work to do around the farm than talking late into the night. But since John's return with the boys, it's been impossible to ignore. Whenever they are alone, he's always trying to talk her into revealing Betsey's state of mind, and what she's up to.

'But we don't see each other very often these days,' Elizabeth says, trying to fob him off. 'And when we do, we mostly talk about the children.'

'But surely she's told you something of what's going on in Government House?' he persists. 'What are their plans for the future? I've heard talk that they've been considering moving back to Scotland. Have you heard anything about that? Has she not talked to you?'

'No,' Elizabeth replies, staunchly. 'We prefer to talk about Lachie and Emmeline and the new fashions arriving from London.'

When John finally gives up, she always feels a wave of relief wash over her. For while he knows she sees Betsey in Sydney, he has no idea of the number of meetings and the frequency of the letters that pass between them, nor of the true depth of their friendship. If he did, she suspects he would press her even harder for information. As a result, she tries to hide how close their relationship has become, or move the conversation in another direction, rather than having to tell more lies.

As she oversees the preparation of lunch, John comes into the kitchen and starts his now-frequent harangue about how much more land they need and his annoyance that the Governor seems to have no insight into the concerns of farmers.

'Lizzie looks so well now, doesn't she?' Elizabeth says, as though she hasn't heard him. 'It's such a shame there is no husband for her on the horizon.'

'I'm sure someone will come along,' John replies. He'd originally approved Lizzie's engagement to her first suitor, Lieutenant John Oxley, and then cancelled it in the face of the young man's debts. Oxley had gone on to become the Surveyor-General of New South Wales, but had never managed to redeem himself in John's eyes. Her next suitor, the explorer William Charles Wentworth, had also fallen short of John's expectations, as his father, the colony's former surgeon D'Arcy Wentworth, was discovered to have been charged with highway robbery not once, but three times, at the

Old Bailey. He was acquitted each time, but still John refused his son's overtures. As a result, Mr Wentworth's become a life-long enemy of the Macarthurs.

'There'll be a good man for her, you mark my words,' John tells Elizabeth. 'When the Governor goes, we can start confidently planning for our future. Freed from his yoke, that's when life can finally improve in New South Wales.'

Elizabeth feels herself growing impatient. 'But John, look at the colony now compared to when we arrived!' she says, trying to suppress her annoyance. 'Surely you agree it's in a much better state than it was then? Sydney is an infinitely more pleasant town, and there have been so many positive changes in Parramatta, too. The Governor and Mrs Macquarie have done a great deal that is worthwhile and they have also been very good to me. They helped me greatly while you were away and have been most kind—'

'Yes, yes,' John cuts in impatiently. 'They aided you no more than you deserved.'

Elizabeth turns on her heel, saying she needs to talk to the kitchen maid to make sure she has everything properly prepared for Captain and Mrs Piper's visit in the evening.

Elizabeth takes delight in catching up with the Pipers whenever she can, partly because it's the one time she can be assured John will be happy. Captain Piper is always entertaining and tonight he regales them with tales of his most recent trip to England in 1811 with Mary Ann, their two young sons, and his daughter by another woman. When Captain Piper claims he and Mary Ann were the toast of London society, John roars with laughter to think of his friend cavorting around London with a much-admired woman, who happened to be the daughter of a convict once banished in disgrace.

Elizabeth flinches, hoping John won't say anything gauche. She knows he doesn't entirely approve of Captain Piper's choice of a wife, but the pair have been good, loyal comrades over such a long period, and Captain Piper has been so firm a friend to Elizabeth during his long absence, there is no way he should jeopardise that bond.

Thankfully, John doesn't comment and only laughs uproariously when Captain Piper says, 'And marriage, I think, suits me,' while grinning and preening himself for comic effect. 'Mary Ann has proved herself an excellent wife, more than equal to the task of looking after me.'

Indeed, Elizabeth admires her energy. Mary Ann bore two more sons for her husband while in England, and then has had two more since, and yet still enjoys a full social life keeping up with Captain Piper. 'Who would have thought I'd have six boys to take up any time she has left over from me?' he says.

John turns the discussion to Captain Piper's work, asking if he's enjoying being a magistrate and collecting taxes.

'*Duties*, you mean,' Captain Piper replies. 'As a Naval Officer, I collect customs duties, harbour dues and excise on spirits. I'm finding it a most profitable occupation and one most befitting a man of my position.'

They all laugh at that. It's well known around the colony that Captain Piper is not a man who likes hard work, but one who still feels entitled to its rewards. Regardless, it's impossible not to like him. He can be so pompous, yet also attractively self-deprecating, funny and charismatic.

'We owe you dinner next at Henrietta Villa,' says Captain Piper. 'It's going to be the most magnificent home anyone here has ever seen. I'm hoping my land grant will be formalised early next year, and then I can begin work on it. It's so tiresome to have to keep delaying it.'

One evening, a stranger with his hat pulled down low over his eyes turns up at Elizabeth Farm asking for John. Elizabeth waves the maid away and enquires what business he has with her husband.

'I have a letter for Mr Macarthur, ma'am,' he replies gruffly.

'Well, you can leave it with me,' she says. 'I'll make sure he receives it when he arrives home.'

When the man looks unsure of what to do, Elizabeth says, 'You can wait for him, but I have no idea how long he'll be. It'll be perfectly safe with me.'

The man hesitates, before saying, 'I need to be paid.'

'Of course. How much?' asks Elizabeth, glancing at the envelope he's holding. She frowns when she sees it has a British Government crest on it and that it's addressed to the Governor, not John.

'That's between me and Mr Macarthur,' the man replies gruffly.

Elizabeth is taken by surprise by his manner, but recovers quickly. 'Yes, of course. You're welcome to wait—' she says as the man tucks the letter back into his coat and turns sharply on his heel.

She goes into the living room and looks out of the window to see him crouched by the front fence.

Perplexed, she decides to have a cup of tea. A few minutes later, she hears the sound of John's horse and peers out into the gloom to see John slow down as he catches sight of the man. He then bends down to speak to him, takes the proffered letter and tosses him a small bag, presumably containing the payment, before getting off his horse.

Elizabeth opens the front door before he reaches it. She's just about to ask him what's going on when he glowers at her and walks straight past to the drawing room. She follows him, entering the room in time to see him tearing open the envelope and bending over to read the letter by the light of a lamp. His demeanour changes immediately, and a grin slowly spreads over his face.

'What is it, John?' she asks him. 'Good news?'

He jumps, not realising she's been watching him. 'Yes . . .' he says, distractedly. 'I think so.'

'I thought I saw someone else's name on the envelope . . .'

His smile vanishes. 'It's none of your business,' he barks. 'Anyway, have you not got better things to do than to spy on me?'

'I . . . I . . . I . . .' she stammers, lost for words. Despite his erratic moods he has never spoken to her in that way before.

Before she can say any more, he tosses the letter into the grate and storms out of the room. Furious, Elizabeth throws the rest of the tea onto the fire and watches it sizzle and die. Then she takes the tongs and carefully eases the singed letter out, placing it on the table and unfolding it. It's a letter from Lord Bathurst to the Governor saying he acknowledges receipt of the Governor's letter of resignation, but the British Government does not want to accept it and wants him to stay on for just a few more years. The Governor is doing important work, it says, and the Government would like him to agree to extend his term.

Elizabeth immediately understands her husband's joy. The Governor and Betsey are beside themselves with uncertainty over their future, fearing the British Government is against them. And now John, in obviously bribing someone to intercept the letter, has prevented them from being reassured about their role. He and his co-conspirators plainly intend to continue to stoke the fires of their insecurity here, in the hope it will induce them to leave . . .

Elizabeth crumples the letter up and puts it in the pocket of her smock. Though she will destroy it later, she is appalled at John's dishonesty. Elizabeth knows she daren't not tell Betsey what John has done—it is yet more evidence of his treachery and would lead to God knows where for him—but at the same time she feels she has to find a way of reassuring her friend.

The next day, John doesn't mention the letter but seems to take enormous pleasure in updating Elizabeth about what friends in London are saying about the colony.

'The British Government is deeply worried about what's happening here,' he tells her loftily. 'The House of Lords has been told that since 1808 the number of crimes in Britain has trebled and the number of criminals convicted has doubled. They believe people are no longer afraid of the kind of punishments that are being levied. Judges are less keen to execute bad criminals, the prisons are more about accommodating prisoners than punishing them and transportation to New South Wales . . . is a joke!'

This is a speech Elizabeth's heard many times before. He's told her repeatedly that Britain is struggling with the waves of soldiers returning from the Napoleonic Wars, unemployment, political tensions, bad harvests, a rising population, riots and a growing crime rate. The British Government is also having to pay a huge percentage of its revenue on interest on the national debt, while still having to fund its far-flung colonies. It seems to her that it's looking for anything to distract attention from its own problems.

But John is adamant that it's all the fault of the Governor and his emancipist policies.

'Once, people used to be terrified of being sent over here to serve out their sentence with hard labour in difficult conditions,' he says. 'But now people are seeing convicts in the colony being treated better than the free settlers, and being rewarded with positions in government and grants of land. There's talk of traitors being made magistrates, and felons attaining well-paid office. Now convicts want to come here. It's an utterly ludicrous situation.'

Elizabeth switches off as she thinks about whether she can truly sit by in good conscience while so many people are conspiring against the Macquaries. She knows how worried Betsey is, but the Governor sometimes seems completely unaware, to the point of naivety even, about what is going on all around him.

She looks up as John changes tack again, and she is startled when he says friends back home tell him further that Lord Bathurst has given Commissioner Bigge a detailed brief to look into the Governor's mismanagement of the convict system, profligate spending, corruption and unauthorised program of capital spending on public works.

'He will have little patience for Macquarie's benevolence towards the convicts,' John declares. 'Bigge's last posting was in Trinidad, where he was also charged with writing a report on the running of the colony and the registers of slaves. As an expert in the slave system he will have no time for indulging convicts.'

Elizabeth's heart sinks for Betsey.

'Oh, and apparently Jeffery Bent has been telling Reverend Marsden that if Governor Macquarie ever returns to England he will prosecute him!' John says with obvious glee. 'He told Marsden he intends to pounce on him within six hours of his arrival!'

Elizabeth winces. After Ellis Bent's death, everyone expected his appalling brother Jeffery to go home to England, but he remained in the colony, causing all sorts of mayhem for the Macquaries. He consorted openly with their enemies and criticised them constantly in letters to the British Government, and although he did finally leave, he continued his campaign in London, with John, no doubt, egging him on. So much for John's undertaking before he left England that he would no longer play any role in public affairs in the colony! Though she loves her husband dearly and admires him for his inventiveness, his dogged determination to get things done and his steadfast devotion to his family, Elizabeth can't understand his seemingly insatiable appetite for trouble and chaos.

If only he would just relax and enjoy everything he has after his long exile. He has a good home, a wife and children who love him, and a profitable business. Why can't he be happy with that?

'But listen to this,' John continues. 'Jeffery Bent also says Mr Bigge will bring about the downfall of Governor Macquarie by revealing to them, with his report, just how badly he's managing the colony. Jeffery Bent told Captain Piper he has also heard that the plan is for Mr Bigge to unseat Macquarie and replace him as Governor.'

At that, something within Elizabeth finally snaps. She rises to her feet. 'I have to go out for a few hours,' she says. 'Don't wait up for me.'

Chapter 22

MORE BAD NEWS

Betsey Macquarie

15TH OCTOBER 1819, PARRAMATTA

There is a sudden pealing of the bell and I look out of the window to see Elizabeth Macarthur's carriage arriving outside. It's late in the evening and most unusual to have visitors at such a time. One of the servants opens the door and shows Elizabeth into the drawing room. We welcome each other warmly, but I notice she looks pale and nervous.

'Elizabeth!' I say. 'Is everything all right? You look as if you've seen a ghost. Please take a seat.'

She drops into a chair by the table and says, 'I just felt I needed to see you. I had a bad feeling . . .'

'What kind of feeling?' I ask, my heart lurching. Elizabeth is obviously close to tears and I'm beginning to feel panicky at how distressed she is. I sink to my knees in front of her. 'Elizabeth, please tell me what's going on,' I implore her. 'I beg you. If more trouble is coming for Lachlan, I need to know.'

'Please do not let on I have confided this to you,' she says, looking tormented.

I nod, my heart racing.

'I've been told that Commissioner Bigge has been specifically instructed to write a report on Lachlan alleging mismanagement, overspending and corruption in the colony,' she says.

I reel back on my haunches in horror. Good God! It just doesn't bear thinking about. How dare he! I neither like him nor trust him. I can see straight through him into his embittered greedy, grasping soul. But Elizabeth continues.

'And Captain Piper has heard from Jeffery Bent in London,' she says.

'Captain Piper? But he is a good friend of ours,' I say. 'Why would he be receiving letters from Mr Bent?'

'You know how much the captain loves gossip and relishes every opportunity to find out what's going on behind the scenes,' Elizabeth says. 'Mr Bent told Captain Piper he is preparing a prosecution against Lachlan the moment he returns to London,' she adds, looking utterly wretched.

I gasp, but Elizabeth still hasn't finished. 'And he says he's heard something else from highly placed sources in London.'

'What?' I ask dully, dreading the answer.

'He says that Mr Bigge,' she continues, 'will be replacing Lachlan as Governor.'

My hand flies to my mouth in both surprise and horror.

Elizabeth stands. 'I am so sorry to bring you this news,' she says. 'But I must go before the servants notice I'm not at home.'

She bustles back out of the house, leaving me still kneeling on the ground. Slowly, I get back up and walk to the bedroom, where Lachlan is in bed reading. I tell him what Elizabeth has said but, to my shock, he just laughs and dismisses it.

'Oh, people love the idea of a little scandal and will stir it up even where none exists,' he says. 'You really shouldn't worry, my dear Betsey. Mr Bigge won't be able to find any mismanagement, overspending or corruption, as there's none to find.'

'But Mr Bigge is already displeased about your arguing with him over Dr Redfern,' I remind him. 'And you've found disagreement over many issues since.'

Lachlan reaches out for my hand. 'I appreciate you looking out for me, but it was just early teething problems,' he says. 'I am quite sure that our record in New South Wales and everything Mr Bigge is seeing in the colony will speak for itself. I believes the Commissioner will write a glowing report back to the British Government. Now come to bed, my dear. You look so tired.'

After Lachlan falls asleep I slip out of bed and reread the letter I received yesterday from my sister Jane. Her son, our drunkard nephew John, had been posted with three other officers of Lachlan's 73rd regiment for duty in Ceylon and, still infuriatingly hot-headed, he'd ridden into a heavily forested area, ignoring warnings about the danger of hidden marksmen. He'd been shot dead with a single bullet—a victim of his own folly, according to our great friend, his commanding officer, Lieutenant Colonel Maurice O'Connell, Mary Putland's husband. Jane was still, obviously, grief-stricken.

I scroll down to reread what she wrote about Mr Bigge who, according to Jane, told some friends of his that he met Lachlan and me at a British consul dinner in Madeira on our way out here. He claimed we barely acknowledged him. I cast my mind back to the dinner but can't recall his face at all.

'I've heard he thinks very highly of himself,' Jane has written. *'His grandfather was the high sheriff of Northumberland, then so was his father, and later his brother Charles. Bigge instead chose to go down to London to serve at the Bar and run his own law firm in the Inner Temple, but was always agitating for a foreign posting. He was eventually sent to Trinidad as Chief Justice to examine the workings of the courts there and came back after four years. Apparently he is a great admirer of the Reverend Marsden, which may not bode so well for you, my dear sister . . .'*

I slip back into bed but am unable to sleep, though I try to reassure myself that, as Lachlan claims, Mr Bigge won't be able to find any evidence of wrongdoing during our time in Australia.

On the contrary, we have done so much. Right from the very start Lachlan ordered that the streets of Sydney be upgraded and initiated a building program. Over the years he has also put countless new laws in place to protect people against fraud, to license boats and carriages and to ensure proper records are kept everywhere. And despite devastating droughts, floods and bushfires, he's established several schools, including the Male Orphan School to house destitute boys aged between seven and ten in George Street and the Female Orphan School in Parramatta. He initiated new markets, created a Post Office, and we've recently agreed to become the patron and patroness of The Benevolent Society, which helps the destitute, mostly the aged and pregnant women.

Despite the increasing flow of convicts arriving from England almost every month, Lachlan has managed the colony so it can feed, clothe and employ all of them, many within our building program. Last year Lachlan also laid the first stone for a new Parramatta Female Factory to replace the old one, so female convicts can live safely and learn everything from weaving cloth to knitting, straw plaiting to needlework and laundry. We even finally have a real currency now as well as our very own bank, the Bank of New South Wales. I am proud to be the first woman in the colony to have shares in a public company.

Naturally, Lachlan has had to spend funds to pay for the fine buildings and roads that befit a colony with such a promising future. We're especially proud of the new Hyde Park Barracks, which Lachlan opened recently, pardoning Mr Greenway as he'd promised. However, we certainly could never be called profligate.

Many of our public buildings have been erected using convict labour or funded with spirits licences, tolls or money from the Police Fund. In fact, the hospital is now known as the Rum Hospital because of the way it was financed.

I glance at the wall by our bedroom window, which is missing some masonry because our funds for making Government House liveable ran so low. I've even been writing some of Lachlan's letters to save on staff costs. Meanwhile, Mr Bigge, I've been told, has a salary one thousand pounds higher than Lachlan's, and with not a smidgeon of his governing responsibilities or cares.

But Government House in Sydney is so run-down now, we've had no option but to start work on a new one in the Domain, with plans drawn up by Mr Greenway from sketches I made for a grand court of offices and stables at the entrance.

I've also planted many of the trees and shrubs that have been given to us as gifts amongst the native trees of what I see as my botanic gardens. It is around these gardens that I finally achieved my dream of having a scenic pathway built all the way to my rock at the headland, which Lachlan calls Mrs Macquarie's Chair.

Since Lachie was born, we've both preferred spending more time in Parramatta, however, because we think it's a much healthier place for a small child. I worked with our architect, Lieutenant John Watts, to draw up designs for extensions, additions and a transformation of the look of Government House in Parramatta. Mr Greenway added a portico on the front to give it an appropriate sense of grandeur.

We also extended the gardens of the Domain that it sits in, pulling down a number of convict huts that spoiled the view of the river. I had a wonderful time landscaping the grounds and planting both native and English trees and flowers, as well as a kitchen garden and a corridor of lemon trees. I suggested to Lachlan that we have convict labourers harvest hay there, and it is now the first time such an experiment has been undertaken in Australia.

In the town of Parramatta itself, I was not a great admirer of the old barn that served as St John's Church and was struck by the idea of adding twin spires to it like the stunning St Mary's Church high on a clifftop near Reculver in Kent, where I'd go for holidays with my closest schoolfriend Henrietta Meredith to her aunt's house.

I brought one of my pictures of it to New South Wales with me, and showed it to Lieutenant Watts, asking him if he could design two spires like this for St John's.

He looked at my watercolour and smiled. 'I am sure we could, Mrs Macquarie. What an excellent idea!'

The twin spires proved a wonderful addition to the church and I think everyone was most impressed by our vision.

But my pride and joy is the Female Orphan School which looks startlingly similar to my beloved Airds House. Every time I see it, my pride is tinged with just a touch of homesickness for my ancestral home. On its opening day last year, the sixty girls who were moving in arrived on government boats. It was quite a parade, with all of them dressed in their new uniforms of blue gowns, white aprons and bonnets.

My heart went out to the girls, some of whom I chatted to on their arrival. One of them, Mary, said she only had a mother, who didn't have enough money for them both to eat. Another, Sarah, had only a father and he often couldn't care for her because he had to labour on farms in far-off settlements. A tiny girl called Amy was a true orphan. Her mother had died on the ship coming over to Australia and her soldier father had been killed in battle.

'This is your new home,' I told them. 'And you will be quite safe and cared for here. By the time it's your turn to leave, you'll have learned the kind of skills that will allow you to make a decent living, and be a good wife.'

I would love to have a little girl and sometimes wonder what my daughter Jane would be like had she lived. Of course I'm extremely grateful to have Lachie. And though Elizabeth still frequently scolds me for babying him, I just can't help it. He's never been particularly robust, and, even at five years old, I can't resist hovering over him.

It's two weeks later when Elizabeth drops by again unannounced. I take one look at her face, then kiss Lachie and ask his nanny to take him away, before ringing for tea.

'How are you?' she asks. 'And Lachlan?'

'I think you might know the answer to that,' I answer, my spirits dropping when I see she's clasping a small Bible.

She looks haunted. 'I picked up my Bible this morning and it fell open at this page,' she says, passing it to me, with her finger on Proverbs 18:24.

'*Some friends play at friendship but a true friend sticks closer than one's nearest kin*,' I read aloud.

I smile at the sentiment, but she doesn't. She looks deathly serious. 'I've learned something more that I have to tell you,' she says. 'Just before Mr Bigge came here, he had a meeting with my son John in London, who had recently been called to the bar. John took him to dinner and apparently told him all about what his father sees as the problems in the way the colony is being run. Dr Bowman also met my husband when he was sailing back here after his long years in exile. Dr Bowman turns out to have been the surgeon on his ship and you know that Dr Bowman spent much time with Mr Bigge on their voyage here . . .'

I realise then that if Mr Bigge and Dr Bowman had met with members of the Macarthur family, no good would likely come of it for Lachlan and me. I should have known better than ever to have trusted Mr Bigge. It's clear he came here planning ill for us from the start. I should have warned Lachlan more forcibly to keep him at arm's length.

I feel the walls of the room start to close in as Elizabeth continues. 'I'm so sorry,' she's saying. 'I had no idea that my husband and my son might have been able to influence Mr Bigge . . .'

I feel sorry, too. It would be tragic if the family of my dearest friend turns out to be my most deadly enemy.

The room swims around until, thankfully, everything goes black and I feel no more.

Chapter 23

STIRRING THE POT

Elizabeth Macarthur

2ND FEBRUARY 1820, PARRAMATTA

John seems in such a good mood that Elizabeth Macarthur can't help feeling nervous. Since his return home nearly two and a half years ago, he's been suffering from what she can only call melancholia, and she's become used to him moping around the house whenever he's not instructing their sons on what to do on Elizabeth Farm. Elizabeth badgers him to go out himself and enjoy the fresh air, but he insists he prefers to stay inside with his letters and books and papers and plots.

So why, she wonders, has he suddenly recovered his bounce and good humour? When she asks him, he laughs and puts an arm around her waist. 'Why shouldn't I be happy?' he replies with a now unfamiliar jocularity. 'I have an accomplished wife and so many fine sons and beautiful daughters. Come on, take a break from your Bible and let's go out for a walk.'

As the pair stroll arm-in-arm through the gardens, admiring the growing vines, the olive saplings taking root, the peach and apricot trees in full blush, and the profusion of roses in blossom, Elizabeth finally realises the reason for his ebullient mood.

'I'm going to Sydney tomorrow,' he says. 'I have an appointment to see Mr Bigge.'

The breath catches in Elizabeth's throat. Why would he want to see Commissioner Bigge? What are they cooking up? She thought her husband was deliberately avoiding all overt contact with Mr Bigge, nervous of what the Colonial Office's attitude might still be towards him becoming involved in political matters. Despite his contact with Dr Bowman and their son's dinner with the Commissioner, John has also previously voiced his suspicions that Mr Bigge could be the kind of strict establishment man who'd be keen to toe the official line on everything and would no doubt disapprove of a wild card like himself. Moreover, John knows that Mr Bigge is an admirer of Reverend Marsden, who is certainly no friend of John's. So what can he be up to now?

He looks at her and smiles, as though reading her thoughts. 'I've become good friends with his secretary and brother-in-law, Thomas Scott, whom I've seen on numerous occasions now,' he says. 'He came to me with a letter of introduction from a mutual friend. I took the opportunity to tell him all about our merino wool industry here and how hard we're working to make sure it earns the kind of money to help make the colony self-sufficient one day. He was very interested and said he'd put in a good word for me with Mr Bigge. I think that, between us, we are slowly changing Mr Bigge's attitude towards me.'

'But you said nothing to me of this,' Elizabeth says.

'I didn't want to worry you,' he replies. 'You've had to deal with so many of our problems over the years I was away, now it's my turn to look after you.'

'Look after me?' she asks, trying to keep the incredulity out of her voice.

'Yes, I think it's important for us to have a good relationship with Commissioner Bigge. After all, if he's to become the next Governor, it will be good for us to know him.'

'But Governor Macquarie . . . Betsey—' she begins.

'Yes, I know you regard them highly, but we have to think about the future,' he says in a tone that brooks no argument.

It turns out that during one of his meetings with Mr Scott, John discovered that Mr Bigge was a good horseman and had a strong interest in fine horseflesh. As a result, John had offered him the use of his Arab stallion, Derwent, while he is here, also offering Mr Scott the use of one of their good mares. To his delight, Mr Scott got back to him to say his offer was gratefully accepted. Now Mr Bigge has agreed to a meeting. And John is going to Sydney to woo the commissioner.

'I think I should accompany you,' Elizabeth says. 'Captain Piper is having one of his gatherings on Friday so we could attend after your meeting.'

John looks displeased at her suggestion but seems to be trying hard to disguise his irritation. 'My dear, that would be wonderful,' he says.

The next day, Elizabeth and John leave for Sydney early. Elizabeth goes straight to their cottage while John heads to

Commissioner Bigge's office armed with files about the sheep they've bred, his records and the papers he has written about the merino wool industry. Maybe I shouldn't be so suspicious, Elizabeth thinks. If John sticks to business, this could be good for them and not affect the Macquaries at all.

But when John returns flushed and looking enormously pleased with himself, she fears the worst. 'How did he receive you?' she asks. 'And what did you say?'

'He was most impressed with what I had to tell him,' John replies, beaming. 'I told him about the enormous potential of the merino wool industry, and how it will not only help make the colony self-funding, but also provide a good income to England. I told him about all my plans to increase our fine wool production, and he was very interested. I'm sure he'd love to be the person who saves the British Government money, which he can do by helping us develop such a profitable industry! I also told him about the sheep I'm proposing to give Macquarie to send to Van Diemen's Land to improve the production of wool there, in return for a grant of more land—'

There's a knocking at the cottage door and he stops abruptly before striding over and opening the door. Standing there is Mr Scott, looking just as animated.

'Come in, come in,' says John. Mr Scott enters, looking ready to burst with excitement, and takes the chair John proffers him. Elizabeth watches them warily. They seem so comfortable in each other's company, they look like—she hesitates to use the word—conspirators.

'You made an excellent impression on Mr Bigge,' Mr Scott tells John. 'He took everything you told him about the potential of the merino wool industry on board, and he was most interested also to hear about the hurdles and challenges with Governor Macquarie you've been facing.'

At that, Elizabeth looks sharply at John. He ignores her.

'Commissioner Bigge views what you said as the key and touchstone of the truth of all we have heard . . .'

John grins, and pours two generous glasses of rum. 'I told him I'd provide him with as much information as I can about the colony,' John says, settling into his chair. 'I know he's leaving for Van Diemen's Land in the morning, and I've already written him a full proposal of things that need to be done to ensure the future of the merino wool industry here. I'd need around fifty thousand acres to make sure our sheep can graze all year round without any risk of being contaminated by the coarse-woolled animals on neighbouring properties bred for meat and for making rough blankets and clothing. I'd also need a lot more convicts to watch them. We need to concentrate on fine wool because it's the one thing produced here that can be exported profitably . . .'

The two men are so deeply engrossed in conversation that neither even notices Elizabeth slip out of the room. Though she'd love their business endeavours to succeed, she suspects her husband is incapable of pursuing his ambitious schemes without making trouble for those he considers his enemies.

It's a great shame, given that everything else is going so well for them. James and William have embraced their work on the farm more quickly than she'd ever imagined and often even live out rough in the paddocks. She's gratified that they've continued many of the methods she pioneered for looking after the sheep, and are improving some of them. Instead of just washing the sheep, for instance, they've devised a method of soaking them over and over to clean their fleeces, by building a series of wooden pens over the waters of the Nepean River. Afterwards, teams of men scrub the sheep with soap and in warm water heated in boilers set on open fires. After shearing, the fleeces are inspected and cleaned again if necessary before being laid out flat to be baled for shipping. It means the fleeces are in almost perfect condition when they reach the London markets in order to garner the best wool prices.

Despite being a busy barrister, their son John in London examines the bales as soon as they arrive and supervises their auction. He seems to have the ear of many men of influence, which serves the family well. Though Elizabeth worries about Edward in the army and had hoped John would come back to Parramatta, she knows how important it is to have someone so reliable in London.

But it's hard. Despite his assurances he wouldn't get involved in the politics in the colony, John is clearly becoming more deeply enmeshed. She often worries about the girls, too. While Lizzie is now thriving, she does not have any more suitors, and although she is quite happy with her books, Elizabeth wonders if she'll ever know the joy of grandchildren.

Hearing more rapping on the front door, she bustles out to investigate and is surprised to see Hannibal standing there.

'Come on in and join the party,' she says, pulling her cloak off a stand by the door. 'They're in the drawing room.'

After a moment of indecision, Elizabeth goes outside and calls for a groom to fetch her horse and carriage. He races off and returns within a few minutes.

'Where are we going, mistress?' he asks her as she climbs on to the seat beside him.

'We're going to the lighthouse at South Head for a party Captain Piper is giving,' she says.

'The master is not coming, too?'

'No, he's in the midst of a business meeting.'

Half an hour later, as they approach the round white tower of the lighthouse, set on high ground back from the cliff edge, Elizabeth can't help but be awed by the classically grand building, with its oil lamps revolving like clockwork to guide ships. Getting out of the carriage, she sees a cluster of half a dozen ladies being entertained by Captain Piper.

'Mrs Macarthur!' he shouts, breaking away from the group and striding over. 'I'm so glad you could make it. But no John?'

'I'm sorry, he's been detained in a business meeting,' she replies.

Captain Piper arches an eyebrow and says, 'Ah, well, all the better for us to have fun without him. I'm just about to climb the tower. Will you join me?'

'I would love to, sir,' she says, laughing.

Linking his arm through hers, he marches her over to the bottom of the lighthouse stairs. 'Have you been up before?' he asks.

'No, never. But I've always wanted to,' Elizabeth replies. 'I've long been curious about the view from the top.'

'It's splendid!' he declares. 'And well worth the climb.'

Elizabeth starts ascending the stairs, with Captain Piper a couple of steps behind. 'Keep walking!' he calls encouragingly after about twenty stairs. 'There are only another eighty to go!'

By the time they finally reach the platform at the top, they're both out of breath, but Elizabeth gasps at the views of the open ocean, the jagged coastline and the harbour right across to Sydney Town. 'It's so beautiful!' she exclaims. 'You're right! It is worth the climb!'

Just then a woman and child emerge onto the platform and Elizabeth is delighted when she sees it's Betsey and Lachie. 'Hello!' she exclaims. 'How lovely to see you. And Lachie. How big you are now! You must be close to your sixth birthday!'

As Elizabeth leans down and tickles Lachie under the chin, he smiles shyly back up at her. With his blonde curls, fine aquiline nose and thoughtful expression, she can see Lachlan in him more and more. He's always been a precocious little boy, but Betsey still spoils him terribly and over-protects him, despite Elizabeth telling her how much good it would do him to be allowed to play more with boys his own age. Not for the first time, she thinks she has to do more to persuade Betsey to give him more freedom. But when she looks closely at her friend, she sees how pale and pinched her face looks.

'And it is wonderful to see you, too,' Betsey says. 'The view is truly glorious, is it not?'

'It is indeed,' Elizabeth replies. 'The Governor is not with you today?'

Betsey shakes her head, looking even more drawn. 'No, he has been here numerous times before and he has so much on at the moment. With Mr Bigge's commission of inquiry . . .'

Elizabeth nods her understanding.

'And John? He's not with you?' asks Betsey.

'No, he is dining with some friends,' she replies.

'Now come along ladies,' says Captain Piper. 'We have lots of beautiful food and a particularly delicious punch downstairs, and I myself would love a drink!'

He takes Lachie's hand and starts to lead him to the top of the stairs. Betsey moves as if to take his other hand, then stops herself. Elizabeth notes this with some satisfaction as they follow Captain Piper down.

Back down on the ground, they eat slices of pies, serve themselves from silver platters of kedgeree and oysters, and sip at the punch. Betsey smiles at several women who greet her, but doesn't join in much of their conversation.

'Is everything all right?' Elizabeth asks, pulling her aside. 'You don't look your normal self.'

'Lachlan and I are both just very worried,' she replies. 'Mr Bigge is prying into every aspect of our lives, and every initiative Lachlan has taken with regard the colony. He wants to know everything he has done, and everything he has not. Lachlan tries not to be anxious but I know he's starting to become so. I just don't know where this will end. And we still haven't heard back from Lord Bathurst about Lachlan's resignation. We've started believing he must be very displeased with Lachlan's performance, and it's corroding our souls. It's making us second-guess our every move and doubt everyone's allegiance. And Lachlan even worries about how it will affect his pension.'

Elizabeth takes a deep breath. 'Betsey, you can't ask me how I know this and you can't tell Lachlan I've said this . . .'

Betsey nods, mystified, and gestures for her to go on.

'Well, I have reason to believe that Lord Bathurst did reply but the letter was . . . lost on the way. And the English Government do want Lachlan to continue for the time being . . .'

Betsey looks shocked. 'But how . . . ?'

'As I said, I can't say,' says Elizabeth. 'You just have to trust me . . . this trouble will all die down. Lachlan has been a very good Governor, anyone can see that, and you have done so much, too. Do not worry so.'

Betsey stares into her friend's face, then takes her hand. 'Oh, thank you, Elizabeth,' she says. 'You always speak such good sense. I am probably just being silly.'

Elizabeth smiles at her friend as warmly as she can, but in truth she is also weighed down with worry about her own husband.

When she arrives back at the cottage that evening, loud, drunken guffaws are coming from the drawing room. The crashing and blundering around of three rum-soaked men makes her feel absolutely wretched.

Chapter 24

UNLEASHING THE PASSION

Betsey Macquarie

13TH AUGUST 1820, SYDNEY

It starts out such a lovely morning. Lachie and I are staying a few days in Sydney while Lachlan works from Parramatta. I'm relishing the chance to visit my gardens and see how they are faring in the run-up to spring and am also looking forward to spending some time down on the promontory. Elizabeth Macarthur happens to be in town, too, so I've invited her for morning tea. It's a shame I can't see her so often these days, but it's just too awkward with Mr Macarthur around. I know she doesn't tell him where she's going when she comes to visit me at Government House in Parramatta. So it will be much more relaxing seeing each other here for a change, while our husbands are away.

She arrives with her youngest child, twelve-year-old Emmeline, whom Lachie adores, allowing Elizabeth and me to swap news of what we've been up to while Emmeline entertains Lachie, teaching him how to play jacks. Elizabeth is clearly loving the greater freedom afforded by the return of her husband and sons, and I remark that she looks ten years younger.

'Oh, get away with you!' she says, although she looks quietly pleased. 'I am now an old woman! Tomorrow on my birthday I will be fifty-four—well into my dotage!'

'No, no, not at all,' I reply—and mean it. Elizabeth moves much more lightly these days, as if the weight of the world is no longer on her shoulders. Her eyes shine and a smile is never far from her face. I know many other younger women in the colony with only a fraction of her energy. And although she now describes herself as 'retired', her retirement involves supervising the dairy, keeping an eye on their hogs and continuing to look after their vegetable plots, herb gardens and orchards.

'The vines are now going very well,' Elizabeth tells me, changing the subject. She is always far too modest. 'William thinks our next harvest will be even better than the last and we should be able to produce a much greater quantity of wine next year.'

'Really!' I say. 'Those boys of yours are very clever. I wonder who they take after?'

'John, of course!' says Elizabeth with a laugh.

'Oh, I don't know about that,' I reply.

'How is your health now?' Elizabeth asks. 'And the Governor's?'

I shrug. Lachlan and I have lately experienced far more than our fair share of illness. Lachlan was sick and confined to bed for almost a month around the end of last year with a mysterious illness which gave him terrible dysentery. He lost so much weight and was so weak that at one point I worried his illness might be life-threatening. I also wondered if it might be his syphilis advancing and showing more symptoms, but that was something I dared not mention to anyone, not even Dr Redfern.

Much to my relief, he finally rallied under the care of the good doctor, though he is still a little fragile. My own health hasn't been good, either. I'm not nearly as strong or energetic as I used to be. Sometimes I suffer such severe bouts of fatigue and weakness that I can't leave the house. My whole body has gone into spasms a few times as well and I can't help speculating that maybe I've been infected with Lachlan's syphilis. As for Lachie, he still tends often to be poorly, sniffing and coughing and wheezing at night. The climate here doesn't seem to agree with him at all and I hope it'll improve when we return to Scotland.

'A lot better,' I reassure her. 'And with spring on the way, hopefully Lachie's latest cold will clear up. We've been so busy, and the strain of Mr Bigge's inquiry is almost insupportable.'

'Yes, I am sure,' Elizabeth replies, looking thoughtful.

Changing the subject, I tell her a funny story about a group of Russian officers we've been entertaining in both Sydney and Parramatta, but I can see she's not really listening.

'Elizabeth, is there something the matter?' I ask.

She leans closer to me. 'Betsey, my dear,' she says, looking anxious. 'John would be angry if he knew I was telling you this . . .' she begins.

'Don't worry,' I say. 'He will never hear anything from me.'

'John says Commissioner Bigge has been deliberately seeking out the people who have negative things to say about you and the

Governor and is writing every word down in his report on the colony . . .'

'But why?' I ask. 'Surely he is just—' I do not finish the sentence.

Elizabeth looks haunted. She's always so faithful to her husband and rarely says a word against him, though I'm sure he can be very difficult to live with. To break his confidence in something like this, to tell me what's happening, is an enormous step for her to take.

'John has been talking to Mr Bigge,' she adds. 'And I don't think he's praised the Governor to him. Quite the contrary. In turn, Mr Bigge appears to be compiling some sort of negative dossier. By all accounts, it's growing by the day. I really think you need to warn Lachlan about it. He needs to view this seriously, and take action as soon as possible.'

I feel my hands tremble but try to control my emotions. 'Thank you, Elizabeth,' I say. 'I cannot tell you how much—'

She stops me by putting a finger to my lips, then calls, 'Emmeline! Say goodbye to Lachie now. It's time to go.'

'Happy Birthday for tomorrow,' I tell her as we say goodbye.

She grimaces, then kisses me on the cheek and whispers, 'Good luck,' as I show her out.

As soon as I've closed the door I call the nanny to look after Lachie and order my carriage. I don't want to burden Lachlan with all I've learned until I can find out for myself how serious the threat is.

First, I visit Captain Piper who, despite being a terrible gossip and liking to stay on the right side of everyone, is both an honest and shrewd judge of people. He says Lachlan's and Mr Bigge's visions of the future of colony are diametrically opposed and, yes, Mr Bigge certainly does seem to be going out of his way to see the kind of people he's been led to believe will back up his own views and preconceptions of how the colony is being run.

Next, I drop in to see Dr Redfern and Sarah. I already know Dr Redfern resents Mr Bigge for bringing out the surgeon who robbed him of his post, and for further casting a shadow over Lachlan's pledge to elevate him to the magistracy. He confirms my fears, saying that he believes Mr Bigge is out to harm Lachlan, as he had harmed him. He's heard about the kind of questions Mr Bigge has been asking people, and how clearly he leads the types of answers he'd like to solicit. One of his first questions is always, 'Have you any complaints to make against Governor Macquarie?'

'Just be careful of him, Betsey,' Sarah warns me as I leave. 'He looks to be a very dangerous enemy.'

I make a visit to Edward Eager next. He's one of the emancipists Lachlan provided with a full pardon. He was a lawyer before being transported to the colony for forgery. As well as serving as a magistrate and teaching Bible classes in Windsor, he has written numerous letters and petitions to London complaining about pardoned convicts not being allowed many of the civil rights of everyone else, including being able to give evidence in court. He is also agitating for trial by jury to be introduced in the colony. When I ask him if Mr Bigge has visited him to follow up these concerns, he suddenly looks stricken.

'Yes, but I told him my focus was on the rights we are denied by the Government in London,' he says. 'I hope he hasn't somehow twisted my concerns into criticisms of Governor Macquarie . . .'

My spirits sink and I'm feeling totally despondent by the time I call on our architect, Mr Greenway. What he says turns my heart to ice. Yes, he has been interviewed by Mr Bigge. Yes, he has been quizzed about the numerous buildings we've worked on together. Yes, Mr Bigge has been critical of many of them. When I ask Mr Greenway what he said in response, he looks abashed and his answers are so evasive I cannot help but imagine the worst.

As I mull everything over on the journey home, my emotions change from weariness to indignation and anger. I've never heard anything so preposterous in my life as that man trawling for dirt on Lachlan in every dark corner of the colony. I'm furious that he's been seeking out anyone who thinks they've been slighted or refused the land grants they've wanted or not been given their rightful dues by Lachlan.

And Mr Bigge appears to be intimating his own bias, with questions expressly designed to elicit certain responses, gilding the answers with his own imprimatur, and preparing to make a damning report to London to throw in Lachlan's face. What has Lachlan done to deserve this? He has faithfully served this colony for over ten years, doing everything in his power to grow it from a derelict dumping ground for Britain's worst felons into a colony of which our homeland can be proud, and this is what he receives in return.

So Mr Bigge is choosing to take evidence only from those with something negative to say or report. It appears he isn't talking to our supporters, upstanding officials, well-regarded magistrates or our friends in the clergy. When Lachlan originally heard who Mr Bigge was talking to, he tried to balance out the situation by contacting the more respectable citizens of our society and asking for their opinion on how the colony has fared in the last decade. But oh no, Mr Bigge did not want to hear from them. In fact, he lashed out at Lachlan for having the temerity to have 'interfered'.

Mr Bigge clearly doesn't want to be bothered with anyone in any position in the colony who favours Lachlan at all. It is only Lachlan's enemies he courts; only those who feel they have been thwarted or disappointed in their personal ambitions. No one would ever expect a servant of the Crown to expressly seek them out, listen to them uncritically, and then repeat every scurrilous assertion as if it were God's own truth.

Surely, if Mr Bigge is taking their petty complaints and malicious imputations as 'evidence', then he should be writing it down as a formal deposition and asking them to swear it on the Bible just as any respectable evidence would be taken in a courthouse? He refused, when he first came here, to be sworn in as a magistrate so he could go about his work 'without any obstacles or inconvenience'. But the British Government is likely to have no idea about this. Yet as a barrister in London, he would expect his clients to give sworn evidence for a court case. So why on earth is he not requiring it here?

I can only think there is one reason, and one reason only. The scunner wants to discredit us purely because, as I have been warned by Elizabeth, he may be in line for the post of Governor himself. In that position, as both prosecutor and judge, he can hardly be considered a dispassionate, objective or impartial diviner of the truth.

By the time I reach home, I'm full of rage.

Is Lachlan expected to stand by and do nothing while he is insulted, denigrated and defamed? He is becoming the victim of vicious, vindictive slurs from a small-minded, evil cabal intent on vilifying him, on sheeting blame to him for every tiny, insignificant problem here.

What does Mr Bigge know of this place and its people anyway, fifteen thousand miles from London? He's been here but five minutes. We have lived here for over ten years. Besides, if he really is positioning himself to take over from Lachlan, will not everyone he interviews try to ingratiate themselves with him and feel almost duty-bound to supply the dirt he so clearly wants—and make it up if they have none?

In the drawing room, I notice the bow of my violoncello sitting on a chair and I seize it. Maybe an hour's diligent practice will help me focus and its sweet sound will calm me down.

So I sit down, position the instrument between my knees, caress the rich, wine-coloured wood and place my left hand lightly onto to the fingerboard. I take a deep breath and swing my bow down and round, towards the strings. But my hand is obviously too heavy. As I pass the bow over the strings, one of them snaps and coils away.

'Damnation!' I shout, flinging the bow to the corner of the room. 'Damnation!'

I sit hunched over the violoncello, my head in my hands. I can feel tears trickling down my face, through my fingers. I see one drop on to the varnished surface and wipe it away in case it causes damage. If only I could so easily avert such damage to our lives!

I have to attend a committee meeting of the Female Orphan School in Parramatta, and it doesn't go well. Despite my position as patroness, the other members—urged on by the Reverend Marsden—decide to ignore some of my suggestions for the better running of the school. I see red; I have contributed so much.

It was my idea that we keep ewes at the property to provide wool for spinning and manure for growing vegetables, to present each girl with a cow when she marries as a contribution to her future as a farmer's wife, and that we appoint a professional superintendent to guarantee the farm's long-term management. I was also the one to ensure the farm was fenced so neighbours' livestock did not stray on to the school's ground and pastures, and to enable us to lease out small plots to earn income towards running the school. When the problem of workmen stealing the farm's cattle arose, with the larcenists claiming they'd been given cattle in return for their labour, I also initiated payment in currency only. Yet having played such an active role, the committee members now see fit to wave my ideas away. As well as Reverend Marsden, I have to suspect the influence of Mr Bigge.

By the time I return to Government House, Lachlan has finished his work for the day. When he finally walks into the drawing room, he takes one look at my face and comes to my side.

'Betsey!' he says, folding me in his arms. 'My Betsey! Whatever is the matter?'

To my shame, I burst into tears. He holds me silently as I wail and shudder until my rage and distress are both spent.

'Now tell me,' he murmurs, 'what has caused all this?'

I look up into his kind, concerned face and try to bring myself under control. This is ridiculous. It should take far more than a few ill-intentioned foes to reduce me to such a quivering wreck.

'Lachlan,' I say, forcing myself to breathe slowly and deeply. 'We are in trouble. I've spoken to some trusted friends who've told me that Mr Bigge is out to destroy you and all you've built here.'

Lachlan goes to say something, but then stops as I continue.

'He is travelling around the colony seeking out anyone who has ever had a grievance with anything you have done here, which he is putting it into his report on the colony. He is presenting all their complaints, whining and allegations as fact. He is asking leading questions and searching solely for criticism, not praise. He is choosing to speak only to those people who will back up his own political prejudices, people who might be jealous of you, people you have accused of offences, people you may have spoken out against for corruption who have made their fortunes through illegal trading or speculation.' My voice is growing stronger and clearer with every charge.

'He has approached no one in any position of responsibility who would be better placed to judge what is happening here. One charge against us, for instance, is from Dr Bowman who is angry that, despite being the colony's principal surgeon, no one thought to put up shelves for him in his house.'

Lachlan looks ashen.

'Mr Bigge is a man of very little imagination,' I continue. 'He sees this place as simply a penal colony to dump all the men and women for whom Britain has no use. He sees nothing of the proud future you are working towards for this colony of Australia. He abhors the fine buildings you and I have worked so hard to erect, and wants nothing but small, squat, ugly, functional blocks instead. He hates that you treat those who've served their time, and have something to offer and give back to the colony, with dignity and respect. He—'

'But how do you know all this?' Lachlan breaks in. 'Who has told you?'

'That doesn't matter,' I say, not wanting to betray Elizabeth. 'We have to concentrate on Mr Bigge. He looks around here and does not see a land like Britain, with a series of farms run by families making the countryside productive; he envisions a new aristocracy with vast tracts of land running sheep and cattle being tended by subjugated convicts and former convicts. And he wants you to stop exploration of this great land in search of new pastures and new opportunities, saying it is too expensive. How small-minded can one man be? I remember he started off wanting to see Port Macquarie to find out if it could support a sugar plantation, yet he still hasn't bothered to go there. If all Englishmen were as limited as he, most of the world would still be unknown . . .'

Lachlan looks stunned. When he is finally able to speak, it is in a slow, gravelly voice I have rarely heard before. 'You speak the truth, I am afraid,' he says. 'I have heard the rumours and have been told that the hostelries of Sydney are full of men boasting of how they have exacted revenge. I did not want to believe it, but I fear he is poisoning Lord Bathurst's mind against us on the basis of a bunch of insubordinate, malicious, vindictive, hypocritical men, who have not been allowed to have everything their own way.'

He stops and wipes his forehead, looking thoroughly beaten. But then he rallies. 'What do you think, Betsey? We've already been here two years longer than we planned. Is it time for us to go home?'

'I don't know,' I say. 'I don't want to leave on this note, being forced out by a man like him.'

'No, I agree,' he replies. 'But then again, is it worth going through this torture with no end in sight? Mr Bigge might be here for many, many months, years even, and I'm not sure I want to spend every day henceforth fighting.'

I'm silent at that. Who knows? Mr Bigge could well be appointed the next Governor and then we'd face the ignominy of having to hand over to him. As well, I'm worried about Lachlan's health. These levels of stress are doing him no good at all. He deserves to take his pension and go home to Scotland to become a Highland laird, as he's always dreamed, and build up his estate at Jarvisfield to leave for his son and heir. Lachie needs to go to a good school and I . . . I . . . I am growing tired. But maybe for him resigning now would feel too much like a surrender. I should make it easier for my husband.

'I think it would be good for Lachie to go to Scotland to get to know his family,' I say, finally. 'He'll need to go to a decent school soon, too. And I think I need a rest from this place.'

At that, Lachlan forces a smile. 'I've already resigned once, to no avail. I will now seek to set the date for our departure.'

I smile at him. 'Yes, I'm ready to go home,' I say. 'I want to settle down with Lachie in the home you and I create together at Jarvisfield. I want to give Lachie a taste of the lives we lived before we came here, and for us to share our homeland with him while we still have time.'

'And I want us to go on that trip around Europe we always talked about,' Lachlan adds. 'Neither of us have been well for some time, nor has Lachie. It would do us all good to go. I will write to Lord Bathurst without delay and tell him we will be leaving late next year or early the next. That will give him plenty of time to receive the letter and appoint a successor.' At that point, he grimaces, and I know exactly what he's thinking. 'As you have said, you and I have achieved a great deal here, but I'm not sure we will be allowed to achieve very much more. And however much I have enjoyed parts of what we have done here, and would like to celebrate the transformation we have wrought, I now know one thing.'

He stops and smiles at the puzzled look on my face. 'Betsey,' he says, taking my hand in both of his. 'What I care for most are you and Lachie. *You* are the most important people to me. And I think we deserve to be able to spend whatever time we have left back home with Lachie, in peace. What do you think, my darling?'

My kiss conveys everything he needs to know.

Chapter 25

A MIRACULOUS ESCAPE

Elizabeth Macarthur

13TH NOVEMBER 1820, PARRAMATTA

A tremendous thunderstorm hit Parramatta last week and John Macarthur is now reading the story about it in that day's *Sydney Gazette.* He's recounting to Elizabeth Macarthur, with not a little glee, how a massive ball of lightning hit Government House in Parramatta, smashing the roof, punching holes in walls on both storeys, shattering windows and leaving an incredible trail of destruction throughout the house. The Governor's office was devastated, with the chair he would normally sit in utterly destroyed. According to the *Gazette*, ceiling plaster was torn down and solid walls were left torn and gaping. The building was thick with smoke and stinking of sulphur.

Elizabeth is already familiar with most of it as Betsey had sent her a note letting her know they were all well, but John quotes the *Gazette*'s account of the carnage aloud. '*Perhaps there never was a more aweful visitation of the kind, than this was: and it is matter of astonishment that no personal harm was sustained by any of the numerous family contained in Government House,'* he reads. *'Most providentially it so happened that Mrs Macquarie, with her darling boy, had that morning breakfasted in an apartment which was the only one in the house not visited by this scourge, and to this cause may be attributed their almost miraculous escape.'*

John puts the newspaper down on the table, and laughs. 'It's lucky for the Governor that he was away at the time,' he says. 'But it must have given Mrs Macquarie and Lachie a hell of a fright. I would not have minded seeing that!'

Elizabeth bristles. Sometimes her husband astounds her. There were times when this big, powerful man was so gentle with her and the children, she was stirred to tears. He could be so kind and considerate and thoughtful and tender. But at other times . . . she barely recognises this callous, brutish side of him. It makes her uneasy but she generally ignores it. Today, however, she cannot.

'That is a terrible thing to say, John. I have heard from Elizabeth about what happened. She and Lachie were terrified and lucky to have been in just about the only room the fireball did not hit.'

John grimaces. Elizabeth can see he doesn't like his wife rebuking him and it's something she's rarely done in their thirty-two years of marriage. She's a forthright woman with her own opinions, but she usually expresses them carefully, in a gentle way she'll know he won't find confrontational. But, now, she's too irate to bother.

'Can you not imagine,' she asks, 'how frightening that must have been for them both?'

'Surely she could see the thunderstorm and knew what was happening?' John responds, trying to make up lost ground. 'There would have been servants around. She could have taken shelter under a table . . .'

'How on earth would she have known what was happening?' Elizabeth snaps back. 'Has this ever happened to you? No, of course not. How would you feel if it had happened to me and the girls when we were all alone here while you were away?'

'I would have been devastated,' he replies, knowing he has been well and truly caught out. If such a thing had hit Elizabeth Farm with his wife and daughters at home alone, he would have been mortified that he hadn't been there to protect them. 'I suppose you are right. I just thought—'

'What?' asks Elizabeth, the coldness in her voice surprising her as much as it does her husband.

'Well, I don't know,' he says meekly. 'I suppose I was not thinking straight at all.'

'I will have you know,' Elizabeth continues, 'that Mrs Macquarie did actually fear for her and Lachie's lives. She thought at the time it might have been a mutiny by the military firing on Government House. She said there was such a terrific noise, it sounded as if there were cannons.'

'But cannons do not sound like . . .' John starts, but then his words peter out as he sees the look on Elizabeth's face.

'Yes, you will know what cannon fire sounds like, just as the Governor would know. But how would Mrs Macquarie know? The only cannons she's probably ever heard were the ones fired when she and the Governor first arrived in the colony and when dignitaries visit. As far as she knew, Government House was under attack by two hundred hostile troops intent on overturning the government and putting someone else in charge. And I think you would know what that looks like.'

John has the grace to blanch. 'But surely she couldn't have thought that!' he protests. 'That is ridiculous.'

'No, not so ridiculous at all,' Elizabeth declares. 'There are so many people plotting against her and her husband, running around to report any perceived infraction to Mr Bigge, why would she not feel paranoid? The poor woman is out of her mind with worry. She has no idea who they can trust at this point.'

John stares out of the window in silence. He looks uncomfortable. Elizabeth wonders if this is the first time she's ever directed such fury at him. She thinks it probably is.

'When the fireball exploded and the place was filled with smoke,' Elizabeth continues, 'Mrs Macquarie thought the whole of Government House was on fire. How on earth would she and Lachie get out if that had been so? And can you imagine what Reverend Marsden is probably saying about the house being engulfed by the stench of sulphur?' She pauses. 'He's no doubt saying, even now, that it is the mark of Satan. You know him. He's never one to forgo the chance of a Biblical reference!'

Elizabeth sighs. Betsey is her friend, and she hates that she's having such a terrible time. After she confided their intention to leave the colony and return to Scotland, Elizabeth tried to persuade her to stay on, knowing how much she would miss her.

Although the two women are so different in many ways, Elizabeth has grown to realise there are also striking similarities.

They both have strong, ambitious husbands who treat them as real partners. They've both had to find their own way of being good wives and mothers, while still retaining their own identities. And they've both been keen to play roles of their own in the wider world. Elizabeth has found fulfilment in building up their merino sheep empire. Betsey has taken genuine pleasure in contributing to her husband's governorship of the colony with her architectural and landscaping work, as well as particular favourite projects like the Female Orphan School and the Native Institution. Elizabeth also knows that Betsey has influenced many of the Governor's attitudes to the emancipists, the natives, and also the Catholics. Betsey once told Elizabeth she persuaded Lachlan to grant land for a Catholic chapel in Sydney, and they also donated a small amount to the building.

While she and Betsey don't see eye-to-eye on many issues, and their husbands have little in common, they've managed to navigate their differences to form a strong and valuable friendship. In a place where there are so few educated women, Elizabeth knows her friend's absence will leave a gaping hole.

She'd tried to reason with Betsey, saying, 'But Mr Bigge will be gone soon. Do not make this choice so quickly. Take a while to see how you feel when this period is over. Mr Bigge will return to London, he will write his report and then everything will blow over again. Mark my words. You are past the worst.'

But Betsey smiled sadly, and shook her head, saying, 'Thank you, my dear. But though I value your counsel, on this occasion I think you are wrong. Mr Bigge is going to do Lachlan real harm with his report, and better we are in England to defend ourselves.'

Elizabeth suspects her friend is right. She knows John has been talking to Mr Bigge on every occasion he can, and how he has recounted their conversations in letters to their son John over in England. According to her husband, their son has been passing on titbits of what Mr Bigge has found to friends and acquaintances and networks of powerful people over there in an effort to prepare the ground for the Commissioner's final report. She's mortified that they both seem so confident they can discredit the Macquaries. For the life of her, Elizabeth cannot understand it.

She knows John wants more land, but what guarantee is there that whoever succeeds Governor Macquarie—unless it does turn out to be Mr Bigge—would be any happier to grant it to him? The new Governor might be someone from London with a set against John, and could well be less gracious towards him than the Macquaries have been.

Furious for her friend, she pleads with John to concentrate on running the farm and keep out of politics, reminding him that doing so was a condition of his return, but he is unreceptive to her entreaties. 'But don't you see, politics *is* about running the farm,' he retorts. 'We need more land to be able to expand.'

'We cannot even manage the land we already have,' she replies. 'Look at this house!' She points to the roughly patched repairs on the walls and then a corner of the ceiling that has come away. 'We need to do more to the house to keep it liveable. And it is not big enough for us all.'

'Yes, you are right,' he says. 'I will draw up some plans. We will repair and extend it.'

Though he sounds as if he means it, in the days that follow she sees no sign of him working on any plans, or talking to Mr Herbert about any repairs. Sometimes John is so busy concentrating on big, ambitious schemes, he fails to see important things right in front of his nose.

Elizabeth has been busy for the last few days overseeing the kitchen staff pickling and preserving the excess fruit and vegetables from the gardens. But now she's had to spend all day supervising a dinner John's arranged, against her better judgement, for Mr Bigge. The greyhounds have been out to bring in some wild duck, the cook has made rosella jelly to accompany them and there's some oil squeezed from the olives.

By the time the bell rings to announce their guest's arrival, she's organised everything exactly to John's satisfaction. Meanwhile, he's assembled the family tableau, with his sons and daughters all in their best clothes ready to receive their visitor. It must have taken a lot of effort from John to persuade James and William to leave their work and come home early, thinks Elizabeth drily, although the girls are pleased at the opportunity to dress up. She just hopes all their efforts will be worthwhile, knowing this image of a perfect family is pure pretence. Since John's return her life has been far from easy, and she knows the children have suffered from having their parents separated for long periods of time.

When Mr Bigge is shown in, John strides across the room to pump his hand vigorously. 'Welcome to Elizabeth Farm!' he says. 'Now meet the family.'

Elizabeth watches as Mr Bigge's eyes flicker around the room and everyone present. She hopes, for John's sake, he's impressed. Though he's giving away little, he smiles and greets her formally with a bow of the head. 'Mrs Macarthur, I have heard so much about you,' he says. 'It is a pleasure to finally make your acquaintance.'

Elizabeth smiles back at him with as much warmth as she can muster. 'And mine yours,' she says. 'I've heard a great deal about you, too.'

The dinner passes pleasantly enough with Mr Bigge asking each of the children about their experiences in the colony. With Edward abroad, all the children present were actually born here, and have no conception of another home, Elizabeth thinks sourly. Of course, the boys were schooled overseas but it never crossed their minds not to return here as soon as they were able. In addition, all but Lizzie—who was born in Sydney—were born in the bedroom here. No, Mr Bigge will not extract any dirt on what the Macquaries are doing in the colony from her children, if that is what all his polite conversation is aimed at.

After dinner is over, John dismisses the children from the room and Elizabeth realises John is about to get to the point of this invitation. 'Mr Bigge, would you like us to show you around the farmlands?' she asks. 'Most of our sheep are at the Cowpastures, but we do have some here, not to mention cattle, horses, goats, poultry . . .'

Mr Bigge looks at her blankly.

'I think you will be most interested to see the quality of the fleece on the sheep,' she continues. 'Most, of course, have already been shorn this year, but we have kept a few to demonstrate how long the fleece can grow with the right breeding and methods, and how clean they can be with the novel way we've developed of washing them.'

Mr Bigge glances at John, who looks at her nervously. She stops.

'Thank you so much, Mrs Macarthur, that is most interesting,' Mr Bigge says in a tone that suggests it really isn't. 'Now, I am sure you have plenty to do. I must not keep you. Your husband and I have lots to discuss about sheep and the colony. Thank you so much for a most delightful meal. I have enjoyed meeting you and your beautiful family.'

Elizabeth suddenly understands. She is being dismissed from the room. John will say nothing about how she actually ran their farm for eight years, how she multiplied the flock numbers, worked to keep the breed pure, introduced ways to keep them safe from predators and came up with the idea of washing the fleeces before they were sent to London. She is the expert, yet he does not want to listen to her.

'Yes, I do have more important things to do,' she says, rising slowly to her feet. 'It has been very informative to meet you. Now I will leave you gentlemen to your business. Good evening!'

And with that she glides from the room, her shoulders square and her head as high as she can possibly manage. There is no way she will give either of them the satisfaction of witnessing the cussed tears that are now stinging her eyes.

Part FOUR

It is time for us to go and, while I will be sad to farewell Elizabeth, I will be happy to be home again. Lachlan's estate has been enlarged in our absence, and I hope it will prove a very comfortable home for our small family. This is a time for us to rest and regain our strength and to enjoy our time together. We will be able to look back in pleasure and savour our proud legacy of helping turn Australia into Britain's finest colony, a bastion of promise, hope and glory.

Betsey Macquarie's journal,
14TH FEBRUARY 1822

Chapter 26

BETRAYAL UPON BETRAYAL

Betsey Macquarie

15TH FEBRUARY 1822, SYDNEY

We are finally leaving Australia! It's been over twelve years since we first landed on these shores, and despite our travails of the last two years, I am proud of what Lachlan and I have achieved. And joy of joys, the contemptible Mr Bigge is not returning to take over the governorship and undo all our good work.

The new Governor, Sir Thomas Brisbane, is another Scot with a scholarly air about him. He has proved himself a kind and generous ally. We recently completed our last tour of Van Diemen's Land and are ready to return and settle back on the Isle of Mull. Lachlan has had his brother Charles draw on all his savings to buy more farming land while we've been away, so we're hoping for a handsome homecoming.

Meanwhile, it is both lovely and somewhat bittersweet to say goodbye to some of the dear friends I've made in the colony. My first call is to Elizabeth Macarthur.

'Oh my dear!' she greets me when I call in at Elizabeth Farm on our way to Sydney. Tears are already running down her face, and they start immediately streaming down mine, too. We both laugh.

'Goodness, I'm so sorry!' she says. 'I told myself I wouldn't cry. I was determined not to. And now look at the two of us!' She sees me glance towards the drawing room and knows instantly what I'm thinking. 'And don't worry. John is out, and won't be back for hours. I told him to stay away on the pain of death!'

I smile. I was dreading this farewell, but dreading even more that Elizabeth's husband would be standing by, glowering at us. I'm relieved, but feel heartbroken nonetheless at having to say goodbye to the woman who's proved, over the years, to be my dearest friend.

'I shall miss you so much,' I say. 'You have been wonderful to me. There have been so many difficult . . .'

'Shhh,' Elizabeth says. 'Let's not dwell on the bad times in our last few minutes together. Let's remember the good. And now you're off back to your beloved Scotland to live on the estate Lachlan has been building up over the years you've been here, to see your family again, and to introduce Lachie to them all. It will be wonderful, so wonderful.'

'Thank you, dear Elizabeth. I do hope it will be wonderful. I am looking forward to seeing my family again, especially my sister Jane, but I won't recognise her children anymore! Twelve years is a long time to be away, especially in a child's life.'

Elizabeth reaches for my hand. 'But how beautiful it will be for you to get to know them again in their adulthood!' she says. 'They will be so excited to see their favourite aunt again. There are many here who will miss you. But be careful. There may be some who you think are friends, but who may well switch their allegiances and curry favour with whom they believe to be next in power.'

I squeeze her hand. So typical of her to warn me of danger ahead, even when we are saying farewell and avoiding all mention of Mr Bigge and his accursed report to come. I take a deep breath. 'Thank you. And one day . . . one day . . . I hope I will be able to come back here and visit you again . . .' I say.

'That would be joyful,' Elizabeth replies. 'But I think we both know that is unlikely. This may well be the last time we ever see each other. I will always carry a memory with me, however, of a beautiful woman who arrived here with no idea of what she was getting into, but who learned quickly, and ended up making a huge difference to this place, and helping, with Lachlan, to found this new Australia.'

'You are too kind,' I say. 'But it's people like you who've really created this colony. You've done so much and will always be an inspiration for me. I will carry a memory of you in my heart.'

We embrace until I have to finally pull away, knowing I have to take my leave. 'I will write to you, and think of you often,' I say, my eyes again wet.

'And I will write, too,' Elizabeth says. 'I will give you all the news of the colony and of the people you remember fondly—and of those you don't!'

I walk out quickly, and don't turn back until I am safely in my carriage. Then I wave to her, as she stands in front of the house, framed by the blossoms of her glorious garden. I will take that image of her with me, I think. But as the horses take off, I feel a terrible grief. Throughout my most turbulent times here, Elizabeth has proved herself a steadfast, loyal friend. I doubt I would have survived my time in the colony without her.

It is easier to take my leave of others. Captain Piper sees Lachlan and me off in his typical style, with a great party on the harbour in a floating barge filled with musicians. He simply does not know how to do anything in moderation. I shall miss his easy company and his wife Mary Ann's good humour. I have left her my beloved violoncello. She admired it once and I'm sure will provide an excellent home for it.

My other great friend, Sarah Redfern, is disconsolate we are leaving, and invites us to dinner with her and her family. Dr Redfern is in England where, amongst other things, he's apparently written an entire book criticising Mr Bigge and his methods. Due to ill-health and, I suspect, legal advice, he has finally decided against publication. Sarah tells us they both hope see us back in Scotland one day. She and Dr Redfern plan to return to Britain so he can continue his medical studies and they can oversee the education of their son William.

Amongst our closest associates, only Francis Greenway is curiously reserved. When we call on him for the last time, he seems nervous and troubled. I ask him if all is well and he replies that he is just over-tired and will miss my guidance and direction enormously. I suspect there is something more behind his diffidence, but any misgivings I have are lost in the general flurry of farewells. Even Reverend Marsden drops by to wish us Godspeed on our journey and a safe arrival. He looks serious and concerned, but I imagine he is labouring to contain his joy.

After we board *The Surry*, we have the traditional nineteen-gun salute and plenty of friends and officials to see us off, but what we hadn't expected are the throngs of ordinary citizens who turn out to wish us well. I feel myself overcome with emotion by the fervour of their farewell and I also see a tear in Lachlan's eyes as he waves to the crowd. We are also presented with five hundred guineas from a collection the people organised, for us to buy a piece of silver in commemoration of our time in Sydney. However much Lachlan's adversaries have tried to besmirch his reputation, many people are clearly grateful for all he's done to transform the colony. And in the end they are the ones who truly count.

I feel very impatient to be home during the long five-month voyage back to England. We have plenty of company with our menagerie of animals, including our favourite family milking cow Fortune and Lachlan's horse Sultan, along with a fair collection of livestock, as well as kangaroos, emus, black swans, cockatoos, pigeons and Lachie's parrots and lorikeets. Lachlan spends a lot of his time finessing his formal responses to the no fewer than sixty-three criticisms of him, his conduct and his regime that Mr Bigge indicated might form the basis of his report. At times, Lachlan is able to laugh them off; at others, I know he is deeply worried and fretting that officials in London might take them seriously.

By the time we finally arrive in London at the beginning of July 1822, we are all exhausted. Many of our precious animals have died on the voyage, my health is not the best, and we are anxious for the money from the pension due to Lachlan to start being paid. We are fearful, too, about what kind of reception Lord Bathurst will give us. No doubt he has been in contact with Mr Bigge during the latter's time in the colony, and will likely know the contents of his report in advance.

In the event, we are cheered by the warmth of our reception. Lord Bathurst is welcoming and gracious and asks about our voyage. Lachlan doesn't even bring up the subject of Mr Bigge's report.

I ask him afterwards why he didn't, saying, 'Surely it would be better to deal with it as soon as possible?'

'No,' he replies firmly. 'There is a time and a place and a formality about such things. I will speak up soon, but not just yet.'

True to his word, three weeks later, after doing the rounds of the dignitaries and being granted an audience by the King, he sends Lord Bathurst his forty-three-page dossier answering all the charges Mr Bigge has levelled against him. It is well-timed. Although it has been an entire year since his return to England, Mr Bigge has only recently delivered the first part of his report on the colony to the House of Commons.

Lachlan reads out parts of his own submission to me, and asks for my comments on some of the sections. It's an excellent rebuttal of Mr Bigge's criticisms. He outlines the state of the colony when we arrived as 'barely emerging from infantile imbecility, and suffering from various privations and disabilities' with the country impenetrable just forty miles from Sydney. By the time we left, he wrote, it had expanded massively west, north and south, and was 'in all respects enjoying a state of private comfort and public prosperity which I trust will at least equal the expectation of His Majesty's Government'.

He recounts how he'd overseen no fewer than two hundred and sixty-five public works, including sixty-seven major buildings and construction projects, ranging from barracks, the military hospital, a hospital, docks, churches, the fort at Bennelong's Point, the lighthouse at South Head to numerous houses and many streets and good roads. The colony now has schools, a bank, institutions for the natives, homes for orphans and the Female Factory at Parramatta for convict women waiting for assignment, their children, and re-offenders, as well as destitute women and others requiring maternity or medical care. He also describes the system of order and justice he initiated, and how emancipists were contributing hugely to the continuing progress of society.

All this had been achieved, he writes, despite trenchant opposition from 'turbulent individuals, generally stumbling on the very threshold of the law, impatient of all restraint'. He did not hold back about his enemies, branding them 'depraved' and 'malignant' with their malice 'beneath my contempt'.

We both wait with bated breath for some kind of reaction from Lord Bathurst. The reply isn't what we were expecting. Lord Bathurst tells Lachlan that the King is very pleased at how well the colony has flourished in population, agriculture, trade and wealth under Lachlan, and praises 'the assiduity and integrity with which you have administered the colonial interests of that settlement'. But he says nothing about Lachlan's pension, and there's no sign of any money.

Still, it is an enormous relief to hear such words, and I am thrilled to see how buoyed Lachlan is as a result. But his cheerful mood does not last for long. He finds out the new under-secretary to the Colonial Office is Robert Wilmot-Horton, a great friend of John Macarthur's barrister son John, who is still very tight with Mr Bigge. I wonder if Elizabeth knows.

But Lachlan does have one great friend and influential supporter in the Government in Lord Castlereagh, who originally pushed for him to become Governor and who Lachlan hopes will help bring others to his side. Tragically, in August, Lord Castlereagh has a nervous breakdown and slits his own throat with a knife.

We hope there will be some respite at home in the Highlands. When we travel to Mull, it is wonderful to see my dear sister Jane again and we shed many tears as we catch up on the key events of the years we've been apart. A number of her nine daughters—she's managed to marry off eight—come to visit their mother and see me.

Everyone makes a huge fuss of Lachie and he's rather overwhelmed by all the attention. He's never known any family but his father and me, and he's bewildered by all the noise and the strange Scottish accents. But his cousins are very welcoming and, after a little shyness in their company, he soon relaxes. I do think he's a little homesick for Parramatta, however. After all, it's the only home he has ever known.

But when we finally leave for the last leg of our journey to our Jarvisfield Estate, things start to go downhill. The Highlands are going through a terrible economic depression and arriving is an awful shock. Charles certainly bought more land with Lachlan's money, and there's now over twenty-one thousand acres. The greater part of it, however, is far too poor and barren for farming. It's boggy and windswept and wild, and the sight of it fills me with despair.

Most of the tenants on the estate are distressingly poor and eking out a living on next to nothing. Looking at the terrible hardship they're enduring, I'm not surprised to learn that few have paid their rents, while most haven't been able to for a long, long time. Lachlan is stricken about not having the healthy fortune he'd anticipated.

I'd been looking forward to my first sight of Gruline House on the estate too but, in the event, it is totally underwhelming. A small oblong house of traditional dark stone, and two storeys high, it is plain—oh, so plain!—with a flat frontage and gabled with verges. It is nothing like I'd so fondly imagined, with none of the charm or grace of my own home, Airds House, on the mainland. Gruline House is in a pretty position, sure enough, at the north end of Loch Bà, which stretches out for around three miles to the south-east, but inside awaits another blow. It's in a ghastly state—damp, cold and in urgent need of repair. It is far, far worse than we were expecting. Lachlan had always intended to build a mansion house or small castle for us nearby, but now we have almost no money and end up having to stay with a neighbour instead. Lachie hates it and cries that he wants to go home. I try to reassure him and tell him that this is home now. That only makes his distress worse. Even the Treasury adds to our worries, pestering Lachlan for receipts for ten thousand pounds worth of

Spanish dollars imported into Australia from India in 1812, which he had the middles stamped out of to create our first currency, the 'holey dollar'.

After four weeks in Scotland, Lachlan decides that instead of spending winter on the estate, where the chill weather will certainly affect us, we will go on a grand tour of Europe—the honeymoon we'd always promised ourselves before we sailed to New South Wales. We find a tutor for Lachie to come with us, and the trip turns into a delightful eight months of travel through France, Switzerland and Italy. We even have an audience with the Pope in Rome, which dazzles Lachie and me. I write all about it to Elizabeth, knowing she'll take great pleasure in hearing of such happy days.

On the last part of our travels, however, we receive another blow. We're in Fountainebleau when we receive a package from Lachlan's friend, Lord Strathallan, containing two more tranches of report Mr Bigge has published while we were away. The total report now numbers more than three hundred pages, and Lachlan immediately sets to reading the whole thing. He grows more and more alarmed as he continues, saying Mr Bigge has taken absolutely no notice of the letter Lachlan sent rebutting many of his points. He has not made any changes despite the additional information and corrections Lachlan provided.

In essence, Mr Bigge has come down completely on the side of our opponents' arguments: that our convict labour policy was misguided, dangerous and wrong. Instead of keeping the convicts in town to build the colony, they should have been sent out of Sydney to help farmers develop their huge tracts of land and manage their stock. He claims this would have cut the British Government's costs of accommodating the convicts and increased the profits of Mr Macarthur and men like him.

Mr Bigge also criticises Lachlan's spending on public buildings, arguing that smaller, more modest buildings would have served just as well, and that much of the infrastructure Lachlan built could not be justified in a mere penal colony.

Echoing the likes of Mr Macarthur, he also opines that the convicts who had served their time did not deserve to be treated with the same consideration as free settlers. He recommends that Lachlan's decree that when a prisoner had discharged his debt to society he should be 'eligible for any situation which he has, by a long term of upright conduct, prove himself worthy of filling' should be overturned, and the handing out of pardons should be massively restricted in future. Lachlan had granted 366 pardons, 1365 conditional pardons and 2319 tickets of leave between 1810 and 1820; by contrast, Bligh had granted just two pardons in his time as Governor. Mr Bigge essentially advocated that New South Wales should be restored to the kind of place that would inspire terror in anyone in England who might face transportation, and misery in those who had.

So instead of the report Lachlan had originally anticipated would provide the seal of approval for his years of work in the colony, it is proving our ruin. Mr Bigge has also criticised me, which takes us both by surprise, enraging Lachlan even more. 'How dare he bring your name into the public sphere through his report!' he fumes. 'And if he was going to do so, then he should at least have credited you with the benevolent character you so richly deserve. This report is simply false, vindictive and malicious.'

We're both devastated as we ponder what some of our inner circle said about us. I now realise, for example, why Mr Greenway was so wary towards me when we said farewell. According to the report, when faced with criticism about the expense and labour involved in many of the great buildings we collaborated on, Mr Greenway deflected all responsibility and blame to me. He must have been trying to ingratiate himself with Mr Bigge in the hope of favour when we were gone, just as Elizabeth had warned. After all we did for him, and the backlash we'd weathered over our decisions to elevate emancipists to responsible positions in the colony, Mr Greenway's actions feel like the ultimate betrayal. I shed tears of both sadness and rage.

After reading Mr Bigge's report, Lachlan spends twelve days writing his response, which he sends off to Lord Bathurst. When we arrive in London on the 31st of July, Lachlan petitions the King, requesting that the report he wrote in answer to Mr Bigge's many charges should also be published in the House of Commons with the same kind of fanfare. When nothing happens it feels like betrayal upon betrayal.

Despondent, we decide to go home to Mull, sailing there in order to save money on the coach fare. Little has changed on the estate in the interim and, to make things harder, we now have debts from our trip to Europe. As we move into the chill and bleakness of the barely habitable Gruline House, worst of all, there is still no sign of any of the pension Lord Bathurst had promised.

Chapter 27

SHARING TROUBLES

Elizabeth Macarthur

3RD OCTOBER 1823, PARRAMATTA

Back in New South Wales, Elizabeth Macarthur is enjoying the friendship of the new Governor, Major General Sir Thomas Brisbane, who served as her son Edward's commanding officer, and his wife Lady Anna Maria Brisbane. They are a sociable couple, and hold weekly soirees at Government House. But Elizabeth knows her card is marked. John has started, yet again, complaining about the new Governor, and she knows her newfound friendships can't possibly withstand that.

She feels Betsey Macquarie's absence far more than she ever thought possible, too. She misses riding over to see her in Sydney or Parramatta, and those wonderful chats they used to have.

The Brisbanes are great company, and have followed the Macquaries' example to spend more time in Parramatta than Sydney but, more and more, they're tending to give her and John a wide berth. Elizabeth suspects the Governor is wary of John conspiring against him and stirring up trouble back in Britain. He's right to be cautious. Already, John is writing letters to influential people in London.

Though John was initially pleased that the new Governor enacted many of the changes Mr Bigge recommended, like tidying up the land grant system and selling off some Crown land, he's now accusing Governor Brisbane of favouring the emancipists over the exclusivists. Just this morning, John told Elizabeth that the Governor is a nice man, but very weak, and there's little he despises more than weakness.

Betsey and Elizabeth write to each other regularly, and even though Betsey is now free of such plots, her letters to Elizabeth are far less cheerful since returning to Britain from Europe, and it doesn't sound as if she's at all happy. It's clear Mr Bigge has caused a lot of trouble for her and Lachlan, and Lachie is having trouble adjusting to a new country. Elizabeth only hopes that when they settle at home in Scotland they'll all find the peace they deserve.

She still tries to keep Betsey up to date with all the news in the colony, telling her Dr Redfern has returned from England after a spell in the healthy climes of Madeira on the way, and he and Sarah are living at Campbell Fields where he's been granted some more land and is growing grapes, and grazing sheep and cattle. He isn't seeing many patients and says he might retire completely from medicine next year.

She also writes that Captain Piper is busier than ever with his work for the Bank of New South Wales—where he's tipped to become the new chairman of the board next year. She says jokingly that, as is always the case with him, he's taken on far too many responsibilities. Besides his duties as a magistrate, he is president of the Scots Church committee, is still involved with customs, wharfage and harbour duties, the collection of taxes on spirits and tobacco and the commission he takes on all moneys paid. She also describes how, since the Piper family moved into their grand ten-thousand-pound mansion in Point Piper last year, he seems to be expending most of his energies on the acquisition of more and more land and property. She describes his magnificent Henrietta Villa—with the domed ballroom he had built in the shape of a St Andrew's Cross—that everyone agrees is the finest house in Sydney, with the most splendid view in the world. '*How I wish you were back in Sydney so we could attend one of his glorious soirees together!*' Elizabeth writes.

When it comes to news of Reverend Marsden, Elizabeth imagines Betsey's delight to hear he isn't faring at all well under the new Governor. In fact, Sir Thomas suspended him from the magistracy for refusing to sit with a colleague he accused of taking a convict girl into his home. That colleague was Dr Henry Douglass, who still has the position Lachlan gave him managing the hospital at Parramatta. Reverend Marsden then sentenced the girl to prison in Port Macquarie—until Governor Brisbane intervened, freeing her and rebuking him.

Elizabeth stops for a moment, smiling, before adding, '*Then, to add more salt to the wound, the Reverend was fined by Dr Douglass over his failure to supervise another convict servant. And when he refused to pay the fine Dr Douglass had his piano seized and sold. It is most unfortunate that the Reverend seems to have taken such a strong dislike towards someone Lachlan so warmly favoured!*'

She also smiles with glee to think about Betsey's reaction to her news of Mr Greenway. Having told Mr Bigge that Elizabeth Macquarie should be blamed for the extravagance of some of his buildings, the tables have well and truly turned. '*When he tried to charge Governor Brisbane huge fees for his building work on top of his salary, the Governor curtailed much of Mr Greenway's autonomy and since then everyone has been changing his designs,*' Elizabeth writes. '*When he railed against this . . . he was dismissed from Government service altogether. What's more, the authorities are now trying to evict him from the house that went with his job!*'

Elizabeth moves on to family news which she's sure Betsey will be happy to hear. Firstly, her dear daughter Mary—the fourth of her seven children and her second eldest daughter—is proving very well-suited to her new husband, the surgeon Dr James Bowman, and they seem very content.

But, best of all, her darling son Edward, who's now thirty-six years of age, has moved back to the colony with plans to build a new mansion at Camden Park. Sadly, though, he plans to leave again in February next year. Lizzie, meanwhile, is still without suitors.

Finally, Elizabeth writes about her husband John. For most of the time Edward has been in the colony, John has sunk deep into another of his depressions and is very unwell. For the first time, Elizabeth starts to confess her fears for his future to Betsey. After all, her friend had to cope with her own husband's ill health and the knowledge he'd probably contracted syphilis. The thought suddenly strikes her that perhaps John has it, too, and that could be what is causing the wild changes in his demeanour. She hadn't before even imagined he might have been unfaithful to her, but after all, he did spend so long in London alone. In addition, he had served as a commissioned officer in the army before they'd met. She muses about the possibilities to Betsey and, as she writes, she feels a weight lifting off her shoulders. It helps to share her troubles with a trusted friend.

In fact, there is no one else on earth she would confide such a delicate matter to, not even Dr Redfern or Captain Piper. Not for the first time she curses John for helping drive Lachlan and Betsey from the colony. She would give anything to be able to sit down and talk to someone who's lived here and understands exactly what it's like to be a woman in this place and to be facing such terrible troubles.

The John whom Elizabeth once loved so unwaveringly seems almost lost to her these days, she writes. Edward has been trying to revive his spirits, talking to him long into the night about his land and their sheep and anything he can possibly think of to try to cheer him. As well as the idea for the new house at Camden, Edward's also been discussing with John the renovations and extensions planned for Elizabeth Farm. Elizabeth has warned Edward it is hopeless, but she's pleased to see him try.

She pauses for a moment, and then resumes writing. She used to believe that when John saw he was surrounded by love from his family, he could not fail to stir himself. But she sees such a blackness in his moods at times and such a rapid decline in his sanity at others, she is truly starting to despair. To see those words finally written in stark black ink on the last page of her letter makes Elizabeth realise just how dire her situation is becoming.

Chapter 28

A KIND OF DESPERATION

Betsey Macquarie

2ND FEBRUARY 1824, SCOTLAND

This winter is one of the worst I have ever known. We've had terrible storms, bitter winds, lashing rain and snowfall. In fact, the rain and wind have been so bad at times that they've swept in forcibly around the door and windows of Gruline House on the Jarvisfield Estate on Mull, even once quenching the fire in the grate. The house joists are rotten, the walls are soaked and the roof leaks in numerous places. We all seem to have colds almost permanently. And in yet another misfortune, our little pet dog was savaged by a neighbour's dog two weeks ago and died soon after. Nine-year-old Lachie is inconsolable and, that night, has a terrible tantrum, screaming that he wants to go home to Australia. It's only when he's completely worn himself out that he finally sleeps.

We couldn't be further from the position of prestige, privilege and power we enjoyed in New South Wales, nor that hot sunshine and bright light that I once found so intolerable—strange as it seems to me these days. But we're still determined to make the best of our new life. I have drawn up some plans for renovating and extending the house, which include a proper study for Lachlan to work in. But alarmed that there is still no sign of his rebuttal document being presented to Parliament, he has decided he should go to London to ask again about his pension—the only news he's received so far is of merely 'the probability' of a pension—and a possible knighthood for his services to the colony.

On a rare perfect winter's day before his departure, he takes Lachie and me out rowing on Loch Ba. The air is brisk but the sky is clear and the water is a glittering expanse of indigo.

'Isn't this beautiful?' he exclaims to us. 'And look over there!'

We all gaze at the shoreline of sand and rocks and grassy heads, dotted with daisies and buttercups. He smiles at us and says, 'That's the extent of your estate.'

'*Your* estate?' I say. 'Surely you mean *our* estate?'

'Yes, yes, of course,' he says, with the strangest faraway look in his eyes that makes me feel uneasy.

Two days later, the three of us go out riding together. After half an hour, dark clouds roll in and it begins to smatter rain.

'Let's go back,' I say, turning my mare homewards. 'This rain is only going to grow worse.'

'No, let's carry on,' Lachlan insists. 'I'm sure it will brighten.'

'But we've all only just got over our colds,' I argue. 'I'm worried that Lachie—'

'Betsey,' Lachlan interrupts, '*please*, let us carry on, just for a few more minutes.'

I fall silent, bewildered at his odd mood and that he would want to continue on in what has now become driving rain. Lachie is shivering on his pony, and icy rain is trickling inside the collar of my coat.

After another ten minutes, Lachlan finally pulls up his horse and says, 'This is what I wanted to show you. This is where I believe we should build a road to, and then I think we should build another path back from here to the shoreline. We also need some fences around here for the livestock. I'll draw up some plans for it later,' he adds. 'I know how much you enjoy landscaping.'

I try to smile, but I am cold and wet and incredulous he has brought us all the way out here in the rain to talk about plans that he could tell me when he's back from London. We trot home on our horses in silence.

In April, the day before he's due to leave for London, I notice he's gathering far more of his papers together than he'd normally take on a trip of just two to three weeks. I put it down to nerves. He is so keen to push for his rebuttals of Mr Bigge's allegations to be aired in Parliament, he obviously needs all his armoury. I wonder if Lachie and I should accompany him to London, but decide to stay and make sure his study is finished for him by the time he returns.

On the day of his departure an even odder event occurs. When Lachie and I go to say goodbye to him, he lifts Lachie up, swings him in the air and kisses him on both cheeks. Setting him down, he turns to me, and embraces me as fondly as he has in all the sixteen years we've been together. 'Betsey, oh Betsey,' he whispers. 'My God, how I love you. You will never know how much.'

I pull away to look into his face, surprised that he's expressing his affections so boldly. His tone of voice suggests a kind of desperation I've never heard before.

'My love,' I begin, then stop as I see Lachlan has started to weep.

I shuffle Lachie off into another room and close the door behind him. 'Lachlan!' I cry. 'Whatever is the matter? What has happened?'

He makes a huge effort to compose himself and wipes his tears away with his handkerchief. 'I'm so sorry,' he replies. 'It's nothing. I'm just being silly. I'm not feeling very well and suddenly everything just overwhelmed me. I'm fine now.' He pauses and smiles to try to reassure me and says, 'Now, think nothing of this. I am just a silly, sentimental old man having to leave his beautiful wife and son at home, and already missing them dearly at the thought of it.'

He takes my face tenderly between his hands, tilts it down and kisses my forehead. 'Now, my carriage is waiting. I have to go. I shall see you soon, my darling.'

I am worried, but try not to dwell on it, thinking it's probably just my imagination. Lachlan has so much on his plate, it's only to be expected that he feels the strain at times.

Later, while Lachie is studying, I busy myself with trying to persuade tradesmen to come all the way over to Gruline to patch up the house. I then draw up plans for three more rooms and a porch to the front to shield us from the weather when the front door is opened, and start plastering the walls—in the hope of either keeping the wet out, or sealing it in, I am not quite sure which.

When Lachie is free, I make a game of trying to clear some of the grounds so we will be able to plant a few vegetables and have something of a garden. He is ten years old now, but a very clever boy and I worry how the events of the past few years may have affected him. Scotland is still proving a shock to his system, and he probably also finds it hard to understand why I am working so hard when once he saw me only in fine clothes, surrounded by servants.

Lachlan writes from London every week, reassuring me that all is well, and he's hopeful of making progress with his rebuttal but it is a slow and frustrating process. There's one piece of good news, however: Lord Bathurst tells Lachlan he will be granted a pension of one thousand pounds a year—double what he'd been promised at the start of his term. It helps dull the disappointment of the Government then rejecting his application for a knighthood.

He's visited a silversmith's shop to price a vase or silver plates to buy with the five hundred guineas from the people of New South Wales, seen lots of friends and been out for many events, although one evening he failed to find a hackney cab and was forced to walk for over a mile in pouring rain back to his lodgings without an overcoat. For the next few days he feels tired and weak.

Lachie and I only leave Jarvisfield once, when I receive a message that my sister Jane is very poorly. When we left to go to New South Wales, she was a vital, dynamic young woman, running around constantly after her brood of eleven. When we arrive this time at Lochbuie House, I am deeply disturbed. She seems to have shrunk and almost faded away, though when our brother John and some of her friends turn up she appears to rally.

Lachie and I return to Gruline House, and a letter from Lachlan arrives saying he has taken ill in the night. He has his faithful manservant George Jarvis with him, but I want to go down to London immediately. My friends, however, advise me to wait for another letter, saying he might have already left London for home and we could miss each other on the road. Far better that I bide my time until he lets me know what he plans to do.

I wait anxiously for three days, and in the wee hours of the third morning, I wake with a start. Lachie has been sleeping with me in my bed because he has yet another cold. Though he's still fast asleep he is shouting out, 'Papa! Papa!' with such a note of terror in his voice it makes my blood run cold. I have never heard him cry out for his father like that, and I have a terrible premonition that my decision to stay on Mull has been a mistake. Lachlan has not really seemed himself for the past year we've been back in Scotland. And, at times, I've wondered whether we will ever be back to normal and happy again.

I tell myself not to be silly and that I must wait for his next letter, though I decide to check his writing desk to see if perhaps he has written anything that reveals his state of mind before he left. When I lift the lid, I'm stunned to find it absolutely empty.

I then open a little casket he had left by the side of the bed, which he said I should keep safe. Inside, I am taken aback to find an array of jewellery I've never seen before. I pluck one piece out and realise, with a sudden shock, that it must have belonged to his first wife, Jane. It's as though he's gathered his most important keepsakes and left them out for me to find.

I decide to leave immediately for London, but as I'm gathering together some clothes for me and Lachie, a messenger arrives with a letter from Lachlan. I tear it open fearfully and barely recognise the shaky handwriting saying he is now so ill, he fears he may not live to see us again.

It takes us four interminable days to get to London. I climb the stairs to Lachlan's lodgings at a run, terrified I might be too late to see him alive. Thankfully, when I fling open the door, he's sitting in a chair by the bed, looking pale and thin, but still—thank God!—very much alive. Lachie and I both launch ourselves at him, but I flinch when I feel his rib cage protruding underneath his light shirt.

'It is so wonderful to see you,' I say, bursting into tears. 'I was afraid . . .'

'No, I am fine now, and getting stronger by the day. I'll be home before you know it,' he says, tickling Lachie, who giggles. I sit on the bed and watch them, to the sound of someone chipping stone outside. I feel a sudden chill on my spirits. Could that be gravestones being chiselled?

'That's the stonemasons,' Lachlan tells me. 'The mason yard opposite is where they prepare the stones for the building work they're doing for the Palace of Westminster.' He winks at me. 'It's not what you think.'

I laugh. He's always been good at reading my mind.

After spending an hour with him, Lachie and I go in search of his doctor, who tells me it will be at least a month before Lachlan is strong enough to travel back to Scotland.

We return in the evening, and Lachlan seems in better spirits. His pension is finally going to be paid, in what he sees as the start of an official vindication of everything he did for New South Wales. All the indications are that the Colonial Office is going to agree to his suggestion that the colony officially be called Australia, too. He laughs at something Lachie says and I feel greatly heartened.

Tragically, that is the last time Lachie and I ever hear him laugh. That night, he takes another turn for the worse and, six days later, on the 1st of July 1824, as I kneel by his bedside, my arm around his shoulders, my darling husband's breathing grows shallower and shallower until he finally slips away. At the moment of his departure, I feel as though my soul is ascending, with his, towards heaven.

Chapter 29

FOR WHOM THE BELLS TOLL

Elizabeth Macarthur

28TH OCTOBER 1824, PARRAMATTA

Elizabeth Macarthur hears the tolling of church bells in the distance and straightens up from trimming roses in her garden. That's odd, she thinks. It's Thursday, not Sunday, and it's not the time for either morning prayers or an evening service.

When the bells keep ringing she wonders if it's a warning of some kind of emergency. But there is no sign of the smoke of any advancing bushfire. In fact, the surrounding landscape looks green, peaceful and quiet, and there is nothing to suggest any native raids or army exercises either. She sees one of the servants making his way to the dairy and calls him over.

'Thomas,' she asks, 'can you hear the bells?'

'Yes, mistress,' he says. 'They've been going all morning.'

'Do you have any idea why?'

'No, mistress.'

'Please could you take a horse and ride into town and find out what's happening?' she asks.

'Yes, of course,' he replies, touching his hat as he bounds away to find a suitable mount.

Three-quarters of an hour later, he gallops straight up to her. 'Mrs Macarthur!' he cries. 'Governor Macquarie is dead! He died in London. Governor Brisbane found out this morning and ordered that all the church bells be rung.'

Elizabeth's hand flies up to her face. No! It can't be true. They've been gone only two and a half years now. Surely fate could not be so cruel as to cut Lachlan down so soon into his retirement? Lachie must still only be ten or so, a terrible time for a boy to lose his father. And poor Betsey will be griefstricken. Elizabeth sinks to her knees on the grass and prays for her friend, for Lachie and for the soul of the man who, whatever one thinks about some of his changes, certainly worked hard for this colony.

When John returns from wherever he's been, he is red in the face, panting, with a wild look in his eyes. One of the sleeves of his coat is torn.

'My goodness!' she exclaims. 'What have you been doing?'

'Have you heard the news?' he asks, brandishing a copy of the *Sydney Gazette*. 'Have you heard? Governor Macquarie is dead. They will blame me for this, I know they will. They will say it is my fault. I must go and get ready. I must prepare.'

'John, John,' Elizabeth says in as soothing a voice as she can manage despite her alarm. 'What do you mean? No one is going to blame you! Lachlan Macquarie's death has nothing to do with you. He's in London and you're here in Parramatta.'

'But they will think I planned it because they know we didn't see eye to eye,' he says in panic. 'They will pin it on me. They will say it is my fault. I must make preparations to return to London to defend myself. I must leave straight away . . .'

'John, sit down now!' Elizabeth orders brusquely.

He looks startled but does as he's bid. She kneels down in front of him, puts her hands on his thighs and looks into his eyes. 'John, you *must* calm down. This has nothing to do with you. The Governor was older than either of us. He was twenty years older than his wife. He was in bad health. Perhaps he had an accident or fell ill. There are one hundred and one possible reasons why this has happened and none of them has anything to do with you.'

John's breathing slows and though he still appears anxious, he no longer has that wild, hunted look she has come to dread.

'Really?' he asks her, his voice suddenly childlike. 'Do you know this? Can you be sure?'

'I'm absolutely sure,' she replies gently. 'You are safe. There is no need at all to worry. Now, maybe you should go and rest for a while. You've had more than enough excitement for one day.'

He hangs his head, then rises to his feet and trots off to the bedroom obediently. Elizabeth watches him, her heart heavy. She hates to admit it, but his moods shifts are increasingly dramatic and he's behaving even less rationally of late. One day he'll sit gloomily in the darkness of his study, brooding for hours about the smallest perceived slights or problems or issues; the next minute he'll be bursting with energy, ideas and optimism and grabbing her waist to swing her around in a dance, laughing brightly and carrying on as if they were youngsters on their first date. And though she always tries to laugh and appear eager to join in, she's just trying to shield the children from how outlandish he is becoming. Though they probably realise some of his behaviour isn't normal, she doesn't want them, or anyone else, to suspect how far beyond normal her husband has really descended.

She picks up the newspaper discarded on to the floor and reads. Lachlan apparently died on the 1st of July while he was in London on business. His remains are to be conveyed to the Isle of Mull for interment. '*Governor Macquarie was distinguished in life and is Illustrious in death,*' the editorial reads. '*From our remembrance the Name of Macquarie can never be obliterated.*'

Lachlan Macquarie's death has a far greater impact on the colony than it has on Britain. Charles Wentworth's *The Australian* newspaper breaks the news with the words, '*The inhabitants of this colony will feel deep grief. Governor Macquarie is no more*', and everyone feels his passing as a significant moment in their history. Many people go into deep mourning for a man they believe modernised New South Wales for the better and was right to give former convicts their freedom. Many are enraged that he died before he'd been able to clear his name of so many of the damning allegations Commissioner Bigge made against him. They see Bigge's allegations as having blackened Mr Macquarie's character by criticising his reforms, his buildings, his financial management, his action and inactions, his very legacy.

But others, like John, are quite unmoved by his death. Apart from his initial attack of paranoia, he seems sanguine about

Lachlan's passing per se. Elizabeth thinks this is deeply ironic given that, if it weren't for Lachlan, Mr Bigge would never have been appointed Commissioner and written his report—which has ended up benefiting their family's fortune hugely. The British Government has since granted their new Australian Agricultural Company one million acres of land, and allowed them to raise around one million pounds, mostly from English shareholders. They will also ultimately be allowed to employ one thousand four hundred convicts, with no rival companies permitted to set up within the next twenty years.

Elizabeth, however, feels the loss of Governor Macquarie keenly, mostly because she knows what anguish Betsey will be feeling, but also because he was nothing but kind and solicitous to her, despite John giving him plenty of reasons to be anything but. She is heartened by the declaration of an official period of four days' mourning, with church bells tolling every day at sunrise and before sunset. She attends a memorial service on the 14th of November, listening to an effusive eulogy delivered by Reverend William Cowper, who served on the committee of the Native Institution and worked with the Macquaries as its patrons.

Afterwards, a procession of mourners walk through the streets of Sydney, led by Lachlan's former aide-de-camp Major Henry Antill, his secretary John Campbell and Dr Redfern, along with army and naval officers, civil servants, magistrates, lawyers, doctors, prominent citizens, professional mourners and friends. As the solemn parade passes, Elizabeth stands in silence alongside a crowd of thousands of ordinary folk, their heads bowed.

She sees tears in the eyes of some of the convicts and emancipists. A few of the women dab at their faces while the men keep their faces firmly downcast, their hats in their hands. As the procession continues, tears slide down the cheeks of more and more people, and someone moans in agony. The news has arrived in Australia that the British Government, along the lines of the recommendations of Mr Bigge's report, is planning to return to the days of transportation as a much harsher form of punishment. By contrast, Governor Macquarie seems even more enlightened and heroic. Many weep for his memory.

Later that day, Elizabeth writes a letter of condolence to Betsey, recounting the poignancy of the memorial service, and the tears, moans and overheard snatches of sad conversation about Lachlan, which she hopes will cheer Betsey somewhat in her hour of need.

'*I have no doubt, my dear, that you are mourning the loss of your treasured husband with all the devotion and strength you showed him in life,*' Elizabeth writes. '*I only hope I can one day mourn the loss of the man I loved with half as much dignity and courage.*'

Chapter 30

MRS MACQUARIE'S CHOICE

Betsey Macquarie

16TH MARCH 1825, ENGLAND

Tears burn my eyes as I re-read Elizabeth Macarthur's latest letter yet again.

I miss Lachlan terribly and think I would fall apart completely if not for the need to keep strong for Lachie, as well as for Elizabeth's encouragement and support.

The days following Lachlan's passing were excruciating. Ten days afterwards, on a Sunday, his coffin was loaded into a hearse and led a long procession of forty carriages through London, with relatives, friends and officials, including the Duke of Argyll, the Earl of Breadalbane, three army generals, and the traditionally empty funereal carriages sent by Lord Bathurst and the Duke of Wellington. The coffin was transferred onto a boat on the River Thames that I chartered to sail to Edinburgh. I originally intended to travel with Lachlan by sea but my good friend Henrietta Meredith insisted I wasn't strong enough for such a journey.

Perhaps it was just as well we were not together. When Lachie and I met the boat in Edinburgh, we were told it encountered terrible storms and only just avoided yet more tragedy. We travelled further north to Perth, where our infant daughter Jane was buried. Everyone there regarded me with enormous sympathy, but I tried to remain as coolly efficient and offhand as I could manage as I arranged for her remains to be exhumed. I knew if I took any of their compassion to heart, I might break down completely and I needed to be strong to take my baby home to Mull so she could finally be put to rest in her father's arms.

I asked my brother John to meet the boat with Lachlan and Jane's remains on the island, which he did, along with some servants and tenants. Then, to the mournful tolling of the chapel bell, their coffins were carried to Jarvisfield to lie in the new room at Gruline House that Lachlan never had the chance to see. How I now regret staying there to have it built, instead of being with him in London when he needed me the most! I keep being tortured by the question of whether he'd still be alive today if I'd gone to London straightaway.

I felt some solace, however, when I laid baby Jane's tiny coffin on his heart, and buried the two together. Their resting place is only a few hundred yards from the house, so Lachie and I would be able to visit them regularly.

Only a few days after Lachlan's burial, a message came with news my sister Jane was close to death. I wondered how much heartache I could take before being crushed by sorrow. I knew

Lachie needed me to stay strong, or at least look strong, so I hid my pain and we rode over to Lochbuie together to say our farewells.

After Jane's death in August, we stayed on in Mull for seven months, but I saw ghosts around every corner. I decided it would be healthier for Lachie to start school, after so long being home-tutored, and get into a routine in the company of children his own age rather than always being under my shadow of despair.

So we've now moved down to the south of England, to live in Surrey, where Lachlan is going to school in East Sheen, and I'm starting to try to come to grips with the woeful state of our finances. Though I've been left the house and farm at Gruline, along with a small annuity of three hundred pounds a year, I do not even own the few cattle we have grazing there, nor the farm equipment, so I make arrangements to buy those. Back in Australia, I have bank shares and some cattle and I had hoped there might be some income from them. So far, however, there has been nothing at all. I instruct our attorney to write to Governor Brisbane asking for a grant of some land for the cattle to graze on rather than having to pay for agistment on another property. So far I have heard nothing.

In the meantime, old friends badger me to ask for the pension due to the widow of a former Governor of a colony. I tell them I'm not interested in doing so until Lachlan's rebuttal is read into Parliament and his name cleared. The under-secretary to the Colonial Office, Robert Wilmot-Horton, a good friend of John Macarthur Junior, also wrote to me saying he feels I should be granted a pension. I write a curt note back, saying, '*No necessity whatever exists on my part for requiring pecuniary assistance from any quarter whatever.*'

Once Lachie is happily settled at school, I direct all my energies to having Lachlan's reply to Mr Bigge's vindictive allegations published. I write to influential friends, to ministers, to MPs, everyone I can think of.

When I finally receive a letter from Lord Bathurst, I am utterly devastated. Instead of offering to publish Lachlan's finely argued letter, he merely offers me a pension.

With Lachlan's death, I think the government feels it is relieved of the embarrassment of admitting parts of Mr Bigge's report were wrong. They fear the shame of acknowledging how poorly they treated one of their most upstanding and popular colonial Governors. It is more politically convenient for them to continue as if nothing has happened than having the courage to concede the truth.

Tonight I am sitting in a chair by the fire, staring gloomily into the flames, contemplating my situation. I am now staying in a tiny house in Putney with my niece Catherine, living almost as a pauper and just managing to scrape together enough money to get by most weeks. To cover costs after Lachlan's death, I even had to sell his military commission for four thousand five hundred pounds.

Lachie's school bills are mounting, and while he's a good and loving boy, he does not like going without, especially when so many of his school friends are from much wealthier families. He has suffered so much already for someone so young, I rarely have the heart to refuse him anything. Meanwhile, I really don't know where the next meal is coming from. And Lord Bathurst has written afresh, now offering me a pension of four hundred pounds a year.

Slowly, very slowly, I take the official British Government letter out of its envelope again, and hold the accursed papers, my hands trembling with rage. Slowly, deliberately, I then tear the thick creamy pages once, twice, a dozen times, until hundreds of pieces flutter to the ground like snowflakes. I sink to the ground amongst them.

Catherine opens the door to the room, and rushes over to me.

'Aunt Betsey,' she asks. 'Please . . . please . . . you are frightening me. What is wrong? This letter . . . What has it said that has upset you so?'

'It's from Lord Bathurst,' I reply. 'He wrote to offer me a widow's pension of four hundred pounds a year.'

'I don't understand,' she says. 'That is wonderful news, is it not? He is officially recognising how important Uncle Lachlan was, and what a contribution you have made.'

I shake my head gloomily. 'No. I was hoping Lord Bathurst was writing to grant me permission to publish Lachlan's reply to Mr Bigge's report, to clear his name of its slanderous lies. But, no, he hasn't even mentioned it. As a result, I can't possibly accept it. I would feel like I were accepting money in return for giving up the fight to clear Lachlan's name. In life, my dear husband gave me so much, and I miss him every day. And, in death, the very least I owe him is to protect and uphold his reputation, the way he always looked after me.'

'So what do you plan to do?' Catherine asks, looking worried.

'I don't know, but I don't want to give up,' I say, standing and starting to gather the shreds of paper which I toss into the last glowing embers of the fire. It flares as it devours its new fuel, the bright flames reflecting eerily against the walls of the small room.

I think about Elizabeth Macarthur's words about devotion, strength, dignity, courage. Well, I've proved my devotion and strength before by accompanying Lachlan to the other end of the earth and helping him turn a ragtag penal dumping ground into a fine colony. Now I need to summon all my dignity and courage once more.

I walk over to the little desk and chair in the corner of the cramped room, pull open a drawer and take out a clean sheet of white paper. Then I sit down, dip my pen in the ink and start writing. I thank Lord Bathurst for his kind offer to grant me a pension, but say I will not accept a penny of it until Lachlan's rebuttal of Mr Bigge's report is published. I say it is monstrously unfair that the world knows what Mr Bigge said about my husband, but only our friends and those few in authority who have sighted Lachlan's rebuttal know that so much of Mr Bigge's report is not worth the paper it is written on.

I am polite and gracious, but I leave Lord Bathurst in no doubt that my determination to see Lachlan's rebuttal published will endure to the bitter end. I imagine some of my friends have written to him about the necessity of a pension, so he will know I have little money. He is also probably aware that I contract flu every winter and am growing thinner and weaker. And he's no doubt been apprised of the costs of Lachie's schooling in Woodford.

I realise this is a fight I am not well prepared for, but I draw encouragement from Elizabeth's words. Her line about my courage touched me deeply. Elizabeth is the toughest, bravest, most resourceful woman I have ever met in my life and if she says she is deriving inspiration from me for her own struggles, then, by God, I have a duty to live up to her expectations.

Perhaps Lord Bathurst will realise he's underestimated how strong-willed Highlanders can be when we see a great wrong that needs to be righted. I wait and wait for a response. But he does not pay me even the courtesy of a reply. It is hard. As the writer of Lachlan's obituary said, despite half a century of faithful service, Lachlan returned to England in 1822 a much poorer man than he'd left it in 1809. The granting of his pension came far too late for him.

I write back to Elizabeth about what I'm trying to do, saying how heartened I was by her generous letter. I thank her from the bottom of my heart for being such a stalwart friend during such difficult times. Then, on a sudden whim, I add a favourite line from one of Samuel Johnson's essays on friendship: '*Life has no pleasure higher or nobler than that of friendship.*'

I wish her well in her own battles and tell her how truly sorry I am to hear of John's troubles—and I mean it. I also say I am confident of my own eventual success, though with every passing month and year, I am becoming less so. I am physically frailer too, but the fight to safeguard my husband's proud reputation and all he achieved carries me onward.

Everyone tries to persuade me to change my mind and accept the pension. My brother John even visits and talks to me long into the night, trying to coax me into taking the money. 'Think of Lachie, Betsey,' he urges me. 'Think of how much more you can do for him with such a sum every year.'

'Lachie has never gone without and never will,' I reply sharply. 'He is always my first priority. But this is something I could never live with, and I am sure when he is older and can understand, it is something he would never wish to countenance either.'

'But you are not well,' John says, trying another tack. 'How much longer can you continue this in your state of health?'

'However long it takes,' I tell him. 'However long it takes.'

In the end, it takes three long years, give or take a few days.

Even though I rarely receive replies to any of my letters, I refuse to be put off. The only person I hear from regularly is Elizabeth, who provides me with unending encouragement and reassurance. Indeed, she is the sole person amongst my friends and family who never tries to persuade me to give in. She tells me there were many times when she was tempted to give up on her mission of building a sheep industry, especially during the long absences of John and her sons, but she refused to abandon her dreams. In the same way, she says that if I feel I am right, then I must never give up the fight.

Finally, in 1827, I take fresh heart when Lord Bathurst is replaced by Viscount Goderich, a good man well known for his campaign for the abolition of slavery.

I write to him nine days into his new post, asking him to make enquiries into the situation, saying it should never be too late to order justice for the memory of a deserving and much injured man. Friends, I know, also write to him on my account.

Viscount Goderich is understanding, but only to a point. He says the fact that Lachlan had been granted a pension, even so late in his life when he could not take advantage of it, shows the high esteem in which he was held by the Government. It is thus unnecessary that any further action be taken.

Though I am downcast at his response, I still refuse to give up. Over the years that follow I write to William Huskisson when he replaces Viscount Goderich and to Sir George Murray when he replaces William Huskisson. Rarely do I even receive a reply.

I move to Middlesex to be closer to Lachie's next school at Finchley, continuing my mission from there. Every summer holidays, I take him back to Mull to remind him of his true home and birthright. Every time I come back to London, I launch myself afresh into my crusade. I am persuaded by friends to ask for ten thousand acres of land in New South Wales since nothing has come of the two thousand acres Governor Brisbane promised me. Then, sadly, my dear friend Henrietta Meredith dies and, much to my astonishment, leaves me two thousand pounds and her small house by London's Fitzroy Square. I move there and continue to petition Parliament.

Finally, I have a quite unexpected breakthrough when the emancipist magistrate Edward Eager is in London campaigning, as Lachlan encouraged him to do, for trial by jury in Australia. He visits Sir James Mackintosh, one of the leading Whigs in Parliament, who also happens to be an old friend of Lachlan's. Sir James presents Mr Eager's petition to the House of Commons and asks for Lachlan's report to Bathurst and his response to Mr Bigge's report.

So . . . almost by accident Lachlan's papers are finally presented to Parliament on the 16th of June 1828. They are then printed as a Parliamentary Paper on the 25th of June.

I am absolutely thrilled and send a copy of the paper to our old friend William Wentworth, of *The Australian* newspaper, who so memorably labelled the report of Mr Bigge as 'nauseous trash'.

I write to our other friends back in Australia with the news that a great man has finally received justice. His prediction that 'my name will not readily be forgotten after I have left it' is at last assured. I finally feel at peace.

It is with a great flourish that I write to the Secretary of State for War and the Colonies, Sir George Murray, to tell him I am at last ready to draw my pension. I then write to Elizabeth Macarthur, saying I could never have held out without her. '*Thank you, my dear friend*,' I end my letter. '*Thank you with all my heart.*'

Chapter 31

EVER YOUR AFFECTIONATE WIFE

Elizabeth Macarthur

5TH MAY 1832, PARRAMATTA

Elizabeth Macarthur folds up the letter that arrived that morning from Betsey Macquarie, desperately worried about her friend's physical and emotional health. She has taken Lachlan's death so hard and Elizabeth seriously wonders if she will ever recover. In one of her letters, Betsey wrote: '*It is no easy task to support life with rational satisfaction after the loss of such a husband. Thus much will I say, that I am beyond the reach of joy or happiness, and I am in a state of indifference to the world and its concerns.*'

Elizabeth knows how hard her friend has tried to keep positive for the sake of Lachie, who's now just celebrated his eighteenth birthday. She is gratified to hear her letter to Betsey, praising her strength, and encouraging her, has helped keep her going. She'd meant those words, too.

The *Sydney Gazette* has also steadfastly supported Mrs Macquarie's insistence on the publication of the country's beloved former governor's response to Bigge's report. One article says that while most of her friends have urged her to take the money, the 'venerated' Mrs Macquarie has continued to refuse.

So when the news finally breaks that Governor Macquarie's reply to Commissioner Bigge's report has been printed as a Parliamentary Paper, and only then has Mrs Macquarie accepted the money she is owed, Elizabeth rejoices. She writes to Betsey immediately to say how relieved and happy she is.

She longs to discuss Betsey's victory with Captain Piper. Sadly, she hasn't seen him for some time. As with John, his life has unravelled. And spectacularly so.

Things started to go awry when his twelve-year-old son Hugh died in a riding accident. After the departure of Governor Brisbane, with whom Captain Piper had been close friends, Governor Darling proved nothing like his old ally. He constantly found fault with Captain Piper's work, and insisted on an investigation into the affairs of the Bank of New South Wales, discovering it had loaned far too much money out to merchant friends of the directors under Captain Piper's watch. An inquiry into Captain Piper's own accounts followed, which revealed they were in a state of complete chaos, too. As a result, Captain Piper was forced to resign his presidency of the bank and was suspended from his other posts.

He dealt with the situation in the only way he knew: by throwing a big party. Inexplicably, he left part-way through, took out his barge and ordered its crew to play music. Then he jumped overboard into the churning waves in a bid to kill himself. A crew member dived in to save him, but by the time they dragged the captain out, he was unconscious and half-drowned.

The fall of the colony's most popular man caused an absolute sensation throughout Australia. As a result, he ended up selling nearly all his property, including his magnificent house at Point Piper. Elizabeth hasn't seen him since he moved to some land he'd retained in Bathurst, where he's raising cattle and sheep.

After she wrote to Betsey about his situation, she heard her friend had asked her Australian agent to offer Mary Ann Piper the gift of a good dairy cow. It's so typical of Betsey that, after all she's been through, she still has time to think of others, Elizabeth thinks in wonder.

Elizabeth walks through the door of Elizabeth Farm to hear a roar of anger followed by screaming and the smashing of china. She races to the drawing room to find the floor littered with shards of broken crockery, while John brandishes both his sword and his pistol at two of the cowering maids.

'You swines!' he shouts at them. 'I'll teach you to try and poison me! How dare you attempt to kill the master of this house!'

'John!' cries Elizabeth, advancing slowly towards him. 'John! Put down those weapons. Can you not see how much you are frightening them?'

John turns to face her, his brow creased in fury and his teeth bared as he stares at her with pure hatred.

She hesitates and tries to regain her composure, then says quietly, 'John, please, *please*, calm down. Now, give me the pistol.' She holds a hand out, beckoning the maids to slip out of the room while her husband's attention is fixed on her. 'Come on, John, give it to me.'

He looks for a moment as if he doesn't know who she is, before a recognition sweeps over his face. She relaxes, but too soon. He suddenly raises himself to his full height, moves the pistol closer to his own body and bellows at her. 'Get away from me! Get out of my house, you brazen hussy. You whore. You harlot!'

Elizabeth stays frozen to the spot. She's never heard him utter such words in his life.

Apparently taking her silence as an admission of her guilt, John says, 'Aha! I know you've been shamelessly taking lovers. And under my roof, too. How did you think you could keep such licentious behaviour from me? I will not be made a fool of in front of my own family, and especially not by you, madam! Go, be gone from here!'

Elizabeth still can't move. She's seen him rage before when this blackness has taken hold but up until now he's never directed the worst of his ire at her. Rather, he's always let her soothe him, and talk him down. But now he seems beyond her reach, beyond all reason.

She starts as he brandishes his pistol again and slices his sword at a display of dessert dishes on the side table. They cascade to the floor with a deafening clatter. Elizabeth turns on her heel and walks out, signalling to the butler and some of the other men who've gathered behind her to take over. There is nothing she can do.

She has resisted acknowledging it, but her husband has been descending into madness for some time now. At first, he just experienced periods of melancholy followed by periods of manic activity. But the melancholy has become deeper and lasted longer—almost the whole year of 1827, for instance—while the highs have become more manic. It has become a common sight to see him striding along the road, muttering to himself, or galloping frantically across the hills on one of his favourite horses. It is not helping his mental state either that he's now facing so much hostility about the preferential arrangements he insisted on for the Australian Agricultural Company a few years ago, before the share price went into freefall. The press has joined in the criticism, and in 1829, with the sheep numbers devastated by drought and disease, a director from England comes out to take control of the company.

Steam engines have just arrived in the colony and in a letter to Edward, Elizabeth likens his father to having set '*a variety of wheels in motion, with a Steam Engine power . . . planning . . . building . . . making believe to do so at least digging up the Earth . . . altering . . . directing, driving about at all hours changing his mind continually and in short keeping us all in a perpetual worry.*'

James is currently in England conducting wool business, taking some of the responsibility for the family company from John. But when he returns home in February 1831, John's spirits seem to revive somewhat. Elizabeth is thrilled with the portrait of John Junior that James brings back for her, gazing wonderingly at his face in the painting. He has now been in London for so many years, with no return visits back, that she can see little sign of the seven-year-old son she farewelled in this image of a strapping man in his thirties.

In September, however, she is utterly heartbroken to receive a letter from Edward saying John Junior collapsed a day after conducting a big case, and was unable either to speak or to move. He died three days later on the 19th of April 1831. Like Elizabeth, John is absolutely inconsolable. John Junior was always his favourite and he'd been immensely proud of how well he was doing in London, hoping that one day his family would become as well regarded in Britain as in Australia.

Despite her despair, Elizabeth writes back to Edward straight away, thanking him and saying she hopes that time will one day allow them to look back without as much pain. John, on the other hand, sinks into a depression that isn't even relieved by the departure of Governor Darling. Darling had been a strict, tough military man keen on banking reform, sorting out the system of land grants and eager to assign convicts to settlers. As a result, Elizabeth had assumed Governor Darling and her husband would find common ground. But John's abiding enmity against those in authority fired again. At one stage, the two refused to speak to each other, with the Governor publicly casting aspersions on John's 'soundness' and branding his behaviour as like that of 'a wayward child'. He is replaced by Governor Bourke who is, much to John's disgust, an avowed emancipist.

By May 1832, it seems that John is once more emerging from 'these mists of the mind' and, not content with the major renovation he's already done to Elizabeth Farm, he starts planning a second big program of improvements. Elizabeth is pleased to see him so much better but is worried by how chaotic his plans are.

Unfortunately, he is then overtaken by a major outburst of paranoia, accusing people of poisoning him, Elizabeth of infidelity again, James and William of abandoning him and his daughters of robbing him. His threats of violence, as he's armed with his pistol and sword, become insupportable.

A formal writ is issued under the lunacy regulations in August 1832, declaring him incapable of looking after his own affairs. Elizabeth moves out to live in the home of her daughter Mary and husband James Bowden. Lizzie and Emmeline move in with Miss Lucas, and the boys, together with the doctor and John's manservant, confine their father to the library of Elizabeth Farm, often having to use restraints. It is an unhappy separation for Elizabeth, but she still writes to John constantly and dutifully, always signing off her letters with, *Ever Your Affectionate Wife*.

Eventually, Elizabeth and her children decide to move John to Camden, where they are building a new mansion, in the hope he might take an interest. It also means Elizabeth and her family can move back into Elizabeth Farm. John shouts all the way to Camden, saying that he is being kidnapped. Emmeline returns to the farm and spends a few weeks clearing away all the breakages and replacing some of the wrecked furniture, before the others follow. Elizabeth is relieved to be back at her home and agrees to see visitors but is too embarrassed to go out visiting herself.

It's during this terrible time in her life that Elizabeth feels Betsey's absence most keenly. They continue to correspond regularly, sharing their pain about their husbands. Elizabeth finds she's able to explain to Betsey the anguish of knowing John is physically so close, yet emotionally a world away.

James and William visit their mother frequently during breaks from looking after their father. Poignantly, the family have every reason to rejoice at their good fortune. In 1834 alone, they export more than four million pounds of fine merino wool to England and their financial futures look assured. But Elizabeth finds it hard not to feel constantly distressed by John's health and never fails to ask after him.

John, on the other hand, does not once enquire after her. In fact, never again does anyone hear her name pass his lips.

Yet Elizabeth never gives up hope that John's sanity will somehow, miraculously, be restored and they can be reunited and grow old together as they always planned. Sadly, it is not to be.

On the 10th of April 1834, Elizabeth is at Mary's helping her after the birth of her fourth child, when she receives the shattering news that John has died. Numbed by grief, she is disconsolate that she hasn't seen him for so long, remembering Betsey's account of being at Lachlan's side when he died, her arm around his shoulder. It's devastating that her own lifelong sweetheart has died alone, unable to love and be loved.

The letter she writes to Betsey to tell her about John's death is the hardest she's ever written. She says she knows Betsey was never fond of John and she can hardly blame her, but she hopes her friend can find somewhere in her heart to forgive him, particularly given he had such a terrible end.

Before she sends the letter, Elizabeth sits down and goes through all the letters she's received from Betsey over the years, from the stiff formal letters Betsey wrote at the start of Lachlan's governorship to the letters where she decried their common enemies, celebrated shared friendships and they both schemed behind their husbands' backs. She smiles as she reads some, and weeps at others.

Then Elizabeth has a carpenter on the estate make her a small wooden box with brass hinges, and ties the letters into small bundles with red ribbon, wraps them in soft white cotton and places them in the box, writing a covering letter.

'*It occurs to me that you may wish to archive your letters as a memory of your time in Australia . . .*' Elizabeth writes. '*Your period here was monumental in transforming Australia into a colony of which Britain could be proud. These letters will one day be part of an extremely impressive history and you need to make sure your work is honoured forever more for posterity.*'

Chapter 32

THE LAST PAPER TRAIL

Betsey Macquarie

20TH DECEMBER 1832, SCOTLAND

It is a cold, grey, rain-spattered day on Mull when my man servant delivers a small box that has just arrived in the post at Gruline House. I look at it curiously and see it is from Australia. Opening it gingerly, I pull aside folds of cotton and find a letter from Elizabeth Macarthur resting atop bundles of letters bearing my own handwriting.

I rip open her letter impatiently. She describes her last months with John, and then his ignominious death. I never had much time for the man, it's true, but my heart aches for my dear friend, now also in mourning. I still miss Lachlan terribly, but I can't even begin to imagine the torture Elizabeth went through with John's madness before his passing.

But, magnificent correspondent that she is, Elizabeth still also manages to write about her children, and the happenings in the colony, including more details about poor Captain Piper's downfall and the new governor. I feel a torrent of nostalgia for my old life in the colony, which is in such stark contrast to my small world here on the island.

I smile, though, as I read Elizabeth's congratulations on finally having Lachlan's rebuttal to Mr Bigge's appalling report printed by Parliament, and the praise for me from the *Sydney Gazette*.

'Venerated'? I don't quite think so, but that is nice to hear.

These days, with my battle for justice for Lachlan over, and Lachie off in the army, thinking about our days in Australia distracts me from worrying about my son. Lachlan and I had always hoped he'd move to Scotland and become a Highland laird, in turn establishing a line of lairds of Jarvisfield, but that hasn't happened. Instead, he decided to follow in his father's footsteps and join the army, and last year I managed to buy him an ensigncy. With him now settled, I've returned to Jarvisfield to live on Mull full-time.

My life here is made easier now I'm receiving Lachlan's pension, as well as regular money from Australia from the sale of milk from my cattle and occasionally the sale of the cattle themselves. It's allowed me more time to invest my energies into pushing for the completion of the work Lachlan started. I am lobbying for fuller rights for former convicts in the colony, trial by jury, and for Australians to have more of a voice in how they are governed, via elected members of a Governor's Council overseen by the Governor.

Progress, however, is slow. Although the new Governor, Sir Richard Bourke, seems much more enlightened than his two predecessors, so far the strength of vested interests opposing him means he's been unable to get many of his changes through.

I am also planning on erecting a mausoleum here for Lachlan's and our infant daughter's remains. I am drafting a magnificent inscription to be placed upon it in honour of the man I intend to describe as 'The Father of Australia', paying tribute to his energies as well as to his benevolence, generosity and wisdom. It is no less than he deserves. But, for the moment, money is just too scarce.

I don't receive many visitors. At first, I was delighted to be told that Dr Redfern was moving back to Scotland with his eldest son William. However, I soon discovered he has become an embarrassing spendthrift and I generally avoid him. Sadly, Sarah Redfern decided to remain in Australia and I still remain good friends with her.

I reread Elizabeth's letter. Her final lines explain why she's enclosed all my letters to her over the years. What a beautiful idea! How terribly thoughtful. I have been keeping all of her letters to me, too. It is so strange that we're much more alike than either of us could ever, at first, have imagined.

I laugh so suddenly that the maid, bringing an armful of holly into the house in a vain attempt to make it look more festive, is startled. 'Sorry!' I say. 'I'm just reading a letter from an old friend.'

I ask her to bring me tea when she's finished with the holly, and go to the bedroom with the wooden casket. Then I settle down by the big window in the sitting room to read all the letters I sent Elizabeth. I start at the earliest and work my way steadily through them. I think back to my nervousness when we first arrived in

Sydney, the things Lachlan did, my anxiety about whether I'd be allowed to play a role and my fears about Lachlan's love for me.

I shake my head and look over to a favourite portrait of him hanging over the fireplace. Later, I had no doubt at all about his devotion and passion, and realise I should never have questioned it earlier, either. He was a quiet man in many ways, not given to shows of emotion and, living back here in Scotland, I see so many like him.

Reading more of the letters, I relive the agony of my miscarriages and the mixed relief of learning of a possible cause of Lachlan's likely illness. If only we'd been able to look into the future and see that we would eventually bring a son into this world! There are also painful memories of the many betrayals we suffered—some expected, like John Macarthur and Reverend Marsden—and others we had never foreseen, such as Mr Bent and Mr Greenway. I laugh and cry at all the scheming Elizabeth and I had to do to protect our husbands, and our cherished ideals, from ruination.

Finally, I read Elizabeth's beautiful lines again, which so inspired me in my final choice of whether to move on with my life and accept Lachlan's pension, or to fight till the death, if necessary, to clear his name. I know I will always owe Elizabeth a huge debt for helping me make the right choice in my hour of need.

At the same time, I realise that if these letters were ever to fall into the wrong hands, they could be used against Lachlan and his legacy, as well as against Elizabeth and hers. Elizabeth's renown is already assured but the letters might show I had far more involvement in Lachlan's decisions, his projects and his political battles than has ever been publicly acknowledged. I spent the better part of my life working hand-in-hand with my husband, so it would never do to diminish him in death.

The room is now dim from the fading light of the short winter's day, and I gather all the letters back together and throw the first bundle into the flames, watching as they're devoured. I toss in the next and another and another until they are all reduced to embers in the grate.

I made my choice and it has turned out to be for the best. My work has been done. Now the memories are mine and Elizabeth's alone.

AFTERWORD

Elizabeth 'Betsey' Macquarie

Elizabeth 'Betsey' Macquarie continued to press for the rights of convicts and a fairer legal system in Australia for the rest of her life.

She died peacefully on the 11th of March 1835 at Gruline House on Jarvisfield Estate at the age of fifty-six. Her remains were interred with those of her husband and daughter in the burial ground on the family's estate.

The ten thousand acres of land she'd applied for in New South Wales were eventually granted by Governor Sir Richard Bourke a year after her death.

Her son Lachie became a Captain in the Scots Greys and married Isabella Campbell in 1836. Reports characterise him as a hopeless drunkard and gambler, and he died in 1845 at the age of thirty-two. Having had too much to drink, he apparently fell down some stairs at Craignish Castle, his wife's family's home.

The couple were childless, so the Macquarie dynasty came to an abrupt end with his death.

Apart from Gruline House and the farm, which he left to his wife, Lachie bequeathed all his parents had left him to his friend William Drummond, the son of Lord Strathallan, to whom he was deeply in debt. His will was challenged by his cousin Charles Macquarie, who argued that Lachie had been of unsound mind when he drew up the bequest. Charles Macquarie's challenge failed, so the estate was lost forever from the extended Macquarie family.

Mrs Macquarie's mausoleum for her family was eventually constructed in the early 1850s, with her inscription placed upon it:

> *Here in the hope of a glorious resurrection lie the remains of the late Major General Lachlan Macquarie of Jarvisfield who was born 31st January, 1761, and died at London on the 1st of July, 1824.*
>
> *The private virtues and amiable disposition with which he was endowed rendered him at once a most beloved husband, father and master, and a most endearing friend. He entered the army at the age of fifteen and throughout the period of 47 years spent in the public service was uniformly characterized by animated zeal for his profession, active benevolence, and generosity which knew no bounds.*
>
> *He was appointed Governor of New South Wales A.D. 1809 and for twelve years fulfilled the duties of that station with eminent ability and success. His services in that capacity have justly attached a lasting honour to his name.*
>
> *The wisdom, liberality, and benevolence of all the measures of his administration, his respect for the ordinances of religion*

and the ready assistance which he gave to every charitable institution, the unwearied assiduity with which he sought to promote the welfare of all classes of the community, the rapid improvement of the colony under his auspices, and the high estimation in which both his character and government were held rendered him truly deserving the appellation by which he has been distinguished, The Father of Australia.

A later owner of Gruline, Lady Yarborough, bequeathed the tomb and its land to the people of New South Wales in 1948. It is now maintained by the National Trust of Australia (NSW) in partnership with the National Trust for Scotland.

Elizabeth Macarthur

John Macarthur's will, penned before the dramatic decline in his mental health, left Elizabeth Macarthur, the woman who had played such a critical role in building the wool industry in Australia, nothing but the use of Elizabeth Farm until her death, along with a small annual allowance.

He left Elizabeth Farm and everything in it to their eldest son, Edward. Apparently, Elizabeth never quite grasped this. She later declared that she would leave Elizabeth Farm's contents to Edward providing he returned to live in Australia, not realising he already possessed everything. The rest of the Macarthur properties and lands John Macarthur divided between the three remaining sons, Edward, James and William.

Edward petitioned for their father to receive a baronetcy for his contribution to Australia, backed by John Bigge, but that was refused by the Prime Minister Sir Robert Peel. Mr Bigge then urged him to seek an hereditary title. This too was refused. Edward stayed on in England to help the family business from there and the three brothers quarrelled acrimoniously about their respective shares and the management of the different estates.

Elizabeth was distraught when she heard of the death of Betsey Macquarie just eleven months after John's passing. One more letter to her friend remained unopened. She spoke of her ever more with fondness. She also never expressed publicly any bitterness towards her husband John for the suffering he had put her through, but remained faithful and loving towards his memory till the end. She was also always close to all her children, and dined regularly with Miss Lucas. Elizabeth Farm has been retained as a museum and is the oldest private house left in Australia.

Elizabeth and John's eldest daughter Lizzie, who never married, died when she was forty-nine. The Macarthur's youngest daughter Emmeline and her husband Henry Parker, the private secretary to a later governor, moved into Elizabeth Farm to look after Elizabeth.

In later years, Elizabeth became fond of visiting Watsons Bay each summer, where she would sit in a chair carried up to The Gap at South Head. Just as Betsey had done all those years before from her own 'Mrs Macquarie's Chair' at the Domain, Elizabeth would sit and dream from her perch while watching the ships from England arrive and depart.

Elizabeth Macarthur died on the 9th of February 1850 at the age of eighty-three and was buried at Camden with her husband.

Mr John Bigge

John Bigge never recovered his health after a fall from his horse in the Cape and started having fits. (It later turned out that the excellent military surgeon, Dr James Barry, who treated him, was really a woman disguised as a man, who'd pretended to be male in order to be permitted to study medicine. Her gender was only discovered after her death.)

Mr Bigge had other anxieties. He worried constantly about his will and who would be the best recipient of his money. In December 1843, he went to stay in the Grosvenor Hotel in London to have a meeting with his solicitor. There, he suffered another seizure and fell into the fireplace of his room where a fire was burning. Doctors tried to save him, but after forty-eight hours of agony he finally died. He was sixty-three years old. He was buried in Fulham Cemetery with, as his will had outlined, no 'ceremony or superfluous expense'.

After Mr Bigge's death two wills were found. He had made one in 1840, which left most of his estate to his sister Grace while cancelling the debt owed to him by his spendthrift brother Charles. His other will had been drawn up in 1843 but was incomplete and unsigned. Charles argued that because the first will was in two pieces it had been torn up, so the incomplete will was intended to be the real will. That meant Mr Bigge had died intestate so his fortune should be equally divided three ways between Charles, Grace and the children of their late brother Thomas.

The case went to court in 1845 and the judge ruled that the paper of the first will had simply split in half from constant reading and folding, and should be considered the final will. So Charles inherited nothing but the elimination of his debt to his brother.

Charles died five years after his brother and left his properties to his youngest son Matthew, the director of his father's bank. But when one of the bank's biggest creditors fell into liquidation, Matthew had to sell their stately home, Linden Hall. The family's fortunes came to a quick and ignominious end.

Mr Francis Greenway

Francis Greenway carried out a few architectural commissions after Lachlan Macquarie's departure from the colony, but was never again to regain the respect and prominence he'd once enjoyed. In 1835, he advertised in the *Sydney Gazette* asking for help from his friends and the public as he was destitute. He withdrew to a piece of farmland he had been granted and continued writing a series of letters to *The Australian* newspaper outlining his grand visions for the colony. He died of typhoid aged fifty-nine while living in a dirt-floored shack near Maitland. He was buried in an unmarked grave.

Dr William Redfern

Dr William Redfern resigned from the medical service after being passed over for the position of principal surgeon and turned to farming instead. He was the recipient of various land grants, including that of a large property in an area of Sydney that later became the suburb of Redfern. He died in Edinburgh in 1833 and has been described since as the 'Father of Australian Medicine'.

The Reverend Samuel Marsden

Reverend Samuel Marsden claimed he was unconcerned at not being given the position of Archdeacon of Sydney but also alleged there was great public anger at the 'injustice' of the move. By then he was out of favour with Lord Bathurst, who warned Governor Darling about his 'vehemence of temper'. Reverend Marsden continued to sit on a number of boards, committees and bodies within his parish. He died in May 1838 in Windsor, New South Wales, aged seventy-three.

Captain John Piper

Captain John Piper ended up entertaining guests like Governor Darling and Governor Bourke in Bathurst, but he was broken again by drought in 1838 and had to sell the property. Friends, including *The Australian*'s owner William Wentworth, came to his aid and set him and his family up on land by the Macquarie River. He died in 1851 aged seventy-eight. His wife Mary Ann outlived him by twenty years.

FURTHER READING

Bickel, L., *Australia's First Lady: The story of Elizabeth Macarthur*, Allen & Unwin, Sydney 1991

Broadbent, J. and Hughes, J., *The Age of Macquarie*, Historic Houses Trust of NSW, 1992

Cohen, L., *Elizabeth Macquarie: Her life and times*, Wentworth Books, Sydney, 1979

Currie, J., *Mull: The island and its people*, Birlinn Ltd, Edinburgh, 2001

Ellis, M.H., *John Macarthur*, Angus and Robertson, Sydney, 1978

Gapps, S., *The Sydney Wars*, NewSouth Publishing, Sydney, 2018

Karskens, G., *The Colony: A History of Early Sydney*, Allen & Unwin, Sydney, 2009

King, H., *Elizabeth Macarthur and Her World*, Sydney University Press, Sydney, 1980

Lindsey, K., *The Convict's Daughter*, Allen & Unwin, Sydney, 2017

Parker, D., *Governor Macquarie*, Woodslane Press, Sydney, 2010

Ritchie, J., *Punishment and Profit*, William Heinemann Australia, Melbourne, 1970

Scott Tucker, M., *Elizabeth Macarthur: A life at the edge of the world*, Text Publishing, Melbourne, 2018

Walsh, R., *In Her Own Words: The writings of Elizabeth Macquarie*, Exisle Publishing, Wollombi, 2011

ACKNOWLEDGEMENTS

Throughout the research for this book, and its writing, I've met so many people who were incredibly generous with their knowledge and their willingness to help.

I will be forever indebted to Robin Walsh, the author of *In Her Own Words* and expert in all things Macquarie, for his wise counsel and unerring ability to lock, like a heat-seeking missile, onto any hint of an error or anachronism. This book would have been all the poorer without him.

I'd also love to thank Sarah Dundas, the owner of Elizabeth Macquarie's beautifully restored ancestral home Airds House at Appin for showing me around. The present-day owners of Gruline on Lachlan Macquarie's Jarvisfield Estate on the Isle of Mull, Nichola and James Harmer, were also kind enough to throw open their doors, as was Patience Corbett of Lochbuie, the home of Elizabeth's sister Jane and Lachlan's uncle and mentor Murdoch Maclaine.

On the Macarthur side, thanks to Rosemary 'Posie' Bowman of the Macarthur family for her insights into Elizabeth and John Macarthur.

I'm also grateful to historian Dr Stephen Gapps who read the chapter on the Appin massacre and offered invaluable advice, and to Louise Thurtell who gave great guidance and help.

Closer to home, I so appreciate my partner Jimmy Thomson's neverending encouragement with this novel when I came so close many times to giving up, and Clare Birgin, Virginia Addison and Jane-Anne Lee who all read the manuscript in its various incarnations and gave fabulous feedback.

Likewise, all my friends and family who doubtless grew sick of me talking about, and agonising over, this book for so many years, as the two Elizabeths became constant companions.

Then there was my indefatigable agent Fiona Inglis of Curtis Brown, who never stopped believing. Or if she did, she didn't tell me.

Last but by no means least, I'd like to thank Allen & Unwin publisher Annette Barlow for sticking by me—even, probably, against her better judgement—and editor Christa Munns for improving the book hugely with her insights. A bow, too, to cover designer Christa Moffitt for her beautiful cover illustration, and to publishing assistant Jennifer Thurgate for her tireless efforts.

Together, they've worked hard to make this book the best it could be. Any failings are totally mine.

COMING IN MAY 2023

THAT BLIGH GIRL

Sue Williams

'Superb narration and engrossing drama.'
Tom Keneally

She's the daughter of the bloody-minded mutiny on the *Bounty* villain William Bligh, who accompanies him on his appointment as Governor to this raw British colony on the other side of the world.

Yet Mary Bligh is no shrinking violet. After an horrific six-month sea voyage, she proves as strong-willed as her father as the pair immediately scandalise Sydney with their personalities, his politics and her pantaloons.

And when three hundred armed soldiers of the Rum Rebellion march on Government House to depose him, he is nowhere to be seen as she stands defiantly at the gates, fighting them back with just her parasol.

Despite being bullied, belittled and betrayed, Mary remains steadfast, staying with Bligh as he's placed house arrest, and then imprisoned at the barracks.

When, however, he's finally given permission to sail back to England, he double-crosses her yet again in his desperate attempt to cling onto power.

But will Mary turn out to be her father's daughter and betray him in pursuit of her own dreams and ambitions?

Sue Williams returns to the untold stories of the women of colonial Sydney with another fascinating, and meticulously researched, historical novel.

ISBN 978 1 76106 588 0

PROLOGUE

26 January 1808

Three hundred scarlet-uniformed soldiers, with fixed bayonets and loaded firelocks at the ready, are marching through the rough dirt streets of Sydney.

Some passing locals stop to stare at the troops being led by their New South Wales Corps' band, playing a rousing rendition of 'The British Grenadiers' on the fife and drums. Others scatter in terror.

It's the twentieth anniversary of the founding of one of Britain's newest colonies and one soldier's bellow that this will be the most glorious day in the Corps' history is met by a cheer from the ranks.

These men in battle dress, with their colours flying and rebellion in their hearts, are on their way to overthrow the colony's governor, the notorious William Bligh. But when they reach the cast iron gates of Government House, they halt.

Standing behind the bars is the lone figure of a small, slim woman, dressed in a black frock and bonnet. Mary Putland does not move to allow them in; she simply stares steadily into the eyes of the man at the head of the battalion.

For a moment, Major George Johnston hesitates. 'Madam,' he says finally, gathering his wits, 'move aside! We have not come for you. We have come for your father.'

'Well, you shall not have him,' she replies. 'Go back to your own homes and your families. Leave this instant!'

Johnston—commanding officer of the Corps, the first man ashore in the First Fleet, and the celebrated hero of the battle against an armed pack of convicts that outnumbered his men ten to one—again wavers. He'd expected the governor to be here himself, with his guards, his staff or a crowd of his supporters. He hadn't envisioned Bligh's daughter being the sole sentry brave enough to face his troops.

He reaches for the bars of the gate but still Mary refuses to yield. He shouts an order, there's a clatter through the ranks and the men ranged behind their commanding officer raise their muskets to their shoulders. Mary doesn't flinch.

Instead, she raises her furled white silk parasol above her head and, as the soldiers push the gate open and jostle their way in, she rains blows on their chests and their shoulders. 'You traitors!' she shouts. 'You rebels! Get back!'

'That damned Bligh girl,' Johnston mutters, his frustration matched only by his secret admiration of her pluck. 'She'll be the end of us.'

1

FATHER, DEAR FATHER

Mary Bligh

5 OCTOBER 1803, LAMBETH, LONDON

Sometimes I hate my father. I know how shocking that sounds, so I don't think I could ever say it out loud. I couldn't even confide in my sisters or my mother, although occasionally I notice her looking at Father with a scowl and I catch her eye and she carefully rearranges her face to give nothing away. But I suspect there are times when she loathes him. She must.

My sisters don't feel the same way as me. They regard him with awe, like so many other people. Captain William Bligh is a national hero, they say; he's a symbol of all that's good and upstanding and courageous about England.

I beg to differ.

Of course, he's clever. That's not in dispute. Remember Captain Cook's terrible murder on the Sandwich Islands? Well, Father, at just twenty-four years old, was the one who took charge of Cook's ship's navigation and brought everyone safely home again. Ten years later, he ferried his loyal crew back over nearly four thousand miles in an open boat following the mutiny on HMS *Bounty*. Both feats were pretty remarkable.

But what of him as a man? What is he truly like in the outside world? Is he kind and caring? Is he a strong leader who carries the hopes and dreams of his men with him? Or is he more of a bullying, blustering braggart?

At home, I find him plainly insufferable and I have no doubt that those *Bounty* mutineers thought the same. And it's not as if they were the only ones to ever stand up to him, either. Later, another crew on the *Nore* mutinied against him, too, over poor pay, calling him 'The Bounty Bastard'—a nickname that's stuck with him ever since. I would have loved to have seen his face as they taunted him, although his challengers paid dearly. The ringleaders ended up hanging from the gallows for their audacity.

But at least I can escape my father. I can go into the bedroom I share with my sisters and hide away from his booming voice and his terrible oaths that make everyone cringe—even the dogs skulk away in terror. I can retreat to the kitchen, where he rarely ventures, and ask the cook to stand aside so I can take out my anger kneading bread. Bread-making is a great way to vent my anger as it silently absorbs all the punishment I mete out.

'Mary, Mary!' Mother says to me when she catches me there, pounding the dough with a ferocity that at times even takes me aback. 'What are you doing? There'll be nothing left of that by the time you've finished. Knead it gently. Look, this is the way.'

I move aside to allow her to take over and pretend to take an interest. 'Thank you, Mother,' I say meekly. 'I see what you mean.'

She frowns as she patiently turns the dough and presses her knuckles into it, rhythmically turning and pressing, turning and pressing. 'I've shown you so many times, but it doesn't seem to make any difference,' she says.

'Sorry, Mother.'

'Are you really?' she asks, stopping what she's doing and looking me full in the face. '*Mary, Mary, quite contrary* . . .' she starts reciting the nursery rhyme that she knows will make me smile.

I can't help myself.

'That's better now,' she says. 'You're so much prettier when you're not glowering.'

'Thanks, Mother,' I say. 'I do try, but sometimes I find it hard . . .'

She nods. She knows me better than I probably even know myself. But after she leaves the kitchen, I seize the dough again and smack it hard with my fist. I don't care about being gentle. I'll often mutter curses as I work the dough, taking care that no one is around to hear. I'd love, one day, to say such things to Father, but I'd never dare. I can't imagine what would happen if I did. The role of dutiful daughter is so much a part of me, I can't conceive of being any other way towards him. I prefer to knead my profanities into the dough, into something that won't answer me back, that won't curse me, that won't deride me or belittle everything I do.

I wonder if those men on the *Bounty* felt the same way. If they did, then really, they didn't have much choice than to rise up and load him into that little boat and send him out to sea. For I know how ruthless and cold-hearted he can be when he considers himself crossed, and how vicious when he encounters what he sees as disrespect. He's never been a terribly violent man, that's true, but the lashings he gives with his tongue inflict far more long-term pain and suffering than any physical beating. I've seen his wrath and his appetite for revenge first-hand. And it terrifies me every time.

Once, when I was maybe seven, I remember walking with him, Mother, my younger sister Elizabeth and the twins Frances and Jane in their pram along the River Thames, close to our home in Lambeth, when a vagrant wandered into our path.

'Move over, sir!' Father said to him. 'Let us pass.'

The man looked him up and down, then sneered. 'Why not ask me nicely?' he retorted. 'This footpath is as much mine as it is yours.'

I felt Mother's hand tighten around mine, and I knew what was coming.

'How dare you be so insolent!' Father exploded. 'Do you not know to whom you are talking? Get out of our way.'

'William,' Mother said in a quiet, pleading voice, 'not here, not now . . .'

I don't think Father even heard her. 'You ill-mannered bugger!' he shouted, stepping towards the man and waving a fist in his face. 'God damn you! If you don't move now, I shall make you.'

Standing stock still, the man looked stunned at the crudeness of Father's language, and I wondered, briefly, if he was as shocked as me by how quickly things had got out of hand. He then glanced at Mother and me and the three little ones. 'For their sake, I will,' he said softly. 'Because they deserve better.'

He side-stepped us and made off down the path, leaving Father ruddy-faced and Mother trembling. I burst into tears. I couldn't help it. The scene had scared me horribly.

Since then, some thirteen-odd years later, anytime he feels he's not being respected as much as he deserves, Father descends into a fit of rage, and almost nobody is safe from his ever-increasing wrath. But strangely, despite his anger stemming from a lack of respect towards him, he has no interest in treating others with the same regard.

I sometimes wonder if it's anything to do with him being an only child. Although he has a half-sister, born before his father married her widowed mother, Aunt Catherine was nineteen by the time he came along, and had left home soon after marrying a naval surgeon. As a result, my father was brought up as the light in both his parents' lives, and indulged terribly, from what I've heard of his childhood. He never had to learn to cohabit happily with brothers or sisters, or to negotiate fairly with equals for favours. Instead, he became used to getting his own way, and threw a tantrum whenever he didn't. In adulthood, he's not much different. What he wants, he's used to getting. And woe betide anyone who stands in his path.

I often ponder what Mother saw in him—still sees in him—but she hushes any talk around the dinner table, even when he's away at sea, of their relationship. But while he's so harsh towards me, and towards nearly everyone else he seems to encounter, to be fair, I've never seen him raise a hand, or even so much as speak sharply, to his wife. She's just about the only person I've seen him treat with absolute respect. That's understandable, too. She's brought him love, a happy home, children and, probably the most important thing for him, contacts for his naval career.

My sister Harriet, who is two years older than me at twenty-two and married last year, is much more forgiving than me. When she visited us a few weeks ago from her marital home not far from ours in London, she took me aside. 'Why do you get so angry with Papa?' she asked. 'He's been a good provider, and he started work so early in life. It couldn't have been easy for him being signed for the Royal Navy at seven, when he was just a small boy, to get the experience he needed for a commission later. These days, he obviously makes Mama happy and he's treated like a national hero. If he's good enough to receive praise from Admiral Horatio Nelson—and not even once but *twice*—why not from you? Most would think we're very lucky to have a father like him.'

I rolled my eyes. 'That's fine for you to say,' I replied. 'But since when was Nelson any true judge of men's character? From what Father's told us of what happened in the Battle of Copenhagen, I bet he was just happy that Father was as pig-headed as him and ignored their commander's signals to follow Nelson's lead instead. Father demands absolute loyalty from his men, yet he followed Nelson rather than the man really in charge. Doesn't that make him the ultimate hypocrite?'

'Mary!' Harriet sighed. 'You're so unforgiving. Papa was so courageous in that battle, and that's one of the reasons England is safe and secure today. Can't you give him a little credit?'

'Of course,' I said. 'You're right.'

But I didn't really believe it. Harriet sees a different side of Father. Like his parents were to him, he's always been terribly affectionate to his firstborn, and has always talked to her and listened to what she says. Since Harriet married, and then named his first grandchild William Bligh in his honour, he's become even more doting. Whenever he's home from the sea and she drops by, his face lights up with pleasure.

By contrast, I can't seem to do anything right. As a small child, I suffered terribly from The Itch, with a rash all over my body that I couldn't help scratching and making worse. Mother used to make an ointment for me by crushing mercury pills, which Father brought back from naval supplies, but he had no sympathy at all. He'd slap my hand away whenever he saw me scratching.

'You'll scar for life if you keep doing that,' he'd say. 'Is that what you really want? To make yourself ugly? You'll have to hide yourself away as no one will want to see you.'

I'd shake my head dumbly, tears in my eyes. 'No, Father.'

'Well then, stop it,' he'd admonish.

I was only about four years old, but I still remember the nightmares I'd have afterwards, of a hideous creature cowering in a cupboard, covered in red scars and pus.

Thankfully, after a couple of years, The Itch disappeared. But Father's criticism never did. He just found other aspects of me to find fault with.

Recently, when he caught me poring over the latest clothing catalogues, he saw red. He despises my interest in fashion and has often ticked me off for glancing at my reflection in a shop window as I pass. 'Why can't you be more like your sister?' he scolded. 'She worked hard at acquiring all the skills she needs to be a good wife and mother and look what a good match she made.'

'But I spend so much time on my music and reading and drawing and embroidery and learning how to prepare meals from Cook,' I told him. 'I think it's also important for a young lady to study fashion . . .'

Father shook his head with disgust and rolled his eyes. 'What frippery! Ridiculous frippery!'

Now that Harriet is expecting his second grandchild, it's even worse. Every time his eyes fall on me, I know he's comparing me, unfavourably, to my sister. And, stupidly, it makes me only crave his approval even more.

I try to please him, I really do. One day, I cooked him and Mother dinner—pigeons in a white sauce, and chicken stuffed with roast chestnuts. He ate it, but said he'd prefer something much simpler. I was crushed. Then, the next morning he said he couldn't sleep as the food had upset his stomach. If I'd intended that, I would have been happy but, sadly, I hadn't.

Another day, I showed him a sketch of our house and garden in Lambeth that I'd been working on all week. I thought I'd made a very good job of it, as my tutor had always told me I had artistic talent. He barely glanced at it.

'Yes, yes,' he said. 'Very nice, I'm sure. Now, I have work to do. Please don't disturb me.'

As he shut the door of his study, leaving me holding my sketch stupidly and fighting back the tears I could feel burning my eyes, Mother came over and put her arm around me.

'Come on, Mary,' she said. 'Your father's a very busy man. He's got a lot on his mind. He doesn't mean it.'

'No,' I said, turning away. 'He never does.'

I went to my bedroom, slamming the door behind me, and sat at the dressing table, staring at my reflection in the mirror. I noted, with satisfaction, how pale and bereft I looked. I understood Father could often be preoccupied with work and his worries about our family. My youngest sister Anne is very sickly and not quite right in the head, and I know he frets about what the future might hold for her. His preoccupations have grown worse since he and Mother lost Henry and William, my twin brothers, just a day after their birth. He'd been so happy when he'd heard he had sons, and so devastated by their deaths.

That is still no reason, however, to be quite so dismissive of me.

But I have a plan, and it won't be long before I break it to him. I hugged myself and my secret tight. As Father might say himself so indelicately, he has a hell of a shock coming to him.